An Irish Wife

An Irish Wife

a novel

Deborah Lincoln

Blank Slate Press | St. Louis, MO

Blank Slate Press
Saint Louis, MO 63110

Manufactured in the United States of America
Cover Graphics: Shutterstock, iStock (Getty Images)
Set in Clarendon Text Pro Adobe Garamond Pro and Exmouth
Cover Design by Kristina Blank Makansi

Library of Congress Control Number:

ISBN: 9781943075690

For Jeff

Main Characters

In Uniontown

Harry Robinson

Agnes Canon Robinson, Harry's mother

Agnes's sisters:

   Mary

   Sarah

   Joanna

   Elizabeth

   Martha (Mattie)

Philip Murray, coal company manager and Mattie's gentleman friend

Harry's friends:

   Rebecca Smith

   Dan Sturgeon

Old Senator Daniel Sturgeon, Dan's grandfather

Dr. William Sturgeon, Dan's father

In the Patch town:

Niamh Kilgariff Gill

Martin Gill, Niamh's husband

Patrick Kilgariff, Niamh's brother

Kate Byrne, Niamh's neighbor

The host is rushing 'twixt night and day,

And where is there hope or deed as fair?

Caoilte tossing his burning hair,

And Niamh calling Away, come away.

~ W.B. Yeats

The Hosting of the Sidhe

February 1930

Harry's wife brings him coffee and gingersnaps before she leaves for her bridge game, wrapped up in the raccoon coat he'd bought her five years ago. It's beginning to look ratty, and there won't be another one. She doesn't want to leave him alone—the part-time nurse who pestered him most days taking a holiday—but he insists. Bridge is important to her. She is fiercely competitive and manages to win two or three dollars every week, her one little vice, she says.

Maybe that's how we'll pay the cook.

She tucks the afghan around his thin legs and puts another log on the fire. She's left him the newspaper and another of the boxes, this one with some of his personal papers. Wouldn't do to leave them behind when he goes, rubbish from a life well lived. He'd rather be at the office, but instead he's swaddled in a dressing gown and slippers at mid-day, watching the snow float past the veranda. He's glad he didn't have to dig out the Plymouth this morning—hasn't driven it for a month and doesn't want to as long as the weather's foul. He shakes his head. His driving days are over and he knows it.

The snow must be two feet deep along the roadside, and it's coming down now in great white flakes The radio says there'll be another six inches before it stops. His wife bought him one of those Zenith consoles for Christmas this year, though he wishes she hadn't. They can't afford such luxuries now. There'll be no new car this year, and if the bank collapses, they'll be hard put heating this cavern of a house, much less buying new cars and radios.

The box is full of old letters and certificates of election, most of which he lost. News clippings. Harry picks up the one where the boys were off to the Mexican border. No one remembers that now, that men fought and died in Mexico, caught up in that mess, chasing Pancho Villa all over hell and beyond. But back then, 1916, all the boys in Uniontown were hot for the army. They all trooped up to Connellsville and hopped on a train and off they went, five thousand mothers and fathers and sweethearts waving and cheering and sobbing. Harry tries to remember how he felt, sending his four oldest boys off to get shot at. He thinks he was proud, no reason not to be. He remembers how his wife beamed. Young Dan was there, too, desperate to go with his brothers but a couple years shy of eighteen. He remembers his wife clinging to Dan's hand throughout, Dan trying to shake her off.

That was in May. By October they were all back again, fit and sun-burned. Two years later they shipped out for France. This time the army took all five of them: John, Charlie, Harold, Bill, Dan. The two littlest boys left at home to fashion make-believe rifles out of firewood and talk about when it's their turn. And young Agnes. No one paid any attention to her at all.

He rustles through the stack of papers for the folder that lies buried at the bottom of the box, one he'd tucked away years ago. He pulls it out and opens it across his lap; it cracks along the spine. There are two news clippings, a letter and a photograph. The headline in the Connellsville paper trumpets THE MOLOCH OF THE MINE: Fourteen Victims of Fire-Damp. The Somerset paper simply reports MINE DISASTER: Fourteen Men Killed. It was what, now, forty-five, fifty years ago? 1884, the clippings say. Nearly forty-six.

He tucks them back into the folder and picks up the photograph. It shows a young woman, no more than twenty-five, dressed in a fashion popular just before the Great War: high-necked, long-sleeved lace blouse, high-waisted skirt, big eyes like a silent film star. Her wavy hair is parted in the middle and cascades down her back and it is dark, black like her mother's. He takes up the letter and reads it through. The words, oddly enough, raise only one sensation, a scent, the acrid scent of coal burning in ovens, slowly turning into coke, the smell of the Eighties and progress and death and dirt.

He folds the letter carefully. The creases are still good; it has lain untouched in the folder for the past twenty years. He slides letter and photograph behind the clippings, closes the folder, drops it to the floor, and reaches for today's Post-Gazette. The paper says business is on the upward trend; a complete readjustment expected in a few months.

Harry stares out at the snow. Maybe we won't lose the cook after all.

1

1870s

Harry was four years old when his mother brought him home to the valley between the rivers where her family had lived for a hundred years. Where the Youghiogeny River wiggled north through folded hills and smoky valleys, crashed into the Monongahela on its way, and joined the Allegheny. Together their waters became the great Ohio River, the highway into that dim west of gold mines and vast distances and vaguely recalled adventures.

South of the Yough Valley, at the point where Connellsville took root around Stewart's Crossing, swept a land of ridges and knolls, rolling farmland and steep forested gorges. Back then, new snow crunched under foot and breath stung harsh and lovely in his child's throat. A place where cardinals, brilliant drops of red, like blood, sang through winter and into spring. Where rills freshened with ice melt and the shadows of mudcats lingered near their rounded rocky nests.

Harry's young world revolved around the Laurel Highlands and Chestnut Ridge to the east, clothed in the cool greens of summer and the blue-white of winter. He loved the way dawn took its time climbing over the summit of the Ridge in autumn. The air changed to a pink and green haze then, and softened just as the maples and birches, beeches and red oaks turned. He'd always loved that ridge, fancying as a small child does without regard for direction or authenticity, that the reward for peeking over its crest would be the sight of paradise. The broad world existed in mystery beyond Uniontown, on the other side of those Pennsylvania hills, maybe even to the wild world of Montana, his father, and his earliest memories.

When his twice-great grandfather built the old farmstead, the low lands as well as the ridges were clothed with silent deep woods of beech and sugar maples, with hickory and walnuts and oak for the nuts that fed men and beasts, with birch and elms simply for beauty. Much of the northern areas of the county were still thick with chestnuts and rich with understories of ferns and fungus, with songbirds and salamanders, land snails and beetles.

The land that had settled into steep-sided, deeply forested ridges and troughs was born out of the violence of continents smashing against one another like the slow-motion movement of a nightmare lasting eons. In the process, ancient ferns and scaly-barked trees were mashed into peat, squeezed until nothing was left but the precious carbon, the rich black stone heart of the hills, buried beneath the fields and pastures. By the time Harry came of age, the chestnuts were doomed to blight, the creeks were sluggish with filth, and the stone heart had turned cancerous.

Harry was always a Canon, though he bore the name Robinson. Canons had a history in southwest Pennsylvania and history meant a great deal to Uniontown folk. His family was a matriarchy because his grandmother bore seven daughters, who survived, and three sons, who did not. When she died with the last son, his grandfather was left to manage seven girls—seven, the number of completeness and perfection, one for each color of the rainbow, one for each day of the week, one for each note on the diatonic scale. Seven headaches, or so old Dan Canon was heard to say. And when he died, only women were left. The second of those women was Harry's mother, Agnes.

Harry learned early on to be proud of his Canon ancestors. The family was related to Abraham Lincoln—yes, that Abraham Lincoln—and the link to a martyred hero secured for it a distinct cachet in the growing folklore of the recent war. And although his Robinson ancestor had shepherded the Mayflower pilgrims, Harry's father, Dr. Robinson, was persona non grata in Uniontown due to his well-known rebel sympathies.

His mother was known not as Mrs. Robinson, but as Miss Agnes, as her sisters were Miss Mary, Miss Mattie and so on. Even when she became a prominent businesswoman—which she did because she was widowed, was forced to provide for herself and her son, and never did anything by halves—she continued to be called "Miss" by the town's businessmen. Harry had always thought the label patronizing, though probably he too was patronizing once he became a businessman, but by then the war widows had for the most part died out and men were back in control, so he didn't give it much thought. Besides, that was just the way things were done in Uniontown.

Harry spent his first four years in a Montana hut with a sod roof, but his first home in Pennsylvania was an eighty-year-old farmhouse built by his Lincoln ancestor. Mordecai Lincoln—great old name, Mordecai—bought a tract of land named "Discord" four miles outside the town of Union. Union's claim to fame was that the first worldwide war commenced in a glen within spitting distance where an inept and befuddled George Washington watched his Indian ally, the Half King (why Half King? Why not Whole King?) sink a hatchet into the head of a Frenchman, then wash his hands in the brains.

Harry and his good friend Dan spent one particularly vicious May night there in the midst of a spring thunderstorm, huddled against the sheer rock face, waiting for the ghosts of the dead Frenchman and his massacred mates to appear. Legend had it that the bones, which had been left to wolves and vultures, maggots and beetles, reassembled themselves each year on the anniversary of the carnage and searched for their scalps, pates bloody and ragged. Turned out they weren't the only ones to hope for a sighting: the Ruddy brothers put in an appearance along toward midnight, rattling dead sticks from behind outcroppings, hooting like owls, effectively scaring the bejeebers out of Harry and Dan until they ran pell-mell for the farmhouse, where they were supposed to be tucked up in bed. They suffered for years after that. The Ruddy boys were their sworn enemies until Malcolm Ruddy died in the Great War.

So back to the tract of land called "Discord." It was aptly named, or perhaps the name was an omen of what was to come. Mordecai built the farmhouse (the very farmhouse where Dan and Harry were supposed to be sleeping on the night of the ghost-watch escapade) on nearly six hundred acres sometime around 1790. The acres and the house were deeded to his daughter, the widow of a Welshman named Jones, who in time became Harry's great-grandmother. The Welsh in old Grandfather Jones appreciated the coal that lay thick on the property, protruded from the ridges, paved the beds of the creeks and rills. He and Mordecai and others of their extended family harvested the black rock and burned it in their fires, cooked their meals, heated their homes, stoked their forges, never appreciating the threat that lay deep inside those enchanting green hills.

❈

By 1868, the year Harry and his mother left the Montana frontier and made their way to Fayette County, coal barons had discovered the land where sat the Canon ancestral home. The country was wild for coal, the foundries demanded it, the cities already befogged with it. Several of Agnes's sisters continued to live in the old farmhouse, as did Agnes and Harry when they first arrived in Pennsylvania, and the question of whether to sell hovered like a wraith for years. When it finally came to a head—in an offer from a local man with connections—"Discord" kicked in with a vengeance.

Early seventies, Harry's eighth winter. He had dragged Aunt Mattie outside after Sunday dinner to build snowmen—snow people, she insisted; she wanted a snow woman, too. Mattie was the youngest of the Aunts, little more than thirty that year. Unmarried, as were they all, ready to play any time, he didn't even have to beg. They used chunks of coal they found scattered next to the coal chute for mouth and eyes; everyone was careless of the chunks back then, so plentiful were they. No one ever went cold in Southwest Pennsylvania, not like Montana. And it was cold, just after the new year; pristine snow from last night's fall lay thick on the hills, bare blackened tree limbs like the bones of crows stark against the gray sky, so cold the snot in his nose froze and his cheeks chapped of their own accord.

Mattie pulled an old cob pipe from a pocket and Harry squealed. He'd never seen it anywhere except in the pipe stand on the mantel and he was forbidden (by Aunt Mary) to touch it on pain of dire consequences. It was Grandpa Dan's, a sacred relic like the silver cross on the alter in church. But fearless Mattie had stolen it and now she stuck it in her mouth and grinned. He leapt at her. "Me! Let me!" She let him pull it from her mouth and lifted him so he could jam it begtween the snowman's coal black teeth. Mattie dropped him none too gently and swept off her headscarf to wrap it around the snow lady's head.

"Good health and every good blessing to you!" She spread her arms and bowed low to the icy couple.

"Good health!" Harry said and he too bowed.

"Inside! I'm for chocolate." She swept him up and tucked him against her side, both of them red-faced and cackling, and marched him to the back door.

Aunt Mary stood at the stove, her face thunderous. She was the oldest and the scariest of the Aunts. She set the farmhouse rules. She never smiled. She wore her iron-gray hair pulled back so tightly that Harry thought her eyes would pop out. She always smelled of lavendar, a smell Harry to his dying day would hate. But she baked cookies every Tuesday and let Harry have two fresh out of the oven, so she wasn't all bad.

Harry climbed out of his wet jacket. He could smell the chocolate she was stirring. He craved a hot cup of that sweet smell and an oatmeal cookie to go with it but he daren't speak up. Mary didn't think much of children being heard. So as soon as she turned to the sisters gathered at the table, he snitched a cookie and curled up next to his pup, while his trousers steamed. Ferdie slept on a cushion behind the stove and softly woofed at a dream rabbit. Rich smells of coffee and chocolate, lingering scents of roast beef and candied yams, the warmth and the exercise worked their magic and his eyes drooped. His mother's voice mentioned coal and in a half-awake dream the snowman's eyes winked at him. But Mary's sharp voice woke him. She was angry and for once not with Harry. Mama had the crease between her eyebrows that meant she was serious.

Sarah leaned back in her chair, her hands draped over her stomach and her lips pursed. Today she wore red, her second-most favorite color, and had pulled her hair back in a band, letting it cascade in curls down her back. Mother once told him that Sarah was as batty as Barney's brig, and Harry for years watched for the bats. She quoted Shakespeare and swanned about, recalling her success as Lady Macbeth in a local production no one else remembered. Now she rolled her eyes at Harry and winked and made small sucking noises with her lips.

Elizabeth and Joanna sat very still. Neither said much when the others were in the room. Harry had a hard time telling them apart, both seemed to fade into the wallpaper when the other sisters were around. Except when Joanna took care of the farm animals and then she dressed in men's clothes and then no one could mistake her for Elizabeth. Elizabeth's gaze darted from one face to another, her fists clenched on the table. Joanna stared into her lap, cheeks flushed. Mary flourished a saucepan and Harry thought for a moment she planned to hit someone with it. He laughed, couldn't help it, and she glared at him.

She turned on Agnes. "You'll not sell this land while I live here. I won't have coal ovens and smoke and those shanty Irish miners crawling all over my farm."

"Our farm, Mary." Mama stood and poured herself more coffee.

"We'll never get a better price than now," Sarah said. "And I for one would like the money. Life is short, may as well enjoy it. Before we all end up like Belle. Dead."

"Sarah!" Joanne's head snapped up. "That's uncalled for." Harry wondered who Belle was.

"We can invest the money," Mama said, "and Harry can go to college."

They all turned to look at him, and he shrank into his shoulders. Mattie smiled at him and dropped her wet gloves and coat on the floor. Mary scowled as if this argument were all Harry's fault. He tried to be invisible.

"I could have a shop." Mattie dished up chocolate. "I always wanted to own a sweets shop. I'm so tired of teaching." She handed the cup to Harry.

Mama turned to Elizabeth and Joanna. "What do you say?"

They looked at each other, then at Mary and both said, "Sell."

Mary turned away and moved the chocolate pot off the flame. She moved slowly, as if she were mightily wearied. She seemed very old to Harry, more like a grandmother than an aunt. It made him sad.

Harry crept over to his mama, careful not to spill chocolate, and tugged at her sleeve. "Who's Belle?" he whispered. "Why's she dead?"

2

July 1872

"Belle would have had these stitched up in half the time it took me." Agnes climbed down from the chair and surveyed the curtains. "She was the best of all of us at sewing."

Harry had forgotten all about Belle, but here she was again. "Who's Belle?"

"She was my sister who died."

He'd wanted to help move into the new house in town and had been allowed to unpack the crate that held Mama's collection of pots and pans though the cast-iron kettles were heavy for him, though he was all of eight years old. He dropped a pan on the floor and his mother jumped.

"Oh, Harry, do be careful. You'll put a dent in the floor."

"You mean there was more?"

"More what?"

"More aunts."

"Just Belle. She died of consumption not long after I left for Missouri."

He wondered what it would be like to have yet one more aunt. His birthday was tomorrow; there would be a party with all the aunts at the farmhouse. And a swim in the creek afterwards. Mattie and Mama and maybe Joanna would swim, too. He wondered if Belle had liked to swim. But she was dead, like his papa.

"Was that in the war?"

"No, it was several years before. 1853."

"Lots of people died." Harry sat on the floor, cross-legged, and piled wood shavings from the packing into a mound. He liked the way they curled around his finger and the way they smelled, fresh and clean. "Papa died."

Agnes knelt and stitched the loose hem where the curtains touched the parlor floor. "That was a long time after. But yes, lots of people died in the war."

"Did Papa fight?"

"No, he was a doctor. He took care of some of the people who were hurt." His mother sat on the floor near him, not working on the curtains any longer but staring out the window. It was almost dark, late, his bedtime, but she didn't seem to realize it and he wasn't going to remind her. It was just nice to have her with him, just the two of them, their first night in their new house and tomorrow his birthday.

They'd sold the land but kept the farmhouse, with a pasture for Joanna's beloved animals and just enough room for a big garden. Agnes had bought a large brick house on Fayette Street, big enough to hold all the sisters. And all but Joanna chose to move into town, Mary leading the way and grumbling incessantly. They'd be closer to the shops, closer to their workplaces. And they'd be there to watch out for Harry, now that Agnes had to work so much. The sisters stuck together, clustering like a covy of quail in the springtime— too often, in Harry's mind, a vexing din. But for the next few days, he would have his mother all to himself, just like they had been in Montana.

He bent over his pile of shavings and puffed on them, enough to make the top ones fly up and flutter back down. "Sometimes I dream about him, about him being dead and under the ground."

She turned to him then and ran a hand over his hair. "You have night-mares, don't you?" She picked up a pan and settled it inside another. She seemed to be looking at something a long way off. "I don't think he's in the ground, not really."

"Where is he?"

Her gaze drifted back to him. "Somewhere very pleasant, I hope. Wherever he is, he's taking care of someone." She smiled and pulled him into her lap. "Did I ever tell you about the time your father helped rescue a miner from a collapsed shaft in California?" She settled him against her and leaned against the wall. "Well. It was eighteen forty-eight and your father had been in the gold fields for only three months… "

Agnes's success at selling the farmland in parcels at a comfortable profit led her to launch a business buying and selling properties for a living. She dealt mostly in homes (more appropriate for a woman) though sometimes she sold business real estate downtown. The Seventies and Eighties were a heady time in the Monongahela Valley, once the coking business took off. The very rich, the Fricks and the Carnegies and such, couldn't be seen to live in such small towns, their wives would never settle for the society. Instead, they lived in New York or Philadelphia or even in Pittsburgh, until the air grew too sooty. But the second-tier coal men sometimes bought property on Fayette Street or Ben Lomond or south where Captain Nutt built a mansion on property he bought from Agnes, her biggest sale.

Harry's mother was not like other mothers, he knew that from before he knew most things. Particularly not like Dan's mother. She, too, had married a doctor, but unlike his mother Mrs. Sturgeon raised a houseful of children, organized Sunday School picnics and oversaw a colored cook and an Irish maid. In the Sturgeons' comfortable house there were lots of men, his grandfather, the old Senator, and Dan's father and brothers. Harry's brick house on Fayette Street, on the other hand, was filled with women. The aunts cooked and cleaned, Mattie taught school, Agnes sold houses. Even in the evenings, she showed properties or finished paperwork in her office downtown. It seemed to Harry she preferred the office to the chirping and bustle of the aunts. It was Mary who met him at home after school and stood over him while he finished homework. Elizabeth who cooked his dinner, Mattie who tucked him into bed. He learned to anticipate the special times his mother stayed home, read to him, told stories, heard him recite his Latin lessons. It seemed to him they were few and far between.

He noticed the way no one mentioned her lack of a husband. The aunts avoided the subject; never blessed with husbands of their own, they seemed to consider the topic taboo. The strange thing was that even though there were so many widows after the war, so many mothers and fathers who had lost someone, so many sisters, brothers, aunts, uncles who grieved, no one seemed to have learned how to address another's grief except to pretend the losses didn't exist. People pretended that a town full of spinsters was the natural order of things, that an entire generation of men hadn't disappeared and left behind other generations of bereaved. No one said his name to her, no one said "Jabez" or "Doctor Robinson," and the few times she mentioned "my husband," they glossed over the subject. The looks on their faces were not pity or grief, but embarrassment.

They were tired of widows, there were too many of them, and besides, Agnes had been a widow for years. That should be long enough, as if there were a statute of limitations on grief. One should not grieve above a year or two at most, then one must get on with it. But as Harry grew older and recognized the deep and abiding grief he carried for what he himself had lost, he knew she would never get on with it, that the anguish would be forever with her if she lived to eighty or ninety or a hundred, like an unhealing scar, raw, but at the same time comforting because no one else had a scar quite like it.

Harry's father had never been to Fayette County, had never met his mother's family or neighbors, but his reputation was well-known in the valley. To the townsfolk he was a Secessionist, even a bushwhacker. To Aunt Mary, he was a traitor. Harry found that out the day before their first Christmas in the new house. His mother had left him in the Aunts' care while she was at work and he'd crawled behind the sofa to draw pictures of birds along the edges of his reader. The birds weren't very good but he drew them anyway because he loved birds. The Aunts were in the next room, just around the corner. Once he realized they were speaking of his mother, he forgot the birds and began to listen.

"I still don't know how she can come back here and hold her head up?" Mary said around the nasty cold in her nose.

"After all that happened during the war," Sarah said.

"This is her home, Mary," Mattie said. "Of course she should come back here."

"How she can look some of these fine veterans in the face when her husband was a filthy rebel sympathizer." Mary again. "More than sympathizer. I hear he actually wrote things in that newspaper of his that were nothing short of treason. He should have been shot!"

"*By treason's tooth bare-gnawn and canker-bit.*"

"Oh, Sarah, hush," Mary said.

"But that isn't Agnes's fault," Mattie said. "She didn't know what would happen when they married. And once she married him, what could she do?"

"She knew from the beginning he was no good. He thought the south should. . ."

". . .just go away." Sarah finished Mary's sentence.

"He was a traitor even then. She knew. Oh, she knew."

"She knew," Sarah said.

"I believe I just said that."

Mattie didn't answer.

Harry's head buzzed, he didn't know he could be so angry. His father was a traitor? He wasn't sure what that meant, but he knew what "no good" meant. And he surely knew about being shot. According to the stories his mother told him, his father was a hero. But Mary said he was a rebel, and a rebel was bad.

3

July 1876

The celebration started with a long line of carriages winding its way west on Main Street, over Cool Lick Run toward Oak Grove Cemetery. A marching troop led the procession, men in Union blue, ragged shirts and thread-bare pants, the red stripe of an artilleryman, the yellow stripe of a cavalryman, but mostly the dusty and well-worn, patched trousers of the enlisted man. The men stared straight ahead, eyes shifting neither to left nor right. The fringed banner of the Eighty-fifth Pennsylvania Volunteer Infantry flew above the first ranks, its thirteen stripes imprinted with the names of battles: York Town, Malvern Hill, Petersburg, Strawberry Plain. An ongoing roll of snare drum, the stamp of boots on packed surface, the creak of carriage leather and the occasional snort of a horse competed with the cheers and sporadic applause of onlookers who lined the streets, but the men themselves were silent. Several marched with the help of crutches, an empty pant leg flapping. There were empty sleeves, too, an arm that ended in a hook, eyepatches. Some were gaunt, as if the intervening years had not been enough to erase the diet of hardtack and wormy dried beef, the wet and chilly bivouacs, the smoke and fire and terror of battle. Colonel McGiffin, in a double-breasted coat with the silver oak leaves of his rank, sat atop a prancing horse at the head of the line, his captain trailing behind.

The Fourth of July was always hot, the height of summer humidity, and it never rained. The regiment had paraded every year ever since Harry could remember; sometimes he would go with Dan and Dan's grandfather, the old senator, sometimes he'd stay home at the house on Fayette Street because his mother refused to commemorate the war at all. "If the people of this town had been in the middle of the war the way it was in Missouri," she would say, "they would do everything they could to forget." By the time he was ten or eleven, though, he had the run of the town, he and Dan, and they wouldn't have missed the Independence Day parade for love nor money.

This year the country had gone mad for such displays. It had been a hundred years since the Declaration of Independence, and neither the British nor the Mexicans nor the Texans nor the Natives nor the rebels in the South had managed to tump over the government in Washington though Democrats muttered that either President Grant or the barons of industry might yet accomplish what war had not.

Harry and Dan teetered on the edge of their teenage years, and the heady mix of warm summer breeze, incipient hormones and military pageantry sent their blood racing. They ran with a pack of boys of all ages behind the last of the buggies, Ferdie prancing at their heels and nosing into horse droppings and the rear ends of other dogs. By the time they reached the cemetery, they were hot and sweaty and hungry. Harry sprawled in the grass next to the Beeson family markers, on a rise above the speaker's stand where the townsfolk gathered. McGiffin climbed the steps flanked by the mayor and Dan's grandfather, the old senator.

"I gotta go cool off." Harry blew a hank of hair out of his eyes. "Let's go down to the creek. We've heard these speeches a hundred times."

Dan, who never went far without food of some kind, pulled out of his pants pocket a kerchief wrapped around a hunk of bread and hard cheese. He broke them in half and handed a chunk to Harry. Ferdie snatched the bread and ran off.

"Hey!" Harry jumped up and ran after his dog, who dodged the markers and the monuments, wound through a grove of elms and streaked for the creek, out of sight behind the rise, Dan and Harry hot on his trail. By the time they reached the creek bank Ferdie had swallowed the bread whole and splashed in the shallows, absorbed in his new game.

Dan flopped to the ground and shared the rest of his bread. "Shoulda brought more," he said. "I always forget about Ferdie." He jammed cheese in his mouth and tossed a stone in the water. Ferdie jumped for it.

Harry lay back on the grassy bank and closed his eyes. The rich, rank weight of summer growth settled over him, the smell of dusty heat stupifying. The sluggish murmur of the creek was punctuated by the sudden call of an annoyed crow, disturbed by movement upstream. Something splashed through the low summer waters. Then Ferdie growled, a low rumble. Harry rolled over, doze interrupted. Dan sat up and stared downstream. "Uh oh. We're in for it now." Ferdie whipped around mid-stream and barked.

Harry swiveled and choked on his bread. Frank and Malcolm Ruddy splashed down the center of the creek followed by two other boys, their posse, Frank called them. The two hangers-on were small, Harry's age or younger; Malcolm and Frank were older. And they were big, they'd begun to put on muscle. Ever since the night at the ghosts' glen Harry and Dan made it a point to keep out of their way. Harry's first instinct was to run but it was too late. He squatted, poised on the balls of his feet, and looked sideways at Dan. His friend's face paled behind his freckles. He'd had more experience with the Ruddys and it was never good. Harry could tell he wanted to run too. But he'd never leave Harry alone.

Frank and Malcolm loped up to them, Frank with a leer on his face. "Well lookee what we got here. Grandpa's little pet and the Reb's boy."

"What do you want, Frank?" Dan stood, fists clenched.

Malcolm brayed like a donkey. "You little pisser. Think you're so good just because your grandpa's a senator."

"Copperhead! Copperhead!" Frank danced around waving his arms. The posse boys aped him.

"Donkey democrat!" Malcolm yanked at his britches, pulled them down to his knees, stuck his bare rear end at Dan. "Here's an ass to kiss! *Kiss my ass!*"

Harry scrambled to his feet. One of the posse boys threw a rock at Ferdie; the dog snarled and dodged. Harry aimed a kick at Malcolm's butt. It mostly missed but Malcolm stumbled and caught himself, pulled up his britches.

The leer on Frank's face turned to a scowl. The posse boys tensed, their eyes flicked back and forth from Frank to Harry. Dan crouched like a boxer, but Frank waved his hand and the posse boys jumped him from behind, pulled him to the ground. One sat on his chest and smacked him in the face while the other sat on his knees.

Frank advanced on Harry. "Your pa was a shit-eating sneak, and you're nothin but a filthy Reb." He swung a fist.

Harry threw up his arms and blocked the punch, but Malcolm came at him from the side swinging a tree limb. The limb caught him in the ribs and broke. He doubled over as Frank's fist crashed into the side of his head. He went down and Malcolm landed a heavy kick on his right kidney. Ferdie, all thirty pounds of him, leaped at Malcolm, full-throated barks mashing with Dan's yells. Frank knelt over Harry, pummeling, snarling "reb, reb, reb" with each blow. Harry's nose cracked and hot blood cascaded into his mouth. Another kick took him in the ribs. Ferdie squealed in pain. The posse boys, from their perch on Dan, threw stones at the dog; Ferdie danced out of reach, howls filling the air. Harry curled into himself, covered his ribs and his genitals when Malcolm kicked him from the rear. Frank sat back on his heals, his breath labored, his face brick red. "Fucking nancy-boy," he muttered. A mist floated in front of Harry's eyes, his sight narrowed. Darkness pressed in from the sides. Just before he passed out, he heard his mother's angry voice.

Harry remembered snatches of being carried through the cemetery and laid on the seat of the senator's carriage, then nothing until he woke up in his room on the top floor of his mother's house. He was still in a fog, and he thought maybe he'd dreamed the beating, but maybe not. A kerosene lamp, turned low, burned at his bedside and the window across from him showed a night sky. His eyes didn't want to focus and his arm refused to move, seemed to be tied down. One by one, various aches began to make themselves felt, first his head, then his ribs, and his nose pulsed. He had to breathe through his mouth which was open and hideously dry. He'd give an arm and a leg for a drink of water. He wondered where Ferdie was, and then Dan. Frank's face floated into his memory and he shivered.

The senator snored in a chair next to his bed, in his shirtsleeves, a lock of snowy white hair shuddering with each breath. As much Harry's grandpa as Dan's, the old man was always there whenever the boys were in trouble.

"Hah!" Senator Sturgeon snorted and started. "You're awake then." He pinched his nose between his fingers, squeezed his eyes shut, then opened them to peer at Harry. "Want your mother? She just now went to bed."

Harry did, desperately wanted her, but it sounded like the senator didn't really want to go get her so he only said, "No, but can I have some water please?"

The Senator fussed and crooned, poured water from a pitcher on the bureau and held the glass to Harry's lips. Harry drank, and his stomach rolled. He couldn't take much. But his mouth felt cooler.

"You took quite a licking," the Senator said. "Want to tell me what happened?"

"Is Dan all right?" Harry blinked to focus.

"Oh, yes, Danny seems to have got off with just a few bruises."

"And Ferdie, did Ferdie get away?"

"He's limping some but he'll do. Danny says he did his best to pull them off you." The old man patted Harry's hand and was quiet for a moment. "Can you tell me what happened, son?"

"What did Dan say?"

The Senator looked uncomfortable and he hemmed. "Danny hasn't said yet. I imagine he will."

If Dan hadn't told, then neither would Harry. Not because he was afraid; for some reason he knew he'd never again be afraid of the Ruddys. But there was a code. You didn't rat out even your worst enemy.

The Senator let it go. "Do you know why?"

"They said my father was a rebel." Harry turned his face away.

"Ah." The old man slumped. "The damn war never will be over."

"Aunt Mary said so, too." Harry's voice came out in a whisper. The senator had to lean over to hear him. "He was, wasn't he? He was on the wrong side."

The Senator blew air through his lips. "Son, he was. He took the wrong side, and he paid for it, and now you're paying for it."

Harry thought for a minute. "Does everyone in town know what he did during the war? Mama says he wrote newspaper articles mostly. He didn't fight."

"Being an educated man is no excuse. You have an opportunity, boy, an opportunity to redeem your name. Grow up to be a credit to your ma and everyone'll forget what your pa did during the war."

"When I grow up, I'm going back to Montana."

"You surely can do that if you want to. But I hope you won't. Your mother needs you." He'd always looked out for Agnes. There'd been whispers that the widowed senator had been sweet on Agnes back in the forties. In spite of the age difference, had even asked for her hand, and that that was one of the reasons Agnes had lit out for the west. Mary once said that Senator Sturgeon had paid for Agnes and Harry's return trip to Pennsylvania. Harry always wondered if she'd thought of marrying him then. Much as he loved the old man, he was glad she hadn't.

Senator Sturgeon heaved himself out of the chair and turned to the window, his back to Harry. "Your grandpappy'd be proud to see you here today. He'd want you to stay here where your roots are and make this a better place. You're all that's left of his line."

Maybe so, but Harry didn't want to be all that was left. His eyes stung, and he was afraid the Senator would see tears on his cheeks. That would be worse than his aches, he was too old to cry over a beating or over shame for his father. He shut his eyes and pretended to drift off to sleep. After a while he heard the old man shuffle out of the room.

He shifted and regretted it. The lump above his left hip complained along every nerve in his body. He thought about the obituary he'd found tucked away in his mother's desk last year. Some newspaper from Kansas called his father a bushwacker, said he was insane, burrowed up in the rebel paradise of Montana. Said his death wasn't a calamity, should have happened years before. But it also said he was extraordinarily talented and an excellent physician. *So how am I to think about him?* Harry squeezed his eyes shut, saw the men in today's parade, armless, legless, flinching at any loud noise. *How is it up to me to make it right?* And take care of his mother. It startled him to think he might need to take care of her. She'd always taken care of everybody else.

He wondered how it was his mother had shown up at just the right time.

4

September 1876

"Nope," Dan said. "That's not it, either. Blast the stupid thing." "It has something to do with the square root of two being an irrational number."

"It's all irrational, if you ask me." Dan threw down his pencil. "Why would anyone want to know what a quadratic equation is anyway?"

Dan hated algebra and Harry wasn't much of a fan of it either, and both would rather have their noses in the *Odyssey*, which Harry thought was great fun, or even decline Latin verbs. Anything but algebra.

Harry looked up. A tall, skinny girl finished washing the slate board and stood by the next desk over, listening. His face grew hot. She was the new girl in school, the one who always knew the answers in class, and the teacher beamed when her hand went up. He wriggled so his back was to her and lowered his voice to read from his textbook: "'What are the proportions of a piece of foolscap and how do you express them in a quadratic equation?'"

"Fools is right," Dan muttered. "Who cares?"

"It gets you the Golden Rectangle, what the Greeks thought was the perfect shape." The girl pushed aside a desk and pulled up a chair. "If you fold your paper like this"—she pulled a sheet from her satchel and folded it so she made a square of the bottom half—"you get two rectangles with the same proportions."

"Who are you?" Dan said.

"Rebecca." She took Harry's pencil from his fingers and scribbled on her paper.

Dan looked at Harry and Harry looked at the girl. "Yeah, so?"

"So then you have—"

$$\frac{x}{1} = \frac{1-x}{x}$$

She tilted her head at the boys.

"So?" Dan said.

She wrote:

$$x^2 + x = 1$$

"The n its solution, is: $x = \dfrac{\sqrt{5} - 1}{2} = 0.61803\ldots$"

She beamed. They stared back.

Harry bent to the paper. "You make a lovely square root, ma'am."

She smirked. "Thank you, sir. I practiced."

"What are the dots?" Dan said.

"It means the number goes on forever. It's the Golden Ratio." She leaned forward, twitched the pencil between her fingers and tapped the end on the desk. "It's the shape of windows. It's the way leaves on plant stems are arranged. There are all sorts of patterns in nature that connect to this." She looked back and forth between them. "You can predict the population of rabbits."

Harry gawked at her. "Rabbits. You made that up."

Her right eyebrow twitched. She had very dark, expressive eyebrows that arched in a point over deep-set black eyes. The eyes twinkled. "No indeed. Fibonocci did. Three or four hundred years ago."

Dan snickered. "And field mice."

"Elephants," Harry said.

"Kangaroos." Rebecca grinned.

Harry guffawed and then they were all laughing. She laughed with a snort that made them laugh even harder.

"Fibonocci Fibonitchy Fibonocci makes me itchy," Dan sang. He stood and stretched. "C'mon, let's go to my house. My mother's baking today, and I can smell it from here." He couldn't, but his house *was* across the street from the school. "You come too, Becky."

Rebecca stared at him hard with those dark eyes. "You'll never call me that again."

"Yes ma'am." He grinned and swept her a bow. But he continued to call her Becky.

LaVerna Rebecca Smith, who refused to be called either LaVerna *or* Becky, could out-organize Melville Dewey. The algebra episode happened the autumn after the Ruddy fight, their eighth-grade year, and if it hadn't been for Rebecca, neither of the boys would have made it through geometry, much less trigonometry.

Harry and Dan stood all of five-feet-six in their boots, and she topped them by another couple of inches. She was gangly and bony, her elbows like splitting wedges, good for carving a path through a crowd or poking the student next to her when he dozed. Her brother Henry, who walked with her into town every morning from their farm in South Township, was a year ahead of Harry and Dan, one of those upperclassmen they idolized and didn't dare speak to. Rebecca had been silent and watchful the first few days of the school term, self-contained, slow to make friends. The other girls thought her stuck-up, but Harry thought she was just shy with them. She got along better with boys, able to throw a snowball or twenty with a right arm that rivaled the second-string pitcher in his summer league, had posted a respectable third in the Christmas ice-skating races. When summer vacation rolled around, she cajoled her parents into letting her walk into town on her own, and she roamed the fields with them, Becky Thatcher to Harry and Dan's Tom and Huck. Which is how they happened to explore the mine.

5

Summer 1877

"Becky won't go in. She'll be scared."
Dan leaned a hand on the cross beam and peered into the hole. It pushed into the hillside like the throat of a monster, breathing out dank, acrid breaths that reached Harry in odd puffs from the depths.

"Pshaw." Rebecca gathered her skirts. She ducked under the beam and crouched in the entrance. It was too low for her to stand upright.

"Do you think we should?" Harry looked around. The mine yard was deserted on a late Sunday afternoon, but the detritus left behind by digging coal littered the ground. This was a primitive mine, a single entry framed by massive beams, rutted lanes clogged with mule droppings and rock waste, dusty in the heat of a dry summer. Ferdie whined.

"You're not going to let a girl show you how to do it, are you?" Dan ducked his head and followed Rebecca into the mine. Harry shrugged, looked around once more, and plunged in. Ferdie whined again and followed.

The chill was immediate and welcome, the heat of the early July sun parching the hills that cradled the mine. Inside, the walls dripped moist and slimy under his fingers. "We're not going very far without a light," Harry said. "It's darker than Hades in here."

"I can fix that." Dan knelt at the entrance and pulled matches from his pocket. Lanterns swung from hooks just inside like small kettles. Dan swished three or four before he found one filled with oil, the wick protruding from the spout. "I think you light this, here." He struck a match.

The flame, when it caught, put out a greasy smoke but enough light to see several feet ahead. The shaft cut into the hillside and for twenty yards or so was nearly level. Dan led the way, crouched almost double. Rebecca followed, holding her skirts out of the muck. Harry brought up the rear. He glanced back as the square of light that was the entrance grew smaller. Ferdie sat abruptly, whined, and would go no farther.

Harry frowned. "What about gas?"

"What about it?" Dan's voice was faint, muffled by the mass of rock around him.

"An open flame like that can set it off."

"We won't go very far in," Rebecca said. "I've heard it pools back in the different rooms." She straightened; the track had begun to slant downward, and she could stand nearly upright. "And the air's still moving."

It was. Harry felt a breeze against his cheek, issuing from deep in the earth, smelling of damp rot and rich decay.

An angled turn cut off daylight. The only light now was the lantern and it didn't reach Harry. He followed the shadow that was Rebecca, who gripped Dan's shirttail. She walked into him when he stopped without warning.

"It branches here." He swung the lantern in a semi-circle. "There's a room off to that side."

"And another one over here." Harry'd been running his hand along the right wall when the wall disappeared. He had the strange sense someone—or *something*—might grasp his fingers, out of the void.

"Look at this." Dan held the lantern to the roof. Lace hung from the roof beams, long filaments of snow-white, cottony fungus waved softly in the breeze, fragments of ghosts trapped underground. A moth, disturbed by the light, darted about their ears and finally settled again out of sight.

The light wavered and dimmed. All three seemed to hold their breaths, listening. Harry closed his eyes, the better to feel the blackness around him. The silence was immense at first, and then he began to hear sounds, small bumps and squeaks. The flutter of distant leathery wings, the whine of a gnat. A scurry of paws, rats who'd learned to expect lunch buckets when humans arrived. Then the creak of timbers overhead and a low gentle rumble, as if the mountain itself cleared its throat. The sound was not sinister but detached, impersonal. The three young people inside its belly were of little concern to the ancient rock, not worth the mountain's attention. They would come and go, and the mountain would not take notice. And yet, Harry had the distinct impression it would crush them if it wanted to.

The lantern flared, then died. He heard Dan shake it; the oil was gone.

"Umm," Rebecca said. "Harry?"

He reached out and took her hand.

She pressed up against him. "Do you think we can find our way back in the dark?"

"Sure we can," Harry said. Her hip was against his; he felt the curve of her breast. "We just follow the wall, there's no place we can get sidetracked." He slid his other arm around her waist. "As long as we don't get off in one of these rooms. Dan, where are you?"

There was no sound from Dan. Harry and Rebecca stood motionless; her grip on his hand grew tighter. "Dan?"

"Don't be an ass," Harry said. "You're scaring Rebecca."

There was a low moan from the emptiness to their left. Harry knew better, but still he shivered. The darkness thickened.

Rebecca dropped his hand. "Oh, for heaven's sake, Dan, stop it. We're leaving. You can come if you want." He felt her move up the shaft, sure-footed.

"*Bwaaa-hah!*" A match flickered, lit up Dan's rolling eyeballs. Harry snorted and followed Rebecca.

Ferdie barked twice, then growled low. It was his stranger alert.

"Who's in there?" A shout from the entrance. "I've got a shotgun on you. I'll get this dog if you don't get out here!"

Harry started to run, rapped his forehead on a low beam and swore. "Don't shoot him! We're coming out." The roof had lowered, and he scrambled on hands and feet up the track until daylight stabbed him in the eyes and made him squint.

A man stood silhouetted in the entrance, a shotgun resting on his hip, a second man behind him. Ferdie licked Harry on the nose and darted back toward the entrance. By the time Harry reached the light, he'd recognized the man: Jim Frost, who owned the mine and the land around it.

"Harry Robinson? That you?" Frost lowered the shotgun. "What the hell are you doing in there? Oh, pardon my language," as Rebecca ducked outside after Harry, her face smudged with coal dust and her bodice filthy.

"Danny Sturgeon, your pa'll whip your backside when I tell him where you were."

"Aw, Mr. Frost, we weren't doing any harm. We just wanted to see what it's like down there."

"You go in there with an open flame and you're likely to get yourself blown to kingdom come. And taking a young girl in there ... why, you've no more sense than a monkey."

The second man ticked his head at the boys. "You often get vandals in here?"

"Not much. Usually too much work going on here." Frost turned to Dan. "This here's Mr. Murray. His company just bought this mine, and you're not showing him the best side of the county."

"You know these children, then," Murray said.

Harry glared at Murray. He could tell the man's clothes were expensive; only Captain Nutt and Mr. Thompson, both bankers and Republicans, wore clothes like that. His eyes, a startling blue, were deep-set in a flat face; one appeared larger than the other and slightly independent of its fellow

"I know their folks. Believe it or not, these are the good kids. Their folks'll take care they don't do this again."

Rebecca slid around Harry and laid a hand on Frost's arm. "Mr. Frost, *please* don't say anything. It was my fault, I wanted to go in, and I made them take me." She smiled and did that thing with her eyebrows that meant she was in earnest.

Murray smirked. Frost melted. "Well, I guess no harm done this time." He broke open the shotgun over his arm. "You all scat on home, and don't let me see you messing in mines again." He stepped back. "All that grime on your clothes'll give you away anyway. Your mothers will know."

Rebecca's smile this time was brilliant. "Oh, *thank* you!" She grabbed Dan's hand, pulled him up the path that led to the main road. "Good-bye Mr. Frost." She waved. "Nice to meet you, Mr. Murray."

By the time they were over the hill and out of sight they were howling so hard they collapsed on the roadside. "*Thank* you, Mr. Frost!" Dan squealed.

"Nice to *meet* you, Mr. Murray." Harry sat up. "Should have had you there when we got jumped by the Ruddys. You could have sweet-talked them out of anything. Saved the day."

Rebecca sat up and brushed at the coal dust on her skirt, smearing it into true filth. "I *did* save the day," she said primly. "Who do you think fetched your mother?"

6

October 1883

"My name is Niamh Kilgariff." She pushed her hair behind her ears, filthy from eight days in steerage and a week on the road before that. With barely enough water to clean her face and hands, there hadn't been enough to wash it.

"Spell it." The man behind the desk didn't look up. He dipped his pen and held it poised.

"N-I-A-M-H. K-I-L—"

He looked up. "N-I-A?"

"Yes. M-H."

"What kind of name is that?"

"Irish. It's pronounced *Nee-ev*."

"*Neeve*." He looked down. "Better Americanize this, girl. No one here wants to twist a tongue around that. Place of birth?"

"I will then." *Neeve*. A new country, a new name. Already, a piece of herself lost. No, she would never change it. "Ireland, County Galway."

"Age?"

"Twenty-one years."

"Who paid your passage?"

"My intended." Niamh glanced around the cavernous interior as if Martin might appear out of the horde, but of course he did not. Thank the Virgin. Better to put that meeting off as long as may be.

"Your fiancé." He looked her over. He might have been judging whether she was comely enough for a sweetheart or he might be puzzling out if she told the truth.

"Aye." She ducked her head, hoping she looked submissive instead of angry, which is what she was. It was nothing to do with him, what she planned once she entered this country, so long as it was not villainy.

Pádraig slipped his hand in hers and squeezed. He ever knew her moods and was quick to settle her when her temper flashed, which was often.

The man at the table lost interest in her and waved to Pádraig. "Next."

"Patrick Kilgariff," the boy said. "P-A-T-R-I-C-K. Fifteen years. County Galway." Ah, Patrick then. No more her dear Pádraig.

The man looked up and squinted. "Smart one, eh?"

"No, sir. I'm only after helping you with the line here." He waved to the crowd behind him, the bulk of the passengers from the *City of Richmond* who had shared their distinctly cramped quarters from Queenstown.

The fellow nodded at Niamh. "Relationship?"

"I'd be her brother, sir, and Mr. Gill, that is her intended, he paid my way as well."

"And what do you propose doing here in this great country?" The man appeared to be enjoying himself now.

"Coal mining, sir," Patrick said. "Along beside Mr. Gill. He's fixed it already."

The man jotted something more, leaned back and inspected his work, made another mark and twiddled his pen between fat fingers while he looked up. He smiled. Patrick could charm the rainbow off a *luipreachán*.

"See you do your job, then, son, work hard, and make your sister here," he nodded at Niamh, "proud, and you'll be welcome in my country. That way." He pointed, peered around them. "Next!" he hollered. They'd been dismissed.

But not yet finished. A disorderly line had formed, bordered by officials in sack coats and wing tip collars who swirled their hands in a desultory effort to move the line along through a maze of barriers toward an open area ahead. Niamh was minded of her father and brothers at shearing time, guiding the Roscommons into the pens. She let go her breath, hadn't realized she'd been holding it. Not that she particularly wanted to inhale; the malodorous crowd that filled the great be-columned interior of Castle Garden reeked even more than the steerage compartments below decks. With the inquisition finished, she was free to look around her at the vivid collection of humanity that filled the rotunda.

She thought she identified Slavs and Germans, their women in colorful kerchiefs and short skirts that gave a scandalous view of top-boots almost to the knee. Russians sported woolen gray overcoats in spite of the stifling autumn heat that lingered late into the evening. She recognized Italian and Norwegian, languages she'd listened to day and night on the boat and caught the familiar cadence of Scots, the spitting and spluttering of Welsh, the Scouse of Liverpool. It was a babel and a show, more people than she'd seen in one place in all her life.

The great round building loomed large as Binn Dhubh. It was dark when she'd first seen it, coming on eight in the evening when the ferry pulled in close to shore, and it was her first sight of America. Lit up, it was, brilliant lights like the sun spearing the shadows. And the streets as well, lined with poles that held glowing globes turning the night into day. She'd never seen anything like it, not even in Cork or Queenstown. If America could transform the dark, sure it could turn Patrick from a sheep-shearing farm boy into a gentleman of means.

She touched her fingers to her rosary, hidden beneath the bodice of her dress. It had been her grandmother's, made of fine green polished beads with a small heavy silver cross, badly tarnished. Her grandmother felt even farther away now. Niamh had often felt Granny's presence in the fields around Killiny long after she'd passed on and in the churchyard where she lay next to the grandfather who'd died during the lean years. Granny had watched out for them all from the land of the Sidh. But Granny had not yet found her in this new country.

It would indeed be a long wait this night. The outer gates would not be opened until all the passengers had passed through the lines and been sorted, the fortunate ones to be loosed on the city and the unfortunate ones, those with no means of support in this new country, to be penned into a large cage to one side. Niamh dropped her valise to the floor and sat on it. She'd hoped for a space along the wall to lean against, but they were all taken, so many women with babes in arms but also strapping men with beards and dark looks, propped with hands in pockets. Patrick carried two valises, one for his clothing and one with the bedding and utensils they'd required on ship, and he set them next to her with a word about keeping them safe from thieves.

"I've seen nothing of that sort yet," Niamh said. "Though Mrs. Bagnoll told me you'd never see the deed done until too late." She watched as the family of a woman traveling without a husband but with eight children was herded into the pen. She'd wondered, during the trip, whether they'd be allowed in, the gossip was the woman had no means of support over here. Likely she and her brood would be sent right back on the return voyage.

Mrs. Bagnoll's family settled with a great deal of fuss and squabbling in the space next to her, pushing a group of Slavs to the side. They planned to move in with to relatives in a neighborhood called the Bronx, not far from Castle Garden. Niamh wished she were going with them, to be at the end of the journey with only a short walk ahead. Fifteen miles, not hundreds. She hated to say good-bye to them, she'd grown fond of the three daughters through the long hours on the ship. They were bright and curious, cheerful. It would be a relief not to have their mother's voice going without stop day after day, but it was the sound of home and she found she would miss it.

The night hours crawled, and the noise did not abate. Patrick slept through it, curled on the floor with his head on a valise, but Niamh fretted about the next step. She went over Martin's instructions in her head, no need to read them again, she'd read them a thousand times. Walk along the water on the west seven blocks to the railroad station, take the ferry to Jersey City, then the morning train toward Pittsburgh. If they missed the following morning's train, they'd have to stay the day in the station. Her stomach fluttered. It was all so new.

"Anois teacht an Earraigh." She closed her eyes, shut out the crowd, the smells, the sounds. Retreated. *"Beidh an lá dúl chun shíneadh."* Da would sing to her, soft and slow, in the summer evenings as the late light faded.

"English," Patrick murmured. He sat up, hair wild, and glanced around. "It must be English now we're in America." He stood and held out his hand to haul her to her feet. The crowd was astir, the doors opening onto pre-dawn blackness.

"I'll not lose my Irish so soon," she said, but he paid no heed. The excitement in his face was mirrored in those around him. Mothers gathered bundles and infants, fathers hoisted toddlers to their shoulders. A mumur like the rush of a creek swelled, anticipation crackling through the crowd. Weariness forgotten, the long voyage behind them, the mass of immigrants prepared to take their first step onto true American ground.

The first step sent Niamh into a dream world where night was day and the world was mad. Even at this hour the city pulsated, the rattle of horse-drawn carts fading into streets like canyons, the hurrying steps of newsboys with bundles beneath their arms. The doors of Castle Garden opened onto a swath of green, a park-like space lit by the lights of the building behind and by globes lining the streets that bordered it. Patrick scurried across the grass and Niamh followed more slowly, the damp seeping through the thin soles of her boots.

"It isn't gas." He pointed to the fixtures above him. "It must be electricity, surely then?" He stared up in fascination and surveyed the street to left and right. "It's all lit with the electric, Niamh, just fancy!"

"And so it is. They said it would be so." She peered into the dimness at the end of the street. "Turn left," Martin's instructions had said, and to their left water glinted in patches beneath a forest of masts and the shadows of hulking barn-like structures stretching into the river, gaping doors like maws facing the city, massive bulk disappearing into the darkness of the water. She could scent it: like a hound, her nose picked up the smells of garbage and offal, the fusty odor of damp rotting wood and rank fish, and the underlying, barely-there whiff of sea brine. All of it the smell of home, of Kinvara, of the boats her brother built, of the bay and beyond it, the sea.

Patrick hadn't finished. "And will you look there?" He pointed to the far side of the street, craning his neck even more. "Count the floors, will you?" And he did. "One, two … five altogether, five rows of windows and others taller. It's like Cork, it is, but so much grander." A wall of brick and stone faced them and truly the buildings went up to five stories and higher yet farther beyond that. The windows, several of them, were lit as well and Niamh wondered that anyone in America ever slept, so light was the night.

The crowd around the Castle thinned, new arrivals scattering to find their way in the great city, searching out friends, relatives, jobs, a roof, a meal. Niamh's tired head refused to grasp the magnitude of it all, so she concentrated instead on the hollow in her stomach which demanded food, and the hurry in her gut that said they mustn't miss the morning train from Jersey City. Which stood, she knew, on the other side of the river.

"Martin said we must walk along the river there." She tugged at her brother's arm. "Have a care with the valises, we can't afford to lose them now. I'll not arrive at Mr. Gill's without my bedding."

Patrick snorted.

"Ah, don't be thinking that, you know my meaning." She picked up her valise and marched off toward the docks.

Niamh never could remember quite how they did it. Through a fog of exhaustion and wonderment she found the ferry, bought their passage, crossed the river, and boarded the train meant for Pittsburgh, Patrick trailing along and commenting on every new and fantastical sight with the exuberance of the country boy he was. Niamh felt the gulf in their ages much broader than the eight years.

Once aboard the train she slept, knowing Patrick would never shut an eye along the way, so keen he was to see it all. He'd be sure they'd not miss their stop. But her sleep was hampered by the hard wooden seat—someday, when Patrick was a fine gentleman, they would travel first class, on cushioned seats—and her thoughts wove into her dreams and her dreams turned into phantoms from the old fireside tales, and in them Martin stood before her, silent and strange.

She woke when the train stopped in Philadelphia, neck cramped and feet a-tingle. Patrick begged to be allowed to step out onto the platform to see what he might, and she let him go with a warning to stay close and a coin to buy a bite from the hawkers. There were but few coins left; if anything happened that Martin did not meet them at the end of the road, at the place called Connellsville not far from the mines, she and Patrick would be desperate altogether. Oh but they were strong and they would find work, they would, in this grand country, just the two of them. It had been a long while since she'd heard from Martin, just the last letter with the money for the journey and the instructions.

Before that it had been over a year since she'd laid eyes on him, himself sitting in the only good chair in her mother's small front room, hat balanced on his knee, silent and smoking and trying not to stare at her as she tried not to stare out the window. A widower he was, and he confessed, when he asked her hand, that his age was much above hers, though it was only some dozen years, not so wide a gulf as many marriages. He was not ugly, not marked nor deformed in any way, and a woman might be, if not proud to walk beside him, at least content. It's just that she knew so little of him, their conversation when he came courting limited to the weather and the fortunes of those neighbors who'd managed to eke a living from the stony fields by the sea. Nothing about the future or what dreams he had if he had any, nothing about whether God watched over the Irish or whether home rule was reasonable or what the current land wars meant or what was her favorite flower or if he preferred apple tart over bread-and-butter pudding.

None of that. Only that he was a cousin of her father's and her father favored the match. And that he had gone into the mines at Ballingarry when the new landlord raised the rents on Kinvara Estate and ruined old Gill and many others. It was there he learned the mining trade and there he took the notion for America. Then his wife had died, and so he asked Niamh to go with him to America, and she'd said aye but only on the condition that Patrick would be welcome in his household.

He left in the summer of '82. A letter had come to say he'd fetched up in a place called Connellsville, in Pennsylvania, and her father said it was a good sign, a town named for the great O'Connell, the Liberator. Then not a word for eight months, then the money and the directions, and that was more than two months ago. Much could happen in that time. Perhaps he'd changed his mind and married someone else. Perhaps he'd got cold feet, left the mines for the American West and disappeared. She shivered. Perhaps there'd been an accident, and he was dead.

She crossed herself hurriedly and said a Hail Mary. It was a sin, it was, to think such a thing and she surely didn't wish it. She'd chosen him for a husband and it was a fine choice. Their life might be hard at first, but this was America, the golden America, where any man and aye, any woman could fashion a new life and raise a family to be better in every way—better housed, better clothed, better educated. Where a young man like Patrick could be anything he wanted to be, a businessman, a lawyer, a physician, even president of the country like Abraham Lincoln, born, it was said, in poverty such as the Irish knew back home.

Through the grimy window she spotted her brother on the platform. He carried in his cap several small packages wrapped in newsprint. He must have found cabbage rolls or whatever it was this country provided. She smiled at him watching the crowd, his head bobbing back and forth like a baby bird, excitement and joy in every line of his body. His coat was shabby and his trousers too short, but he was a fine-looking boy for all that and the pride of herself and all her family. He would make something of himself over here. She would see to that if she had to marry a dozen Martin Gills she never knew, and a bargain it would be. They would bring over the old folk, then, and maybe the two brothers left at home and maybe someday the brother who'd gone to Australia. Then they'd all be together again. Some day.

They traveled through rolling countryside brilliant with autumn. In Ireland, the colors were mostly low to the ground, the heaths and mosses turning red and ochre and gold, the trees along the river holding their green for the most part, and she loved their fine smoky softness. But here the hues rose to the sky, glorious, like columns of flame reaching for the heavens. The sharp radiance ran up the hillsides as the land rose in rounded ridges into shadow and mist against intense peach and purple. The farmlands, too, were rich with ripened crops or the thick stubble of harvest, fields of pumpkins left behind like great orange cobblestones. Not like the west of Ireland, its poor stony fields good only for sparse grasses and furze and rangy heathers. The houses that flashed past in villages and towns gleamed bright and large, two-storied and glass-windowed, shaming the shabby homes she'd known in Galway.

Then the light faded into crisp darkness and the train sped through a land lit only by a half-moon dipping in and out of cloud banks or the distant flickering glow from a farmhouse window. They changed trains in Greensburg, groggy and disoriented, and by the time they arrived in Connellsville, it was early morning hours, the moon had set and a gray wash tinged the eastern horizon.

He was there, Martin, waiting on the platform in the dark silent village, tall and dressed in his Sunday best, ragged enough but clean. She let out a breath—thought she must have been holding it since New York—of relief and maybe a little disappointment. By noon that day, October 8, 1883, they had seen the priest and were married.

7

Niamh was seven years old when Pádraig was born, and she didn't understand why Mammy kept to her bed with her face turned to the wall for such a long time. Her da said Mammy was sick from the baby and so she, Niamh, must take a hand with the housework and the cooking. She was also to care for the baby, bathe it and rock it, though a neighbor, Mrs. MacInerny, who had just had a healthy girl child and was up and tending the garden two days after, came and fed the child for the first weeks.

The three older boys, Conall and Robert and Aedan, who worked long hours to milk the cows and mind sheep, were big enough to need a great deal of feeding. Niamh's days were toilsome, and she spent a great deal of time stirring the stew pot and mixing the bread. "At least we have bread and stew," Da would say when she complained. "Not like when I was the age of that lad there," he pointed to Robert, "and we had naught but praties to eat and a bit of milk which is more than most had back then."

Da brought in a doctor who could do nothing for Mammy, said she needed to make up her mind herself. Then he brought in the priest, who read over her, but he could do nothing as well. Then he fetched home Biddy Early who lived on the other side of Sliabh Eachtaí, between Freakle and Tulla. She was a shaky, cranky old woman who frightened Niamh when she stepped down from the cart outside the cottage door. But she leaned over Mammy and let a spit fall on her and rubbed it in, then she burned a bit of petticoat in the fire and rubbed the ashes on her. She went away after, on her own, refusing a ride in the pony cart, and Niamh never saw her again. But two days later Mammy sat up and looked around as if she'd been gone for some time, and from then on, she took to her chores as before. Mrs. MacInerny told Niamh that if you spit on a child or a beast it's as good as if you said, "God bless it." There was something strange about spits, but

Niamh thought with her seven-year-old logic that it was the petticoat's ashes that brought her Mammy back.

But Mammy never truly warmed to the baby, Pádraig, and though she fed him and minded him, it was up to Niamh to mother him. It was a task she enjoyed, rocking him to sleep at night, tickling him to make him laugh, teaching him to count his toes and fingers as he grew. She sang for him the ballads she learned at weddings and wakes and at the evening gatherings in neighboring cottages by the turf fires while the men shared their bit of illicit *poitín*. She sang the songs in Irish because that's how she learned them, and as Pádraig grew he picked up the rhythms of the language that was disappearing into remote dells and islands along the western shore.

This was a time of relative calm, the estate of Ireland having been cleared of cottiers by the hunger, the Fenians subdued after 'Sixty-seven. The landlords had supplanted the Irish not with their own English folk but with cows and sheep and pigs, with pasturage rather than with tillage, but enterprising tenants were still able to put together a sizeable leasehold. The small farmers, those such as Pádraig Mór, Niamh's father, had the leisure of a winter's evening to gather in one another's cabins and tell the old tales and always in the Irish. Pádraig Mór Kilgariff saw to it all his children understood the Irish and had at least a bit of the speaking of it, though the National School no longer thought fit to teach it. "Robbed the young ones of their birthright," he'd say, and feisty he was about it when he was in his cups. Her father insisted the older boys accompany him to these *airneán* for the sharing of the *béaloideas*, the folklore and traditions that lived in memory and song alone. But Niamh trailed along whenever she could slip away from chores, and as long as her knitting was in her bag and the number of stockings prescribed daily by her mam completed before the evening was out, no one made objection. Sometimes Mam would come, too, and the other wives, and the women would cluster together in the back room, some with infants, all with knitting or sprigging at hand, for the needlework kept their families in tea and sugar and paid the rents. Niamh listened to the gossip, learned the secrets of the old folk ways, came to know the artful practices women used to manage their men.

When the story-telling began, she would tuck herself into a corner where the shadows flickered, the smell of peat pungent and acrid, black tea in a cup by her side going cool. And in that way, she came to know the stories of the Tuatha Dé Danann and the Fianna, Lugh of the Long Hand and the sons of Tuireann. *Why*, she would wonder as her needles clicked, *would Cian turn himself into a pig and hide from his enemies among the herd? Why didn't he just use his magic rod to turn his enemies into pigs? That's what a woman would do.* But the tale tellers never explained those things.

She loved well the stories told by old Margaret Mulkere, a *seanchaidhe* of renown, who favored the romances of Morrigu the Battle Crow, and Eadon, nurse to poets, and Brigit, a woman of song. Her favorite was the history of Etain who was to be queen in Tara. In her imagination she saw the soft purple cloak edged in silver, felt the swish of a green silk gown against her legs, heard the song of the water as she dipped it from the well. Niamh fingered her own black hair and wished it were in long red-gold plaits like those of the princess. Her needles went silent as she listened to Biddy Mulkere sing-song the speech of the stranger who wooed the lovely Etain.

O beautiful woman, will you come with me to the wonderful country that is mine? The young never grow old there, the fields and the flowers are pleasant to be looking at, there is no care and no sorrow on any person.

To be in such a land, if only she might find it out—

Though the plains of Ireland are beautiful, it is little you would think of them after our great plain. There are treasures of every color in the Gentle Land, sweet music to be listening to, the best of wine to drink. There are three times fifty islands in the ocean to the west of us and every one of them three times more than Ireland.

She liked it best when the men pushed back what little furniture there was, and Thady Gormaly started with his high alto lilt, and Andrew Cahill would beat with a spoon on a wooden bench a cadence that seemed to flow from the ancient hills. The women would put down their needles and shake out their skirts, kick off their shoes, and take to the floor. Bare feet on packed earth beat a rhythm that spoke volumes, more so than any words, fluttering light from lard candles and peat flames transforming the whirling figures into phantoms, graceful and lovely as they never were in life. Niamh would watch from her corner, half asleep, as the figures and the music faded in and out, dreaming of *that tilled familiar land where keening is not used, or treachery, there is nothing hard or rough, but sweet music striking the ear.*

✳

They took the 3:37 train from Connellsville toward Uniontown. Niamh was logy from lack of sleep, Patrick dithery with excitement. When the tracks crossed the Youghiogheny River at White Rock Station, he marveled out loud at the trestle bridge and remarked on every barn and farmhouse. Niamh let him run on though his chatter gave her a headache. Her nerves jittered anyway, with Martin sitting silently next to her, staring straight ahead, pinching the brim of his hat. He'd said very little in the time since they'd first seen each other at the Connellsville station. She'd not been sure she would recognize him, it had been so long, but she did. He seemed smaller and more wiry than she remembered, but his shoulders appeared to be filled out and his hands were ropey with muscle. His thick mustache—she'd never seen his lips—was newly threaded with stiff gray, there were nicks on his cheek and throat that showed a dull razor. He had doffed his hat and ducked his head, hesitated, then leaned in to kiss her cheek and she smelled the oil that coated his thinning hair. She tried a smile but could not quite meet his eyes. He shook hands with Patrick and asked the boy how the trip went; he seemed not to want to address her directly. He picked up her valise, said they'd get a bite of breakfast and then meet the priest at the Catholic church, if that met with her approval.

He had continued silent during the early meal, tea and rolls and bacon, and she thought both of them were relieved that Patrick could not be still, went on about everything he saw in the bustling town, the gas lights, the horse-drawn street cars, the finery on passers-by.

"Lots of money here," Martin finally said when Patrick commented for the fourth time on a flashy coach-and-four forcing its way through the crowd on the street. "Don't expect it to trickle down to us." He smiled, though Niamh thought it more of a grimace.

"Will we live here?" she asked him then. She liked the looks of the place, but not for now would she want to live among all this grandness; she would need to become accustomed to it first. Grow into it. Oh, but that shiny deep blue dress passing by was lovely. Stripes on the jacket and a bustle.

Martin snorted. "Not likely. We live in a place called Youngstown, near the mine and the ovens. Eight, nine miles south of here. We'll take the train, 'twould take all afternoon in a wagon which I'll not have at hand in any case."

Niamh could see Patrick was disappointed, but she was relieved. She understood living in the countryside, even in a small village. She could ease into the ways of this strange, fast country.

The wedding ceremony was brief, the priest kind but distant. The claddagh ring that had been her grandmother's, worn on her left hand with the point out since she'd been promised to Martin, was flipped around, point in, and they were wed. Following that, there had been time for another brief meal, this time soup and bread and tea, little enough as a wedding lunch. Martin seemed embarrassed for funds and counted out coins with care, but Niamh was satisfied.

Now exhaustion crept in and the hypnotic motion of the train lulled her into a stupor so she scarcely noticed the stops at White Rock and Dunbar. She woke in a place called Mt. Braddock Station where the air was thick with grit and smoke. Fire beamed from a row of those odd-shaped ovens that Patrick called bee-hive and Martin said were used to cook the coal into coke. The smoke gathered in the valley of the nameless small creek that ran alongside the tracks, to the point that the sun was blocked out. Or she thought it was smoke. Maybe the clouds had moved in. In any case, the brilliant autumn sunlight had faded and the gold on the hillsides had tarnished.

The fourth stop was a place called Frost's Station which was no more than a platform fed by a dusty road paralleled by a spur of track that disappeared around a low hillock.

"This is it," Martin said without looking at her. He stood and pulled their valises off the overhead rack, handed two to Patrick, and swung Niamh's over his shoulder. He limped a bit with the weight, and she wondered if he'd been hurt in the mine. She busied herself gathering her belongings, her small bag, and the shawl she'd pulled out early that morning against the chill, and didn't think to look about her until they were standing on the platform and the train rolled away.

The smoke was thick. At first, she thought something was afire, the forest or the houses. But Martin was unconcerned, and so she decided it must be coke ovens. The grit that settled on the sleeve of her jacket was not the ash she'd seen from wood fires. They faced east with the lowering sun at their backs. Ahead rose a steep ridge clothed in the brilliant hues of October—golds and reds, the deep green of conifers, and oranges of every hue; the drifting smoke couldn't dim the riot of colors that spread ahead of them. She turned in a slow circle, taking it all in, stunned by the menacing beauty of encircling ridges. This was not County Galway where the land stretched flat and low and wet to hazy distant hills. Even Patrick was quiet. Martin watched them with dark eyes and said nothing. Behind them, on the other side of the tracks, pastureland covered rounded hillocks dotted with grazing cattle. The road ahead was a single dirt lane, dusty from summer drought. It rose gently into a cleft between two higher hills, along a stream that wound its way down from the forested ridge beyond. In the late afternoon shadows, the stream appeared black and murky; a rainbow sheen, oily and unpleasant, floated on the water where it pooled against its banks.

Martin led the way up the road and through the gap. On the other side, a second, smaller valley opened up and the road forked to the right, leading south around the knob of the hill they'd just passed. Here the trees stopped, and a second stream sulked southwest, this one stripped of anything growing. And here was the source of the smoke: two long rows of brick and sandstone ovens, one a double row with ovens back to back. A ramp with tracks slanted to the top of the ovens, mule-drawn wagons loaded with coal plodded across the roofs, empty wagons disappeared down the far side. At every third oven, men with long-handled hoes and forks pulled a glowing heap from the mouth and tossed water over it; others loaded the slag into wheelbarrows and open cars set on a spur of track that ran down the middle of the valley. The hiss and crackle of steam rose and added to the murkiness of the air. Niamh, watching the figures silhouetted in the gloom, thought of a cuckoo clock she'd seen in Queenstown while she waited for the ship. The tiny figures, stiff armed and mechanical, had emerged, bowed, jerked, and retreated again and again.

Along the east side of the valley two benches had been carved into the hillsides, one above the other, paths winding their way at a steep pitch up their sides. Identical houses perched on the benches, like boxcars sidelined in a rail station. In the smoky shadow of late afternoon, they looked grand: two stories, broad porches, painted red or soft gray. And built of wood with shingled roofs, so unlike the white-washed stone and thatch cottages of her tree-starved island home.

Martin nudged her on with a nod of his head toward the lower bench. "That would be ours there, then, the third one in."

"And is it all ours? The entire thing?" Niamh strained to see details in the gathering dusk.

"Ah, no, lass." Martin gave a short laugh. "Just the far side. We have half, two rooms down, two up."

"Oh." Niamh nodded. "That's grand, then."

She could see now the houses were doubles: two front doors, two chimneys, two upper windows. The yard along the front of the houses was packed dirt; between the houses, though, were large garden plots, fenced, with the detritus of the summer's crop littering the ground. Women stood or sat on several of the porches, and now men emerged, too, and children; a crowd gathered on the footpath in front of Martin's house. A fiddle started up, chirping a jig she thought was something about a washerwoman, her da had played it, and for a moment in the deepening dusk lit by the fanciful glow of the ovens, she was home in Killiney, warm and safe and all to rights. The thump of a drum wrenched her back to America, then catcalls and the clang of spoons banging on pots. A crowd appeared round the end of the row, twenty or thirty strong. It surged toward them, young boys racing ahead, back and forth until it engulfed the newly-weds.

"It's the Drag!" Patrick said. "You'll be wed proper then, Nee!"

One of the men handed Martin a bottle, and he took a long swig, handed it on to Niamh. She stared at it, then took a sip herself. The hot liquid burned her throat, made her dizzy, or maybe it was the exhaustion. Faces swirled around her, Irish brogues in her ears, and Welsh, too. She was aware of being danced down the path between two grinning redheads, so like they might be twins. Martin was off in the midst of another group who whistled and clapped him on the back and made rude noises. Patrick disappeared into the crowd.

Then a woman appeared next to her, pushed off the twins, and put an arm around Niamh's shoulders. "It's tuckered you look, dear, and why wouldn't you be? I'm Kate, Kate Byrne. I live in the other half of your house. The boys will have their fun, they've been waiting this day for months. Let them celebrate, and I'll see they don't keep at it long."

Niamh breathed deep and managed a smile. Another woman, younger, appeared at her other side. Niamh thought her name was Ellie, but she couldn't hear well for the noise. Ellie, if it was she, whispered that there would be more, but the rest of the Irish were in the mines or at the ovens in the evening shift; this was just what the day shift could shake loose. Niamh silently thanked the Holy Mother for that small blessing.

"We've a wedding supper for you," Kate said, "since there wasn't a time for the breakfast. You'll be wanting to tell your Mam you were wed in the proper way."

They were at the porch now, and the crowd surged in through the front door, Martin and Niamh in its midst. She first glimpsed her new home between heads and feet and waving hands—it appeared to be lit with oil lamps and freshly whitewashed and scrubbed inside. Furniture was sparse, but it was hard to tell with so many people jammed in. A long table made of sawhorses and planks ran the length of the inside wall. It was covered with crockery full of potatoes and slaw, bacon and bread. She saw a roasted fowl, goose possibly, and fried chicken before the twins fetched her, lifted her off her feet and placed her in a rocking chair raised on a low platform. She feared the platform would collapse, it was so plainly cobbled together out of scrap.

Martin was next to her in a wooden ladder-backed kitchen chair, a bottle in hand and a grin on his face that she had never seen before. He waved the bottle at someone in the back and hollered "Play us a tune!" before upending it and polishing it off. A young girl stood behind her and she felt something fall into her hair. She recoiled. At first she thought it must be insects dropping from the ceiling, but it was bread crumbs that cascaded over her shoulders—breaking the bread over the bride's head; she'd watched it done herself at weddings back home. She let herself breathe.

The fiddle and the drum sounded from the porch and already one or two couples were dancing where there was scant room to dance. Plates of food went from hand to hand, and Niamh found a platter in her lap filled with more food than she could eat in a week. Martin's chair was empty; he was in a corner with a full plate in one hand, another bottle in the other, and a crowd of burly men around him.

Through the open door and window onto the porch, Niamh could see the sun had disappeared, and the dark and smoke in the valley were lit by the glow of ovens, flickering out of sight below the bank of houses like flashes of silent lightning. In the doorway appeared a fantastical figure, the head a cone of straw. Straw protruded from wrists and neck and trouser legs. The apparition peeked around the door, ducked back, then slid into the lamplight and stood, motionless. A second one crept in behind it, then a third. She shuddered; it felt like a spider had crawled over her heart.

"Strawboys," she heard. The scene began to fade at the edges; she was nearly asleep. "Strawboys!" someone close by called out and the fiddler started up again with a tune even livelier than before. One of the figures moved toward her, another toward Martin, and then she was in the middle of the room with a straw-encrusted arm around her, poking into her back, scratching her bare neck, making her sneeze. The strawboy danced her up and down the short length of the room, out the front door, onto the porch and back again, clumsy enough. Another danced Martin in circles, a mug of cider held high and spilling across the bystanders. Someone rang a cowbell and a clamor arose. Sweat dribbled down Niamh's cheeks, muddying the straw dust. She gasped; it took all her wits to keep to her feet. Then she was back in her chair, not remembering how that happened, and someone handed her a cup of something strong. She took a sip to be polite and closed her eyes. *Fágaim le huacht é, go n-éiríonn mo chroí-se, Mar a éiríonn an ghaoth, nó mar a scaipeann an ceo*, she murmured to herself. After that they left her alone.

Later, much later, she awoke to deep stillness and darkness. The reek of spilled cider rose from the floorboards, an owl hooted from somewhere close by. The only light in the room was from the glow of the coal stove in the kitchen just visible through the connecting door. She was on her back on a straw tick, rough sheets beneath her, and Martin's face hung over her, inches away. His eyes were closed and he was puffing and grunting, and she felt him shoving into her in that secret place. She knew what it was about, she'd grown up on a farm, and her mates at home had told tales and conjectured. She'd hoped it would be grand. She hadn't thought it would be like this.

8

When the treacherous waves of winter calmed, the *leathbhád* ferried peat across the bay from Barna, west of Galway to Kinvara. Though the western waters, even inside the mouth of Kinvara Bay, rarely stilled entirely, and the horses of the sea were said to dance as boisterously in spring as in the heart of winter. Niamh often wandered to the harbor edge in the village, Pádraig in tow, to watch the boats come in, crimson sails against a leaden sky. Not just the loads of peat but the herring and cod, turbot, clams and mussels. Gulls shrieked overhead, dove in and out among the masts, fought their own battles over scraps and offal and the occasional whole herring thrown to ward them off.

Niamh loved to find the rare spot of sunlight against a white-washed wall, her empty net shopping bag at her feet, Pádraig poking into nooks and crannies with the endless curiosity of a small boy. She would close her eyes and breath deep, taking in the sharp smells of salt water and fish, the lovely sour smell of turf burning in a dozen stoves and fireplaces. And she'd listen to the ruckus of the bayside, the calls of women greeting their men home from the sea, the barking of dogs, the never-satisfied gulls.

She would rouse herself when the bustle began to subside, take Pádraig's hand and fill her bag with fresh herring wrapped in paper from Dan O'Rourke's stand on the dock, pay her respects to Mrs. Hanrahan at the bakery, and tuck away a loaf of brown bread and sometimes, for a treat, *bairín breac* heavy with sultanas and raisins. Then she and Pádraig would wend their way home through the lanes and the fields, under vast crowds of cloud or wide blue skies. The fields, impossibly green and dotted with white flecks of sheep, stretched on either side of the lane to disappear in mist. To the east the hazy foothills of the Slieve Aughty Mountains hovered. Halfway home the land roughened, the gray stone outposts of the Burren intruding into the farmland, bordering the fens and bogs too wet for pasturage. In spring the meadow pipits and skylarks went about their mating, clouds of early dam-selflies burst from fen mosses and sedges lining the edges of the bog. Turf cutters silhouetted against the leaden sky swung *sleáns* in rhythm, tossing turves, black and dense over their shoulders, pulling the ancient vegetation, compressed into peat, from deep in the earth for fuel to warm their evenings.

It was a place for the *daoine sídhe,* the fairy people, the fallen angels, those not good enough to be saved nor bad enough to be lost. For keeping a wary eye out for the *púca* and the *uaisle.* "Up the airy mountain, down the rushy glen," she would sing to Pádraig, and he would search beneath rocks and thorn trees for evidence. Often as not he found elf-stones and fairy-darts, stones with the tracks of fairy fingers that were said to cure a cow or keep its milk from bewitchment. Mam would scoff at him and tell him to throw them away, but Niamh knew he kept them hidden away in the sheepcote. By the time they reached the cottage in Killinny, Pádraig and she were both hollering at the tops of their lungs, "Wee folk, good folk, trooping all together; green jacket, red cap, white owl's feather!"

The fairies, she soon discovered, had not followed her to America. But she searched for traces anyway in the fields and foothills to the west of the grimy patch town. Patrick laughed at her and she laughed back, saying only that wouldn't it have been nice to be real, those fancies of childhood? Martin was, as usual, silent but he smiled, sometimes, listening to their chatter. She hoped he was pleased that she recalled the tales from home, that he enjoyed hearing them.

"I always thought America was the isle from the poem, would you be remembering, Patrick, the isle of the blest," she said. "'*From year unto year on the ocean's blue rim, the beautiful spectre showed lovely and dim.*' It's all I can bring to mind."

"As I remember, the isle keeps receding in the distance. The sailor dies at sea, never gets there," Martin said. He lifted a branch of hemlock so Niamh could pass. It was late October, no more than two weeks since they'd arrived, and already he and Patrick had worked twelve ten-hour shifts deep in the mine. They worked the second shift, mid-afternoon until after midnight, had the mornings free. Patrick was ever up by nine and restless to explore, though Martin often slept late. But this morning he surprised them both by asking, diffidently, to accompany them on their walk, and Niamh was delighted.

"'*And he died on the waters, away, far away!*' That's how it ends, anyway." Patrick turned back the way they came and shaded his eyes. "This late in the year, the sun doesn't come up over the ridge very early."

"And isn't that different from home?" Niamh turned in a slow circle, took in the hills in either direction, east and west. To the south, a small cemetery crowned the next knoll over, shaded by a young oak tree at the far corner. To the northwest ridges of soft green and fading oranges and golds rose rank on rank. "At home the fields are flat as a stone floor and the sun up with the robins."

Martin laid a hand on her hair. She started and he drew back; he had rarely touched her except in the bed. "And are you so homesick, *mo chroí?*" His eyes were soft.

She watched Patrick start down the hill, into a cleft where the trees and brush began. There were tears inside her, but she would not let them spill. She turned back to her husband. "Not so very much."

But she was.

9

March 1884

Rebecca stood at the stove in Agnes's kitchen frying up chicken. How she kept her sleeves free from grease spots Harry could not figure out. He watched her out of the corner of his eye and sliced into his finger instead of into a carrot for his trouble. It bled profusely—he squeezed it to be sure it would—and he let Rebecca fuss. Dan took over the carrots while she wrapped gauze around the wound.

"Who does this for you when you're away at college?" She tied off the ends and flicked her nail against the thick padding. "You've been gone three years and still can't be trusted with a kitchen knife."

"The landlady takes care of all that." Harry was tall enough now to look down at the top of her head, at the rich chestnut hair coiled into a knot. "And besides, only one more term and I'll be back here for good. With all these women around to take care of kitchen chores."

Over the past several years she'd softened, grown tall and slender, though she still pushed her way through crowds. She'd never be plump; Harry figured it was because she never stood still long enough for flesh to attach itself to her bones.

His mother sat at the kitchen table totting up a long column of figures on a lined green pad. She wore her blue silk wrapper and her hair was loose; a coffee cup sat at her elbow and a dish with the remains of a biscuit next to that.

She muttered, wrote a figure, scowled and erased. "Quiet, children. I can't think with you chattering."

Rebecca hushed and returned to the chicken, but Dan grinned. "Need some help, Miss Agnes?" He peered over her shoulder.

"I don't believe I need your help, thank you, Dan." She erased again and ran her pencil down the page. "Ah—there it is." She made a note and dropped the pencil. "Rebecca, when you have a minute, would you check these for me?"

Dan laughed and leaned against the counter, filching a carrot from Harry's pile. "Becky's still the one with the math brain."

Rebecca wiped her hands on her apron and handed a fork to Dan. "Here, be sure that chicken doesn't burn or there'll be no picnic lunch for you." She dropped in the chair and picked up the pad. She could add a column of figures in her head faster than anyone Harry knew.

Agnes stood. "I'm off to get dressed, then to the office. Harry, I'm showing a home on Gallatin Street today, but I'll be back for dinner." She reached up to kiss him on the cheek. "You two are invited, of course. Don't be late, Mattie's bringing Mr. Murray."

Harry's head snapped up. "Murray?"

"*Mr.* Murray. Be polite." She disappeared up the stairs.

"Murray," Harry muttered. He wrapped carrots in a kitchen towel and tucked them into his rucksack. Rebecca folded the chicken into newspaper, and Dan took charge of Mattie's famous walnut cake. They were headed for the family cemetery beyond the old farmhouse so Harry could pull weeds and mend the fence and trim the grass. Rebecca liked to plant flowers in the spring, and Dan tended to stretch out in the sunshine and tell the others what to do. It had become a ritual the past three years when Harry came home for a week every March between college terms, a way to clear the cobwebs left behind from his classes in Morgantown. And it never hurt to have Rebecca and Dan trail along.

The cemetery itself was a beautiful place, unless the wind blew from the east and brought the smoke and soot from the coking ovens. It overlooked the western valley, the pastures greening up, the oat fields waiting for the plow. It was still too early to plant flowers, so Rebecca tackled the dandelions which knew no season. Dan propped himself against Harry's grandfather's headstone and dug into the chicken, though it was not yet eleven.

"So Murray's still squiring your Aunt Mattie around." Dan picked up a drumstick.

Rebecca batted at his hand. "Stay out of that, you'll spoil your lunch." She set the rest of the chicken out of reach, eyes on Harry. "How's the sparking going?"

Harry made a rude noise. "What Mattie sees in the man, I don't know. He's old and fat and loud."

"And rich and generous and she's forty. He's not much older than she is."

"Do you remember," Harry said, "we saw him at the mine that time? When Frost caught us inside?"

"My father would skin me alive if he knew we'd gone in there." Rebecca levered out a massive taproot and waved it. "Look at this one—it'd feed a family of four."

"I remember he called us children," Dan said.

"Mattie would be smart to marry him." Rebecca sat back on her heels and threaded dandelion stalks into a chain. "Your mother and aunts won't be able to work forever. He's rich enough to support them all."

Harry grimaced at the broken tombstone he was trying to set on its base. "That's my job."

"You'll need to do something besides teach school, then." She tossed a clump onto her pile. "Not much money there to support six elderly ladies and your own family."

Dan glanced around as if Harry's progeny were romping on the hillside already. "Assuming he ever manages one. He needs to meet girls, first. You're the only one he knows."

Rebecca snorted, which gave Harry a good idea of what she thought of being the mother of his children.

She dropped the dandelion chain and unwrapped the carrots. "He would be a good man to know when it comes time to find a profession."

"Which, I'll remind you, will be in a few short months." Dan hurled the chicken bone far down the hill. "You can always read law with me. We can go partners. Or get a foot in the door of the coal business. You'll be living in a Pittsburgh mansion before you know it."

"Yes indeed, right alongside Frick and Carnegie." Harry brushed at his hands and dropped to the ground. He wasn't very hungry. "I don't think much of the coal industry. Look what it's done to the valley over there."

"Once we're lawyers we can take 'em to court."

Rebecca laughed. "For what? For making money? For keeping people warm in the winter?" She handed Harry a napkin. "You don't mind the mess they make when it's ten degrees in January and you can read your law books without getting frostbite."

They fell quiet, munching and sprawling in the deceptive warmth of the early March sun. A raspy *fee-bee* sounded overhead and Harry rolled onto his back. The fat little male sat half-way up the white pine shadowing the cemetery, twitching its tail, keeping a beat to its song, checking for rival males. He was the first Harry had seen, a sure sign of real spring. There were robins already, too, a flock spread over the hillside in a search for earthworms still sluggish from the winter. Tomorrow might bring a blizzard, so unreliable was the weather in these hills. The warmth of today was easily lost to the chill of night and the deep-freeze of tomorrow. And then they'd surely be glad of the comfort provided by a sizzling coal furnace.

The farmhouse appeared more dilapidated every time he saw it. The smoke and dirt that blew when the wind came from the east lodged black dust into every crevice. Hard as she tried, Joanna could not keep the windows from filming over with an oily residue or the porches swept of grit. She'd resisted moving into town when the others went, laughed at Mary who grumbled about Irish and hunkies and other undesirables in the Patch town over the hill. "I like my neighbors," she'd say, "I can hear the children laugh even over here."

In her quiet way, Joanna loved the old farmstead and its musty memories. She oversaw the lease of what land was left and the income it brought in, a major part of the sisters' support. She should have been a man, Harry often thought, and she must have thought so as well. She even dressed in men's trousers to do what little farm work was left to her, caring for the buggy horse, the milk cow, the chickens, the garden. She'd pull her well-grayed hair into a messy knot, leave her leathery and lined face exposed to the sun. Soon she'd be forced to move into town, but she told Harry she was determined to put that day off until her fifty-some-year-old joints gave out.

"Your mother's house is more crowded than it was before you went off to college," she said now. Harry and Dan dug into the garden bed, turning in manure. Joanna could get peas and lettuce in soon, maybe spinach. "You're welcome to stay out here for the summer, if you'd rather. All those aunts can get tiresome."

Harry grinned at her. "I just might do that. But Mother expects me to work in town and make some money. It'll be simpler if I live there. I can make myself scarce."

"You can always stay with us," Dan said. "The way people come and go at our house, Ma'll never notice."

"It's only for the summer, anyway." Harry shrugged. "I'll need a regular job next fall. Then I'll get my own place."

Joanna leaned on her hoe and glanced at the house. Rebecca was safely out of earshot, working on a dried-peach pie which was her contribution to that evening's dinner. "You'll be married before spring."

Harry turned red. "Not a chance. She's like my sister. Besides, she's always liked Dan best."

"She's like my sister, too," Dan said. "We can draw for her, high card wins."

"I think your mother is counting on it." Joanna narrowed her eyes.

Harry jabbed his spade in deep. "Mother's never said anything like that."

Joanna laughed. "If she's smart, she'll look to one of those Seaman boys. They'll make something of themselves."

"Like Mattie and Murray." Harry turned the last shovelful and worked apart the sticky clods. "Doing what everyone expects."

Joanna smoothed a row with the blade of the hoe. "There are certainly advantages."

Joanna hitched the placid Mona to the buggy for the ride into town; she and Rebecca rode while Dan walked alongside, entertaining the women with stories of his father's more absurd patients and their rich folks' ailments. Harry trailed along, paid no mind. He thought about what Joanna had said, that his mother was counting on his marrying Rebecca. That was a surprise to him. His mother, when she talked about his future, talked about a career and where he might live. She also mentioned he might like to travel before he settled down, maybe into the West, maybe even Europe. But he knew she assumed he would return to Uniontown from wherever he traveled, marry a local girl, and raise a houseful of children. She just never mentioned who her candidate for the role of his wife might be.

He always figured Rebecca for Dan anyway, something which had rankled once upon a time. Now when he thought about her in that way, which was rare, she seemed like old slippers. Too comfortable. There had to be something more.

He watched Rebecca now. She and Joanna kept up a running commentary on Dan's stories. She was perfectly comfortable with his family, as was Dan.

That's just the way it was in Uniontown, families grew up together, went to church and school together, married each other, blended and increased and buried each other. At least those families that formed the heart of the town, mostly the ones who'd sprung from the early settlers. Sure, there were Negroes and a few new people from parts of the world that spoke a different language, even the occasional Indian like Hanasaw Gibson who did odd jobs for the Canon sisters. But they were servants and laborers. Most of the outsiders lived in patch towns throughout coal country and kept to themselves. Many of the eastern Europeans stayed only until they made enough money to buy a farm back home, declining to be absorbed, unlike the Protestant Irish and English and Welsh who came over in the last century.

Rebecca caught him looking at her and smiled.

No, he would marry, if not Rebecca, someone like her, probably someone he already knew or would soon meet from the surrounding towns. Nothing exciting there, no adventure. The days of roaming the wild empty lands to the west were gone, died with Custer almost a decade ago. He'd always thought he'd like to have lived during his father's time, when the gold fields were raw and the trip across the plains was a gamble and a dare. Where he just might meet a woman—the way his father had—whose own sense of audacity matched his, and they would join up to explore…

Dan snapped his fingers in Harry's face. "Anyone home?" They were staring at him.

"Where were *you*?" Rebecca was laughing.

"In the clouds, I suspect," Dan said. "He can be a dreamer."

Joanna smiled at him. "Dreams are good, Harry. Don't ever let them go." She pulled the horse to a stop in front of his mother's house. "And now, you two take care of Mona and get cleaned up. Dinner will be ready, and the family appears to be gathered."

The family, waiting at home, providing an anchor. A good feeling. Usually.

10

Everything that happened to Harry that year started at dinner that night at his mother's house. The dining room was full, all six sisters, Mr. Phillip Murray and Harry, Rebecca and Dan. A great deal of speculation around the breakfast table earlier in the week led up to the planning of this dinner (once Mattie had left the house). Sarah anticipated an announcement from Murray and Mattie about the future. Mary insisted nothing of the sort would happen, and if it did she for one would be very unhappy to see a stranger permanently introduced into the family. Murray was a catch, Sarah declared, half the unmarried women in town had been angling for the attention of the managing partner of the Youngstown Mine & Coke Works. He could have chosen a much younger companion. And hadn't he just bought a plot of land on Ben Lomond Street to build his mansion? And from Agnes, as estate agent?

"All he wants is a housekeeper." Mary sniffed, her lips puckered.

"I think it's romantic," Elizabeth whispered, but no one paid her any mind.

The dining room in Agnes's house on Fayette Street was Harry's favorite room, painted a warm cream that soaked in the sun's rays from the west and filled with the always-enticing smells from a kitchen graced by Elizabeth's talents as a cook and Mattie's as a baker. His great-grandmother's silver service, a prized possession of the sisters, shone from the sideboard, and the heavy mahogany table, made by an uncle many years ago, stood swathed in lace and set with old and discreetly chipped china.

Elizabeth and Mary hauled platters through the swinging kitchen door; the sisters had gone all out. There was a roast goose as if it were Christmas, golden and moist, nestled on a bed of greens and small onions. Harry smelled cider gravy and garlic stuffing. Rebecca, wrapped in Mary's bib apron, held a bowl of potatoes in the crook of her arm, still whipping the daylights out of them. The scent of Mattie's apple cake leaked from the kitchen in heady competition with the pungent garlic and onions. Murray stood with a glass of whiskey in hand. Dan, who had helped himself to a glass, entertained him, which was the deal Harry had extracted on the walk into town. Harry wanted no part in playing the host. Dan was reminding Murray of the incident at Frost's mine, years ago. Murray had the good grace to chuckle; Harry thought it sounded forced.

Harry was more intent on watching Mattie. Mattie gave no sign that she and Murray would make an announcement. Or even that they were aware of the speculation. Harry suspected she got a huge kick out of stringing her sisters along and intended to keep it up for awhile. Now she snorted at Dan's story.

"Harry never told us that." She grasped Harry's elbow and pulled him close. "I can see you two as Huck and Tom, rafting down Redstone Creek."

"Did he ever tell you about the time we spent the night out at Jumonville waiting for the French ghosts to show up?"

"Dan—" Harry said.

"No, he didn't. I'd love to hear that one, but it will have to wait," Mattie said. "Dinner appears to be ready."

"Pray sit here, Mr. Murray." Sarah pulled out the chair at the head of the table where the goose sat moist and golden and waiting for the knife. Harry stole a look at Mary who shot her sister daggers; as eldest, she usually presided. Sarah appeared oblivious.

"And Mattie, you sit here next to him," she said. Mattie rolled her eyes at Harry. Murray held the chair for her. He was a solid man, his waistcoat straining just a bit at the buttons, his beard long enough that it parted at the tip, two small wings pointing away in either direction, his cheeks florid. He had a high forehead and sandy hair cut close and precise. Harry remembered his eyes, the way one seemed to wander off on its own.

"Do sit," Agnes said, "while it's all hot."

Murray sat and flourished the carving knife. "Shall I do the honors?"

Harry rolled his eyes. *As if he already owns the family.*

"Yes, of course." Agnes pulled out a chair at the table's side and sat, leaving her usual place at the foot for Mary. Mary, casting black looks around the table, took it.

"Now then," Murray said once all were seated. "Who gets the first slice?" He beamed at the sisters and Harry.

"Grace first," Mary said. Harry thought she clenched her teeth.

"Oh, of course." Murray set down the knife and bent his head, winking at Harry, who sat to his left. Harry pretended he didn't see him.

"Elizabeth, I believe it's your day."

Elizabeth bent her head and folded her hands. "*Be present at our table, Lord. Be here and everywhere adored. These mercies bless and grant that we may feast in fellowship with Thee. Amen.*"

"Ah, the Wesleyan grace." Murray picked up the knife again, dug it into the goose. "Very nice. Thank you, Miss Elizabeth."

Harry looked across the table at Rebecca; she glanced back and raised her brows. Dan, next to her, had his teeth sunk into his lower lip, a sure sign he was struggling not to laugh. This was not going well.

"Yes," Mary said. "We are Methodists. And you, Mr. Murray?"

"Well, to be truthful, Miss Canon, I haven't yet settled on any particular church here in Uniontown. Perhaps I'll take the opportunity to drop in on the Methodists soon."

No one said anything. *They're all wondering, why he hasn't already chosen a denomination. You'd think he'd know his religion by now.* It didn't much matter to Harry, but Mary would be quick to judge a lapsed Protestant.

Murray sawed away at the goose, hit a bone with a squeal, and ignored the way Mattie winced.

"Take this one, son." Murray dropped a thick piece of breast meat on Harry's plate. It was half again bigger than Harry could eat.

"I understand," Mother said, "that the coke market is not picking up."

Sarah waved her fork. "Who do you think, Mr. Murray, will be the better man for president? To shore up the markets?"

"Harry," Mary said, "pass Mr. Murray the potatoes."

Harry reached for the bowl. Murray dropped a portion on his plate and flooded it in gravy. He opened his mouth, but Mattie spoke up. "I think Blaine is the man, finally."

"But he's corrupt," Mother said. "I hear the New York governor is being mentioned as an honest man. Cleveland."

Murray's head went back and forth among the women. He opened his mouth again, but Sarah grimaced. "'*Why, you are so fat, Sir Grover, that you must needs be out of all reasonable compass, Sir Grover.*'"

Dan choked into his water glass.

"We needn't be talking politics when we have a guest." Mary frowned.

"Fat doesn't necessarily mean incapable. Certainly, I'll take fat over corrupt," Agnes said.

"Joanna knows about all that," Elizabeth whispered.

"What does she know?" Sarah forked a stack of candied carrots.

"She knows all about the candidates and the parties and all." Elizabeth's face reddened.

"I haven't paid any attention." Joanna took a bite and shook her head.

"I've heard something about the governor's morals," Sarah said with a look at Mary. "That there may be a child. And he a *bachelor.*"

"Sarah!" Mary set her knife on her plate with a snap. "For pity's sake, do watch your words!"

Sarah sputtered. Mattie said, "Well, if that's so, then he'll be hard put to win over the wives." She wiggled her eyebrows at Rebecca. "And we all know who husbands listen to when it comes time to vote."

Murray twitched at that.

"Really?" Mother looked up. "I hadn't heard that. If that's true, and the preachers have their way, he won't get near the nomination."

"The preachers have no business preaching politics in the pulpit." Mattie said. "They shouldn't be passing judgment on—"

"Ladies! Let us have no such discussions at table. It's not fit conversation for young people."

They all turned to look at Rebecca.

"I don't mind," she said. "I think it's interesting."

"We're old enough to talk politics." Harry straightened. "And the morals of politicians."

Murray, who had as yet to get his opinion wedged into the conversation, saw his chance and jumped in, though he'd just taken a bite of goose. "I can't imagine you ladies would need to concern yourselves—"

Harry looked around the table. What would it be like, he thought, to be inside someone else's head? Sarah for example. Now she's cutting her meat into tiny pieces, now she glances at Murray from under her lashes. What is it like to be Sarah? Is she afraid to die? Does she think about dying the way I do? You never really stop to think about what the I-ness of another person is like. And why do they all talk at once? What's important about what they're saying? Why do they bother? Who *were* these people?

And then he thought they all sounded like cackling geese, and he wondered what might be in the mind of a goose at such a moment when every other goose in the flock was making noise. Does a goose think about being separate from the other geese? Everything he'd read said animals aren't aware but how do we know that?

Something prodded him in the ribs; he blinked and shook his head. Rebecca poked him a second time.

"You're dreaming again," she whispered. "What on earth were you thinking?"

He looked glanced around the room. "I was wondering if a goose knows it's alive," he said.

The bell at the front door jangled.

"Oh, for the love of—" Mother laid down her napkin and stood. Mr. Murray pushed his chair back and half rose, but she waved at him.

"Sit, sit. Who on earth can be so rude as to knock at the dinner hour?" She disappeared into the front hallway, only to return shortly and say to Murray, "It's for you."

He went to the door. "What is it, Dawkins? You're interrupting dinner."

Mattie shifted in her chair at his tone.

The messenger's voice was too low for them to hear what he said but they heard Murray's response.

"Just the one killed?"

"Eep," said Elizabeth. Mattie gasped. Mary pursed her lips. The others craned to peer into the front room.

The boy said something else and Murray said, "Damn careless." And "I'll be there soon as I can." The door closed.

Murray returned to the table and sat. He picked up his coffee cup and took a forkful of potatoes at the same time, in no hurry. He smiled at the women.

"There's no sense in letting this excellent meal go to waste." He took the bite.

"Mr. Murray." Agnes peered at him. "Someone's been killed."

"Another accident," he said, his mouth full. He swallowed. "Roof caved in on a fellow who should have known better." He turned to Harry. "How about you boys go along out to the mine with me? Could be interesting."

Harry looked at his friend. Dan nodded, enthusiastic.

"Yes sir." Harry stood.

"You be careful." Mattie fidgeted with her napkin. "If the roof is falling in …"

Murray smiled at her. "We won't be going down in the mine. I leave that for the inspector. My job is to be sure the company isn't at fault."

"It never is," Agnes said.

11

By the time they left the house, the sun had sunk into the Mononga-hela Valley, and the breeze was up, the spring evening chilly. Murray's buggy horse dozed in a pool of gaslight. He turned the reins over to Harry; it was a two-seated phaeton and Dan, throwing Harry an aggrieved look, climbed onto the rumble seat behind. They drove east on Fayette Street, across Redstone Creek, and out of town on the Connellsville Road toward Youngstown. The road ran along the foot of the hills to the east, dark and cloaked in heavy stands of hardwoods just beginning to leaf out. Beyond it, Chestnut Ridge loomed, black against a not-quite-dark sky. Off to the right, in the hills beyond the B&O tracks, a glow rose from a vale like the mouth of a volcano, flickering and spitting, the coke ovens of Lemont Furnace working the evening shift. Harry wondered if they'd heard the news of yet another death. Murray lit up a cigar and didn't speak.

They turned off the road north of Lamont and into a small valley en-closed between a cluster of low hills to the west and the steeply rising ridge to the east and into Youngstown.

"You can pull up over there." Murray pointed toward a squat wooden building to the south. "That's the superintendent's office. We'll start there."

The last time Harry had been on this side of the valley, years ago, thick woods and underbrush blanketed its floor. All that had disappeared, and the superintendent's shack sat at the head of a barren stretch of land along a railroad spur. A bank of brick beehive structures lit up the night with a bloody glow. Above the ovens, halfway up the ridge to the east, the slope had been carved into terraces, a scar slashed into what had been a dense stand of hardwoods climbing the hill. Double houses loomed in the lurid light. Though stars had begun to emerge as they drove along the road, in this valley there were none; they were blocked by smoke, puffing white against the night sky. Harry's throat grew scratchy and he fought an urge to cough. It seemed strange to him that one fuel would be burned to make another, but that was what they did here, burned coal to make coke, a superior fuel for the steel mills. A teacher had once brought a lump of coke into class; it was gray and rough, while raw coal was deep black with a sheen on flat surfaces. Worth its weight in gold, the teacher said. But not really; worth about a dollar a ton, yet worth more than a man's life.

When they arrived, the yard was lit with lanterns and torches carried by dozens of men and women. Harry steered the horse and buggy between them, and they grew silent, backing away, watching, their faces unreadable in the shadows. He heard Dan thump to the ground from behind and in a moment his friend was at the horse's head, leading it through the crowd toward the lighted building. "Is the mine entrance still up at Frost's?" Harry asked.

"A quarter mile that way, other side of the hill," Murray said, ignoring the gathered workers. He waved the cigar stub toward the north. "The mine itself stretches south and west toward Bethelboro." Toward the farmhouse. Harry had always known the valley was honeycombed with mines, but now he was struck with the idea of a hidden world, dark and alien, eating into the center of the earth, buried beneath the familiar fields.

Murray led the way inside as the crowd closed in behind them. Harry and Dan had to elbow their way through to keep up. The office consisted of one big room, cramped with desks and a counter, stacks of papers everywhere, maps pinned to the walls, coal and coke samples littered on every flat surface, a spittoon, and a pot-bellied wood stove going strong. Its heat and the presence of a half dozen men turned the small space into another oven. A fine black powder coated the crevices and surfaces, and the smoke from both the stove and the coke ovens choked the air.

"Look there," Dan whispered, pointing into the room's center. It took Harry a moment to realize that the desks, pushed together under a hanging lantern, held a body. It was covered by an oilskin and two rough gray blankets.

"Thanks for coming, Mr. Murray." A stocky man, lips hidden behind ragged moustaches, separated himself from the group and put out his hand. Murray shook it and introduced Harry and Dan. Superintendent Keighley appeared to be in early middle age, but there was gray in his hair and black dust in the creases of his neck. His eyes held a pained look and his clothes—

open-necked shirt, canvas trousers, shapeless plaid jacket—were caked and filthy.

"Come to see the show, did you?" someone said.

"Let him be, Cole," the superintendent said, his voice weary.

"Let's have a look." Murray turned to the body and lifted the blanket. The man's head was crushed, nothing human left. Harry looked away, hoped he wouldn't puke right there in front of Murray and all these men. Dan drew in breath and gulped, his face green behind his freckles. Harry jammed his hands in his pants pockets to hide the trembling and leaned against the wall, as far from the body as he could get. Dan, son of a doctor, sent him a sympathetic look, but moved closer to the table.

Harry's ears buzzed and he became aware of another noise, one he hadn't registered at first. A snuffling sound came from the corner, and it dawned on him that someone was crying. A woman. Of course. The wife would be here. You'd think they would protect her from that sight, but he supposed she had a right. She huddled on a chair next to the stove, a second woman kneeling beside her, holding her hand and talking low. The wife was young, no older than Harry, pale-haired and thin-faced. Her belly protruding roundly through her thin dress. The woman next to her caught the light. It gleamed off hair as black as Harry had ever seen, black and shiny like virgin coal in the flicker from the lanterns. Her profile showed an upturned nose, a strong chin, and clear delicate skin—an anomaly for women who'd spent any time at all in a Patch town.

The black-haired woman stopped talking and turned to listen to the men. Her eyes were quick, darted from one face to another. He felt their heat all the way across the room.

"What happened?" Murray lifted the blanket and peered down the length of the body.

"Stupid and careless," Keighley said. "Went in to fix up a flat heading. He knew that roof wasn't secure, there were lots of posts right there, he could have shored it up."

"Killed him right away," Cole added. "Near cut him in two. Every rib broken, legs and arms. Mangled."

There was a groan from the corner. The black-haired woman jumped to her feet and whirled on the men, hands jammed on her waist. "Stop it," she hissed. "Just bloody stop it! You'll be tearing the poor woman to shreds with your claver. Where's your decency, man?"

Harry nodded. *Good for you.* She was Irish by her accent; the race was known for temper.

Keighley looked pained. "Mrs. Gill, if you would be so kind as to take Mrs. Finnell home now. She'll want to go with her husband in the morning back to Morgantown."

"You'll be putting him in a decent coffin then, like she asked, will you?"

"Yes ma'am, I've got some men working on it now."

"And you'll have it lined, like she wanted?"

"Mrs. Gill."

The woman turned to her friend who was openly sobbing now and helped her to her feet. She threw one more look over her shoulder—*God save me if anyone ever sends me a look like that,* Harry thought—and hurried her charge out the door. Harry pulled the door closed against the straining crowd.

"She's a feisty one," Murray said.

"She's new." Keighley shrugged. "Come over from Ireland to marry one of the micks. Hasn't learned her manners yet."

"So, you're sending him to Morgantown?"

"He has kin there, seemed best. The wife'll stay down there with them, and we'll get his house without having to evict her. Easier all around."

"You heard from Stinner yet?"

"I sent a wire. He should be here tomorrow."

"What'll he say?"

"Oh, he'll say it was Finnell's fault. Everyone knows he should have propped that roof, even his mates down there said so. No one's going to blame the company."

"All right, good." Murray lifted the corner of the oilskin and took one last look at the ruins of the man's head. He seemed intrigued by it. Then he dropped the cover and turned.

"Well, Harry, Dan, we've done about all we need to here." He shook hands with Keighley and Cole while the other men looked on. None of them had said anything.

"Who's Stinner?" Dan asked when they'd returned to the buggy. Harry, silent, handed him the reins and made his way to the rear.

"Mine inspector. He'll come down and take a look, be sure the company had all the safety rules in place."

Harry climbed onto the rumble seat, his back to the leather hood of the phaeton. He craved solitude.

"Was he the one who told you to use safety lamps after the miner was killed in December?" Dan's voice was faint, muffled by the heavy night air.

"He was. We didn't think it was necessary, not all the time anyway. Still don't, but they made us do it, so we did. If the men would just pay attention to the fire-boss, do as they're told, not be in such a damn hurry, these things wouldn't happen."

The last of the crowd was dispersing, dim figures melting into shadows in the eerie light of torches. The glow from the buggy's dash lanterns bounced off the smoky mist.

"And the woman? Would she have been evicted if she weren't leaving already?"

"Oh, she has options." Harry strained to hear. "She could marry another miner, there're lots of single men here always looking for a wife. Or she could stay and take in borders. But usually the widows are ready to go. They have family someplace, most of them go back to the city, Philadelphia or New York, where there are lots of their kind. The Irish ones, especially, they're in demand as servants, as long as they don't have children."

Harry turned his head and raised his voice. "And if they do?"

"Well, I don't rightly know." He could sense Murray turning toward him. "But the shanty Irish take care of their own, I do know that. Their priests see to it."

Harry turned back. He wanted to ask Murray whether the company gave the widows a pension or even the wages owing to their dead husbands, but he thought he knew the answer. Lights from the houses began to flicker to life, the gables silhouetted against the pale of the night sky and the rest melting into the black of the ridge behind. Dan and Murray fell silent. Once the buggy rounded the knoll and mounted the high road, the only sound was the creak of harness and the muffled thump of the horse's hooves. Stars began to emerge overhead, freed from the smoky murk of the patch town ovens, and the breeze held a scent of new leaves and damp soil. The Evans's farmhouse was lit faintly by a single light in the parlor window but Reverend Hamilton's home squatted dark by the side of the road, silent and sleeping. The road itself was deserted.

Harry thought about the dead man and his crushed head, felt a twinge of sorrow and more than a twinge of repulsion. He was grateful for the sweet dark around him.

12

A brisk March day, cool in the shade, warm in the sun, a southerly breeze tousling new leaves and carrying the pungent scent of skunk cabbage and wild onion. Harry stepped over the cemetery's iron fence and followed the downward slope of the land to the northwest. Tomorrow he would leave for Morgantown and his final college term, but now he wanted the silence and peace of the woods and hills around the old farmhouse. The land dropped gently to a nameless creek, hidden by ancient hardwoods that reached halfway up the hillside and brush just greening in the spring light. His steps in the deep duff below the trees were muffled, as silent as had been those of the Shawnee who slipped among these trees before his own ancestors claimed the land. The creek running clear and warming from spring rains sang to him, an accompaniment to birdsong that filled the air, signaling the business of procreating.

He tried, when he was alone in the woods, to raise the feel of the Montana mountains, the sense of delicious isolation and wildness that had raced through his blood. The feeling had stayed with him as he grew older, connected somehow to his father; it evoked something primordial. The past three years had clogged his system with the dust of old books—which he loved, couldn't get enough of—but he'd missed the freedom to roam the hills and pastures around Uniontown, feel the changing of the seasons, study the birds. His favorite was the bold *tea-kettle, tea-kettle* of the wrens. He wondered how they survived the harsh winters, but there they were, poking into nooks and crannies for spiders, their tails cocked over their backs. He heard the *yank-yank* of the upside-down nuthatch, too, and the drumming of the black and white woodpecker. A couple of years ago, he'd identified a passenger pigeon nest, but there'd been no chicks and since the birds continued to be delicacies in the restaurants of New York and Chicago he didn't expect to see another. The fellows at school taunted him sometimes about tweetie-bird watching, but his skill at third base redeemed him.

Now the trill of a wood thrush vied with the rush of water over rock and brush, and a mink stole silently below the bank. He jumped across the creek and scrambled up a rocky outcrop along a deer trail that he'd discovered years ago and never showed to anyone else, not even Dan. The trail wound along the steep cleft of the waterway, uphill, toward the spring where the creek emerged out of limestone into a bog. There the woods opened up, the top of the hill open to the late-morning sun. The view was to the east, the Connellsville Road and the railroad visible in the hazy distance. Beyond them, a pall of smoke piled up against Chestnut Ridge, spreading north and south over the hidden valley where the coke ovens squatted.

He circled the head of the creek and pushed his way down-hill through a bramble of mountain laurel, skidding his way back to creekside. Mud cats spawned here throughout spring and summer, and schools of fry flashed through the clear water. It was cool again in the shade of the trees and he shivered. He squatted on his heels and poked at the bank with a stick.

It was a few moments before he realized there was someone on the other bank. A girl, so motionless he'd had no notion of her at first. She sat in the shadows on a downed log, hands on her knees, feet in heavy work shoes peeping out from beneath the hem of her skirt. He must have passed close above her on his climb uphill without spotting her, like a newborn fawn hidden in dappled light.

"What are you looking for?" Her accent stirred a memory. She still hadn't moved.

"Mud cats. Catfish." He stood, pointed to the undercut bank. "They spawn here."

"Why do you call them mud cats?" She leaned at the waist without rising to peer into the water as if there might be one to sight. Her long tail of hair swung over her shoulder, black and shiny. He recognized her, then. The Irish girl from the patch town, the one who'd spoken up. Mrs. Gill.

"They taste like mud, mostly." He squatted again and pointed. "They'll hole up for the winter sometimes and stop eating. And then they eat most anything they can find, worms and grubs. They're bottom feeders."

"Sure that's what they call us Irish, sometimes." The girl smiled without taking her eyes from the creek. "Bottom feeders."

"Bottom feeders?"

She didn't answer. Sunlight bounced off dancing water and scattered pinpoints of light over her cheek.

"So lovely here." She stood now and shook out her skirt. He decided she was younger than he'd thought when he saw her with her widowed friend. "I would like to live here, away from the smoke." She waved toward the road and the hidden coking ovens, took a deep breath. "The smell is grand, isn't it?"

Harry studied her. She was like an exotic bird, something he'd never expected to see in his woods. "It is. And it's quiet. And cool."

She didn't appear to recognize him from the night of the accident, and he hoped she wouldn't. She picked her way down the bank, studying the stones that led into the water, and balanced on the log that spanned it. When she wavered he grasped her hand without thinking. It was cool and calloused, but the soft parts were very soft. His thumb rested against the wedding band. He guided her over the log and let go his grip.

"I am Niamh." She bobbed an abbreviated curtsy.

"Neeve?"

"Close enough." She laughed. A laugh, white teeth, a sparkle from dancing gray eyes, a toss of blue-black hair. "Nee-ev, yes. It's said in two syllables. Late of County Galway." She held out her hand, the right one this time, and Harry took it. "And who might you be?"

"I'm Harry." He had the absurd notion that he might kiss her hand. He did not. "Harry Robinson, now of Uniontown. This land once belonged to my ancestors."

"Then you'll be regretting its loss, as did my ancestors when the landlords came and took the farmland away." She crossed her arms and studied him. "Will you work for the Company then? You look quite prosperous, you do."

Harry felt himself redden. He could have wished for holes in the knees of his trousers. "I don't yet have a profession. My mother's family sold this land, partly so I could go to college. I'm nearly finished. With school, I mean."

"Well you're fortunate." She smiled, her eyes still on his face. "My family got nothing for the land they'd farmed for generations, and so I am here and so are my husband and my brother."

Her words were harsh, but her tone was light, practical, her voice a musical lilt. Harry knew little of the Irish who mined the coal, but he'd heard the sad history of the country, had grown up with his mother's tales of the Fenians in Montana and the wild Irish general who'd governed the territory. The Irish held a fascination for him that bordered on the mystical. But he'd never encountered the reality of their exile.

"You shipped over with your husband?"

"I did not. He sent for me. We married in Connellsville. My mam and dad sent us both over, my brother and me. I suspect I'll not see them again, my mam and dad." She looked down, twitched at her skirt. "Or it may be that we'll make our fortune here in America and send for them." She laughed again, and Harry was bewitched. And tongue-tied.

"But you've no interest in my affairs, to be sure, and here I am going on and on." She lifted her skirts, climbing to the path above the creek. "I'll be off home then and leaving you to your wanderings." She looked back over her shoulder. "It was a pleasure meeting you Harry Robinson, and I hope to see you again sometime."

"Yes ma'am." Harry winced; she would think him a complete idiot. He cleared his throat. "I come here all the time. I'll look forward to it." She'd already disappeared around the thickets, and he listened as she moved through last year's dead leaves like a fawn, light on her feet.

A spear of sunlight spiked through the lime-green leaves of a clump of birches. Harry could almost hear it hit the water and send up fireworks. The world suddenly seemed much too complicated, too majestic. Maybe he'd met something supernatural, maybe he'd dreamed it all. Nothing could be that beautiful, that captivating, that alive and intoxicating, and he ran out of superlatives and breath at the same time. Gobsmacked. Knocked on his tail like a yokel teasing a billy goat.

13

Niamh emerged from the edge of the wood and paused on the ridge above the spring that launched the creek. She surveyed the land, new life emerging in its pale greens and sunny song. The fields were strange to her, without the rough stone walls she was used to, but their absence gave a wild, new feel to the countryside that the ancient, long-worked pastures of home did not know. She followed the flight of a hawk as it skimmed the treetops, dipped into a ravine then soared over head, the sun setting its red tail on fire in a russet she'd never seen before. She spread her arms and lifted her face to the warmth, closed her eyes and smiled into the breeze.

But it was the forest that fascinated her. Ireland had nothing like this— the woods gone decades, centuries ago. To sit beneath a leafy roof, the sky obscured, the sun dappled was to be transported to the world of the Others, a world brimming with strange and bewitching life. The variety, the height, the rich scents of pine trees and the flash of brilliant color that here and there invigorated the simple greens and grays. Her heart beat fast and her breath came quick whenever she stepped under the vast canopy, a delicious fear that both drew and repelled her.

A rustle in the underbrush caught her attention; a ground-feeding bird, perhaps a wagtail or whatever passes for wagtails in America. She peered into the woods below her but could not see the creek where the mudcats spawned, the trees too dense even in their partially-clothed state. As she watched, the man she'd met emerged from the brush far down the ravine. In the open, he paused and turned in her direction. She eased behind a tall pine. It wouldn't do for him to watch her watching him. He'd seemed quite taken with her, she could see it in his face. She shouldn't have given him her hand, but there was the devil in her this day, and she did not regret it. Sure and it was nice to be admired by someone her own age, someone not covered in soot.

She smiled to herself. Nothing would spoil her mood so lovely a day. The man had turned south again and began the climb up the opposite knoll toward the tiny burying-ground at the top. If this had been his ancestors' land, that must be where they lay. Her family, those from the last hundred years or so, were buried at the Kilmacduagh graveyard, a good hour's walk from Killinny, but the ancients, so her da said, were in the tiny Killinny burying ground at the village's edge. She and Patrick often spent a lazy hour there, cleaning off the old stones, scratching at the inscriptions to glean their secrets.

Harry—she thought of him as Harry in her blithe mood—stooped to pull a weed from a grave, then another, and tossed them over the fence. As she watched, he lifted his face to the sky. Just then the hawk crested the hill and he followed it with his whole body. He was an educated man, a college student, a man from the town, not tainted with the filth of the coke works. He said he walked there often and if so, she and Patrick might encounter him again. Maybe he would know how Patrick might get an education, an American education. If he'd truly been taken with her, she might use that. For Patrick.

And besides, she'd liked him.

That afternoon she let the fire go out while she sat next door having a blether with Kate Byrne and her girl Eileen as they mended the men's work clothes. The scent of baking bread was strong, the warmth from Kate's cook stove filled her kitchen. The spring breeze that had been so fresh in the morning had blown in the clouds and quick as snap the day turned blustery. March here was no different from March at home.

Niamh thought with the walls so thin she needn't worry herself about the fire on her side, thought she'd save some coal. But she'd left it all too long, lost track of the time in the chatter, talk of the news from home, plans for spring gardens. When she heard Martin rummaging about next door, she knew he'd be wanting his bath and his dinner and she not there to do them up.

"He's early, then." Kate looked up when a door slammed. "I wonder if the others will be out soon, too." She folded the shirt she'd stitched and stuck her needle through it. "Eileen, set the potatoes to boil, there's a good girl."

"If he's decided to be early then he'll just have to wait, won't he?" Niamh said. She folded the trousers she'd lengthened for Patrick. "But I must fetch the water, so I'll be thanking you for your hospitality, Kate." She left humming.

He back-handed her when she stepped through her own door. It wasn't a particularly hard slap, but no one had ever hit her before, not her father nor mother when she was small nor any of the brothers. The sting to her cheek brought tears to her eyes, and she turned to hide them from him. She'd not let him see he'd hurt her.

"You're never to be gone when I get home again." His voice was low and calm. Kate and Eileen would not hear him. It appeared that the slap came naturally to him, it was not something he thought very important. "The fire's out and the water's not hot and my dinner's not begun." He rattled the door of the cook stove, stirred up the ashes, and added kindling. "Go for the water, and I'll try to warm this place up, it's turned into a dank queer day."

Niamh whirled to grab the buckets from the shelf by the door. A sharp needling rain spit into her face, but she ignored that and trudged through the back yards to the well. Others were there, drawing the water for the men's evening cleaning, and she kept her head tilted for fear the sting of her cheek showed red. She carried two buckets at a time and made three trips, since once Martin finished his bath, Patrick would use his water, and then the boarders, one by one, would clean themselves as well as they could in what was left.

The boarders, more of Martin's demands. He expected her to take care of a whole horde of single men and himself and Patrick as well. Seven boarders, now all crowded into the two upstairs rooms, all Welsh or Irish, though Martin said they might need to take in hunkies someday. That would just put the kibosh on it. The hunkies were from someplace in the center of Europe and spoke strange languages and kept strange customs. Several families lived close by already, and Niamh thought them curious, with their noisy celebrations and bright folk dress, but she didn't want them boarding in her house.

The cook stove was well lit now and water heating, the washtub waiting in the corner. Martin stripped to the waist, knelt and leaned into the tub on his hands. She poured the heated water over him and wetted the cloth to scrub his back. It was a fine strong back, toned from digging and hauling coal ten hours a day, but the stoop to his shoulders was pronounced and seemed, to her eyes, getting worse. She was coming to know his body well, what with the washing and the nights in their narrow bed, and sometimes it repelled her, but sometimes when they were together, she felt something inside her that was restless, latent, something she wanted to feel but never quite did.

"Where were you, then?" he asked, not turning. He rubbed his hands in soap and scrubbed his face.

"Next door, talking with Kate and Eileen." She rubbed the creases in his neck; it never did seem to get clean, stained as it was with the black dust like the ink of a sailor's tattoo. "We were after doing the mending and the baking. I thought to save some coal by it." She sounded defensive, even to herself.

He grunted, said nothing further. He hadn't the right to hit her, did he. She was never a slave then. Her cheek still stung, and she wondered if Patrick would see a mark. Such a thing happened, she knew, back home but usually there was the drink involved. Martin hadn't been drinking that she knew of.

She left him to his bath and set a pot on for potatoes. There was nothing in the way of fresh vegetables, it being too early for the gardens and the store having nothing on offer, but there were dried peas and peaches preserved and a bit of fish. She was learning to stretch the boarders' payments much further than she could have managed on just Martin's and Patrick's wages. She sighed. Like home, back in the hard times.

By the time Patrick and the boarders came in and had their baths, and dinner was spread, Martin seemed to have forgotten that all was not as he expected when first he arrived home. He and the boarders sat back and lit their pipes as she cleared the dishes and heated the dish water, and talked about the rumors. She enjoyed listening when they talked in the evenings, she wanted to know what was happening in politics and in business, any-where outside this dismal patch, and she had no one to ask. Tonight, there were rumors that the Youngstown owners might join the operators' pool and agree to shut down the ovens one day a week, restrict the output to increase demand. There was someone named Frick whose company owned many of the ovens and mines around Connellsville and Uniontown, and he appeared to pipe the tune.

And the miners reacted. Jamie Darby said the miners' union called a meeting in Scottdale just after Christmas and that all the unorganized mines were to send delegates. Martin said he'd go and glad of it. "There's talk of dropping the wages up at Trotter, it'll give Murray the idea to do it here, so."

"They've walked out up there," said a coke man named Lewis. "On strike for the wagons as well."

"What, they've stopped weighing them, then?" someone asked.

"Aye," Lewis said, "will be paying by the wagonload, they will, and Stinner says they're all of a size. My brother works up there, he don't believe it for a minute."

Martin leaned back in his chair, crossed his ankles, and pulled on his pipe. Niamh didn't care for the look of arrogance he wore. "We'll be waiting for them with pitchforks, they try such a thing here."

So, it was to be labor troubles. Kate Byrne was always going on about such things, how the Molly Maguires terrorized the state for years, giving all the Irish a bad name, until the Pinkertons broke them and hanged a bunch five or six years ago. Niamh wondered what would happen to herself and Patrick if Martin were to be hanged or shot or beaten to death in a strike. She'd have to think about that, have a plan ready. Oh, yes, he would do it. If he would be after hitting his own wife for almost nothing, he surely would never dither about violence in a strike.

She watched Patrick, sitting to the side of the group and listening to every word. He was a smart lad, someday he'd be a leader of men like these, one who could make the laws that made sure everyone was treated fair, for that's what this country was about. Not like Ireland, where the landowners and the Protestants had all the advantage.

She wiped the last pot, hung it up, and dried her hands. There was bread to mix up and set to rise overnight and knitting to finish; Patrick's old mittens had holes, and Martin needed a warm jumper. The boarders began drifting upstairs, and Martin flapped open a newspaper one of them left behind. She handed him his tea and a cup to her brother.

"Do you think, then, Martin," she pulled out the big bread bowl and the flour bag, "that Patrick might be going to the school in town some this winter?" Her fingers touched her cheek, she could feel the bruise. "He should be learning about the history of this country and its ways, so he can sort what's right for workers and business. He could become a man of business, knowing both the sides."

Martin studied his paper. "It's a fine idea, isn't it?" He looked up. "D'you think I'm made of money, so? He'll be needing to put in a full day's work and earn his way. I don't know how he can manage that, what with having to walk to town and do the studying."

She glanced at Patrick. He raised his eyebrows and shrugged, the look on his face anxious.

"If we figured a way, would it be fine with you?"

Martin folded the paper and stood. "It's of no concern to me what the boy does, long as he pays his way. Just don't be fussing me with it." He swallowed the last of his tea and set down his cup. "I'm for bed." He looked over his shoulder at her. "Don't be long."

After he'd gone, Patrick said, "D'you think there'd be a way for me to get some schooling, then? Could we afford it?" He rolled out the pallet he slept on and curled into it.

"I don't know, *a stór*. I hope so. We'll work on a way."

The boy was silent for some time. A heavy mist rolled down from the east ridge and piled against the kitchen window; she pulled the curtain of sacking across to block it out. But the cook stove glowed, and the soft thump-thump of the dough as she kneaded it, rolled it, kneaded again, warmed her.

"Nee," Patrick said, "how about a tale then?"

"Ah," Niamh said. She settled into the rocking chair, her knitting in her lap. "Well then. *Nuair a bhí sé ina dhiaidh sin, blianta fada ó shin, bhí laoch mór ar a dtugtar Oisín, mac Fionn Mac Cumhaill* ... Once upon a time, many years ago, there lived a great warrior named Oisín, mac Fhinn mhic Chumhaill…"

14

June 1884

Three hours into the six-hour stage ride from Morgantown, Harry was hot, sore, and cranky. The back of his neck itched where the collar rubbed, his tailbone was bruised from the poor springs, and the two women traveling with him wouldn't shut up. The hat on the stout woman sported feathers that nodded and swayed as if they were still alive. They were a sick kind of apricot color unknown to any actual fowl. The thin woman tittered behind her hand every few minutes in a raspy creak. He pretended to sleep. If only someone would build a rail line. Maybe he'd do it someday. When he was rich.

That started him thinking about the job that waited for him when he got home. His mother and Mattie had schemed to set it up and there was no way to back down now. Clerking for Philip Murray was not high on his list of favorite ways to spend the summer, but then neither was minding the counter at Beeson's dry goods or mucking out stalls at the livery stable. He wouldn't have minded doing repairs and odd jobs at the properties his mother took on to sell, but that wasn't steady enough, and besides, his wages would come out of her profits. And Mother wanted him to give the coal business a try. She *had* agreed if it didn't suit, he could look for something else in the fall. She'd paid for his university, and he owed her.

And that started him thinking about how much he owed her. So much. Three months with Murray couldn't begin to pay it off, and that didn't take into account the money. It was a moral debt. If she wanted him to try his hand at business, he'd give it a good college try. What else was he to do with a degree in philosophy?

His last six weeks at university had dragged like a month of Sundays in Reverend Elliott's church. Or worse, if anything could be worse. He slogged through exams with one eye on the blossoming trees outside the classroom window, his mind on a brilliant smile and an Irish laugh. He haunted the library for works on Irish history and folklore. There were few to be found. He devoured the story of the Tuatha de Danaan and the Fianna and tried to wrap his tongue around strange Celtic diphthongs and perplexing consonants. What she'd pronounced *Ne-eve* was actually spelled *Niamh,* and he turned the word over and over in his thoughts when the scents of spring left him awake deep into the soft spring nights.

The stage at long last pulled into the livery stable on Peter Street. No one met him, but he hadn't expected anyone. He arranged to have his trunk sent home, gripped his small bag, and walked the block to Main Street.

Main Street was a mess. As far east as the courthouse, where the street elbowed out of sight, a horde of men—Irishmen, by the accents of those near him, and Negroes—swung pickaxes and shovels. The ditch they dug was deep, heads of those inside popping up when they flung a load over the edge. Horses and carts stood by, tromping up and down, raising dust, hauling tools and rock. Rank after rank of cast iron pipe lay stacked on sidewalks. The water works had come to town.

Traffic threaded its way along the south side of the street. Delivery wagons and buggies squeezed by, wheels on the sidewalk. Pedestrians hurried along with handkerchiefs over their mouths and noses to keep out the dust; fine silt settled on suits and bodices already damp from the June heat. He crossed the ditch on a shaky boardwalk and stopped in the middle to watch the men work below, open-air miners shaping the limestone to carry water for a thriving city. South of Main he passed the bank, full of late-afternoon business, and the Eagle Hotel, where a new chandelier trundled into the lobby on the shoulders of carpenters. Ahead, St. Peter's Episcopal's foundation rose, stonemasons fitting limestone blocks together like a Chinese puzzle. Sleek carriages, blooded horses, patent-leather shoes and dove-gray high-buttoned coats. Professionally tended front gardens. There was money here. He grinned. His town—flush, scrappy, ambitious—boomed.

Next morning, Tuesday, eight-fifty-five a.m., he let himself into the front office of a two-room suite in the First National Bank building. He assumed this would be his space; it had no windows, a thick rug and a small desk on which squatted a new Remington typewriter. From the inner office came the sound of shuffling papers and a whiff of cigarette smoke. He poked his head through the connecting door.

Murray had claimed the building's prime spot, the rounded corner of the third floor. His mother's office, the size of a broom closet, occupied a one-window corner on the floor below, Murray's space dwarfed hers. Warm morning sun flooded three large arched windows that faced Main and Pittsburgh Streets; polished walnut surrounded a green marble fireplace. A massive desk was awash in papers, a heavy library table lay buried in blueprints.

"There you are, Harry," Murray said around the cigarette in his mouth. He stuck out his hand and Harry shook it. "Thought you might want to sleep in your first day home."

"No sir," Harry said. "Might as well get right to work."

"Come take a look at these." Murray set the cigarette on the edge of the library table, burning end out, and turned the blueprint pages to the front cover. "This is the house I'm building over on Ben Lomond. They've finally started working on it."

"So I heard." Harry rounded the table and leaned over the prints. "How far along is it?"

"Cellar's in, they started framing the first floor last week. Should be pretty near done by the time the weather gets bad in the fall." He flipped a couple pages, picked up his cigarette and inhaled. "See, now, here's the first floor, there's a full bathroom down here, two more on the second floor. Gas, running water, central heat, coal, of course. Everything new and up-to-date." He stubbed out his cigarette in a chipped saucer. "Thank Mattie'll like it?"

Harry gritted his teeth and didn't look up. "Has she seen it?"

"No, it's a surprise."

Now Harry did look up. "In Uniontown? You can't keep anything quiet."

"Oh, she knows I'm building it. She just doesn't know what it'll be like." Murray flipped another page. The second floor was a warren of bedrooms, closets, hallways. "The finest in town—marble, wall-to-wall carpets, crystal chandeliers, all glass—only the best." He rocked back on his heels, then clapped Harry on the shoulder. "Now don't give her any details. Don't want to spoil it for her."

"Has she said she'll marry you?" Disappointment speared through him.

"Haven't proposed yet." Murray picked up a package of Three Kings, pulled out another cigarette and struck a match. "But she will." He drew on the cigarette and winked at Harry. "I can tell."

Harry nodded. She wouldn't, she was too smart for that. He knew his aunt better than this man did. Or so he hoped.

"She might like to have a say in some of the details herself." He sounded peevish even to himself. New boss, bad start. He stuck his hands in his pockets. "Maybe you can go over what you'd like me to do while I'm here?"

Harry spent the first week learning to use the typewriter. The previous clerk had been gone nearly a month and Murray's correspondence had piled up. He insisted every letter go out typed. It was more professional, he said. By Friday, Harry'd become proficient with two fingers, hunting and pecking his way over the keyboard, flipping up the carriage to see what he'd written, using a special eraser for errors. He even got the hang of carbon paper, and by week's end left only a handful of smudges on the pages. The contracts were what interested him, though. Dozens of contracts flowed through the office, for the sale of coke, for supplies for the company store, for equipment, employment contracts. They told a story of life in the patch towns, how the operators controlled costs and managed the markets, how the pyramid of businesses depended on the booming steel industry in Pittsburgh and the demand for products created by promoters.

He liked it best when Murray was out of the office, which he was most days. The new house claimed much of the man's attention, and he made frequent trips to West Virginia and Maryland, where the Company prospected, and to Ohio where the Company was headquartered.

Harry read the trade journals and the Connellsville paper so he could type up summaries for Murray, who didn't have the patience to read them himself. He learned the major players in the coke industry: Frick himself, Colonel Schoonmaker, McClure, the Leisenrings. He followed the workings of the operators' syndicate, formed to fix prices, and the Knights of Labor, busy organizing workers. He analyzed the prices of the company stores in the different patch towns, the rents charged to families, the amount they paid for company doctors, the arrangements for schools for miners' and cokers' children. He read letters marked "Confidential" that discussed efforts to recruit unskilled immigrants from Eastern Europe who would work for less and rebuff the unions. And he ordered marble flooring and wool carpets for Murray's new house and a fountain for the front yard. He paid bills for restaurants and hotels in Pittsburgh and Philadelphia and for the Greenbrier. Murray lived well.

He soon fell into an easy routine. In the office by nine, lunch at his desk, lock up by 5:30. Then head for the peace of the countryside. The long June evenings were made for rambling in the woods and across the fields, clearing the dust and details of office work out of his head. Milkweed and morning glory colonized the fallow pastures; the leaves of scattered beeches rustled with fledglings. The creeks were rank with early summer growth and rot, and mudcats persisted in hiding among the shadows. Harry often came straight from work, supper picked up from Mr. Woods's store and carried along wrapped in greasy newspaper. Sometimes he'd get a lift from a farmer in a buckboard, but mostly he walked, keeping to the side of the track and out of the dust until he reached the farmhouse. Say hello to Joanna, turn onto the trail to the graveyard, plunge into the cool of an open grove, sun still high enough to sift through the canopy overhead. He rarely met anyone in these quiet lanes; what he wanted was the slow peace of the fields, the quiet rustles of their habitants, the music of the creek.

And of course, if Mrs. Gill happened to be there, her company would not be amiss.

15

And then one day she appeared. He'd imagined her so often, even carried out long, one-sided conversations with her in his head, that it didn't seem all that unusual. She sat along the bank of the creek that ran below the graveyard, a clutch of black-eyed susans in one hand. She must have watched him stop in the cemetery and clear weeds, then start down the long slope well before he knew she was there, because she watched him with a smile, as if she'd expected him.

"And is it yourself, Harry Robinson? Like a *luipreachán* you are, sliding through the fields of an evening."

"And you would be Titania? Or Queen Mab?" Harry jumped the creek and sat down next to her in the long grass. He did it almost unconsciously, as if it were the natural thing to do.

"*Méabh*, the warrior fairy queen." She laughed. Her hair today was pulled into a bun at the nape of her neck, though wisps had escaped and floated around her face. She pushed a strand back; her nails were broken to the quick and rimmed in black.

"Do you walk here often?" She didn't, or he would have met her before. "Because I do, and I haven't seen you."

"This is a lovely time of the day, and now my husband works the evening shift in the mine, so I have it to myself." She leaned to the left and plucked a sprig of chicory, tucking it into the bouquet she held. "Once the supper is over and the dishes are done, I've not much else to do. Look there." She pointed at the rings spreading in the quiet pool beneath the opposite bank.

"A trout," he said. "The mayflies have hatched."

"Trout. I used to love trout, back home. We had the browns and my dad would poach them when he could. A treat they were for us and more so because they belonged to the landlord."

"He never was caught?"

"Oh, no, he was too canny for that. But my brother was, Patrick was, and got a sound bollocking for his trouble. He was never so clever as Da."

Harry slid down to the edge of the stream and peered into the pool. "I could catch him for you if I had a hook and line. Perhaps next time I'll bring one, or a net."

"Or I could bring one myself and do the catching, for I can, you know. I watched my dad plenty and learned the way of it. And what is it that strikes you funny?" she said tartly at the grin he turned on her.

"Nothing, it's just you sounded like my mother so often sounds when someone offers to do something for her that she can very well do herself."

"Your mother is a capable woman then?"

"Very. Sometimes too much so. She rarely lets anyone do anything for her."

"I do admire a woman who can care for herself, then. No need to be marrying her off to the first gombeen who passes by." She looked up quickly. "Oh, I'm sorry. I wouldn't be referring to your father."

Harry laughed. "My mother didn't marry until she was thirty-three and my father died when I was two. So yes, she took care of herself before she married and has taken care of herself ever since. And me, of course." He turned back to the stream. The trout had disappeared.

They were silent, listening to the ripple of water and the sounds of birds beginning to pipe in the dusk. "The air is so clean here," she murmured. She leaned back on her arms and drew a deep breath.

"Why do you live over there?" Harry said. "I mean, why are the houses built right there where all the smoke and grit are?"

"The men want to be close to their work. They fancy the short walk."

"But the air's so bad."

"It is, but the women have no say. We spend our days cleaning away the grit." She smiled again. "It's a new house, though, almost. Fresh made."

"I haven't been out that way since I came home."

"Oh, university was it? You've come home for the summer?"

"Actually, I've finished, graduated. I need to look for something permanent, some work here soon." He pulled a stem of bracken fern, began to strip the fronds.

"And what is it you're trained for then?" she asked. She sounded eager, as if she were truly interested.

"I'm not settled on any one thing." He heaved himself back up the slope. "I'm a clerk in an office now." He didn't mention whose office. "My mother wants me to learn business, someday take over hers. She's an estate agent, buys and sells land and houses. But I'd rather do something completely different."

"Aye, wouldn't do to be on your mother's patch for long."

He looked at her. "You understand that."

"I do." She smiled at him.

"No one else seems to. They don't understand why I don't just go into real estate and be satisfied."

"And who would these others be?"

"Aunts, cousins, family friends. All those people who hover when you live in the town where you grew up, where your family's been for generations."

She bit her lip. "Ah, you'd be finding it a burden, so. I think I would find it a joy to be in my home-town, even with the hovering."

He squirmed. "I'm sorry, I didn't mean to sound ungrateful. You're homesick then?"

She shook her head back and laughed, though her eyes glistened. "Oh, of course I miss my mam and dad and the ways of Galway, but I'll settle. I have my brother and some of the folk of the patch here are known to me from back home."

"And your husband."

"Yes, him." She drew up her knees and rested her chin on them, staring into the water.

Harry said nothing. He felt they'd crossed a barrier, a very slight one, but something had happened and he didn't want to let it go. "You knew him back in Ireland I suppose."

"I did, yes. He's a cousin of my dad's and almost as old. He spoke for me when I was just a *cailín óg*. There wasn't much for me back there, all the young men were gone to America, and I so wanted to see it as well." She looked up at him now and her smile was gentle. "And it's glad I am that I have. There's so much more here than back there in that sad place. More for my brother, for my husband. For the babes when they come."

Harry looked away. Her words were to him profoundly sad, the sweet-scented summer evening permeated with a deep regret. And then she laughed, not the merry chuckle he'd heard before but a quiet sound that broke the spell.

"And I must be getting back now before it's too dark to find my way." She nodded east to the ridge behind which the cluster of ovens sent up a fug of smoke and cinders into the fine evening.

"May I walk with you?" He climbed to his feet and reached for her hand to pull her up. It was an automatic gesture and she seemed to think nothing of it, but the touch of her hand to his was electric and he thought he might never let it go.

But he did, and they skirted the foot of the rise to reach the road to Connellsville. Beside it ran the raw, raised bed of the B&O railway line, and they stopped to watch the six-fifty-five on its run south. Barney Collier tooted the whistle at him as the locomotive passed and Harry lifted a hand to him. Smoke from the stack floated gently back on the evening breeze and settled around their heads and shoulders like mist. They crossed the track over Cove Run as it veered toward Youngstown, the stream banks muddied and broken where loggers and mules had tramped down to the water, the once-clear creek sluggish in summer's heat. In the growing dusk, a faint reddish glow rose from the unseen ovens behind a low mound. The humidity lay heavy as they drew nearer the coke works.

At the top of the rise they stopped, and he mopped at his face with a sodden kerchief, jammed it back in his pocket. The warmth of the ovens burned through the gray air. The valley's scars were conspicuous in the evening light.

"That one is ours. The third one from this end." Niamh looked at her grimy nails. "It's the cleaning never gets done. Always a nasty soot on everything."

She raised her bouquet of now-limp wildflowers. "Must be getting these into water. It's a fine service they do to cheer up the place." She smiled. "Don't be so downcast, Harry Robinson. 'Tis progress, I'm thinking. The great beast of a machine of America." Her tone was wry, and he thought she had the right of it. It was truly a great beast that hovered in this valley. She lived in its belly, and there was nothing he could do about it. He watched her pick her way down the path and up the steep climb to the row of dingy houses, watched until she disappeared inside the door of her home.

16

Queen Mab—Mab to Harry, Queenie to the aunts—snuffled through knots of wild grass among the headstones. The puppy, a graduation gift from his mother, was a handy excuse for long walks. The graves of his grandparents had become of towering interest to him lately, to the bemusement of his mother. The humid air of summer took the starch out of the leaves by mid-afternoon and left the evenings breathless, still, dense. Harry always carried a book and pretended to read or a pad and pencil to sketch birds and make notes, but more often than not he spent the hours daydreaming, cloud gazing, and generally, he thought, acting like an ass.

Then one evening, the day after Independence Day, he saw her trailing down the hillside across the valley. She followed a trickle of water that wound its way through overhanging pasture grasses, already part-way to the valley floor. She walked slowly, stopping here and there to inspect a flower or watch the flight of a killdeer or peer up at the hilltop where he sat.

She wasn't alone.

Someone—a boy, a man—trailed after her, leaping from tussock to streambank. Harry heard him call to her. The words were unintelligible from that distance, but she laughed in response, a happy musical laugh that started his heart thudding with joy and jealousy.

She reached the valley floor, turned in his direction and waved. She spoke to her companion, then pointed in the direction of the cemetery. The boy, for Harry could see now that he was young, shaded his eyes from the westering sun. He was tentative as they approached, maybe wary of strangers, especially someone not from the patch. Harry wondered what she would say to the boy, how she would explain him, Harry.

He stood and brushed the grass from his trouser knees. Mab, who rarely met someone new she did not immediately adore, caught their scent. She let out a delighted yelp and barreled down the slope, rear end wiggling. Niamh laughed and sank to the ground, her skirts billowing around her. Mab leaped over her with kisses and wiggles. They both squealed.

The boy swiveled between the girl, the dog and Harry. His black hair shone the same way hers did and even from this distance Harry could tell his face had the same heart-shape, the same pointed chin. Harry judged him to be no more than fourteen or fifteen, spindly-limbed with a hungry look to his thin face.

Niamh jumped to her feet and clapped her hands for Mab, taking off at a run with the dog at her heels. The boy followed more slowly. Harry met them half-way down the slope and caught her outstretched hands when she tripped over the puppy. He and she were both laughing, she breathless from her run, he breathless just because. He held her hands as they both dropped to the ground. The boy stood over them, uncertain.

"I was looking for you, Harry Robinson," she said. "And here I've found the most wonderful puppy—what a darling!" Mab rolled onto her side and wiggled her way next to the girl. "What would her name be?"

"Mab." Harry rubbed the puppy's belly. "Queen Mab."

"Ah." Niamh looked at him sideways. "Fine choice." She turned to the boy and took his hand. "But here I've brought my brother to meet you. I want him to know an educated American man of business. Patrick, this is my friend Harry Robinson, a leprechaun I met in the spring. Harry, this is Patrick and he's meant to keep me company, so far from home, and someday he'll be a great man, here in America." She pulled Mab into her lap. "Patrick, if you get your education like Harry has done, you won't be after working underground the rest of your life."

Harry stood and held out his hand to Patrick. The boy hesitated, then shook Harry's hand, his eyes suspicious. "Welcome to America."

The boy looked away, then met Harry's eye. "Thank you, sir."

"And aren't we both proud to be here?" She smiled up at her brother and took his hand to pull him to the ground. He folded his legs and sat next to his sister, stuck a blade of grass in his mouth and stared at Harry.

"You work in the mine?" Harry asked. "Or at the coking ovens?"

"In the mine, yes." Patrick's voice cracked, halfway between child and man, and he reddened. "With my brother-in-law." He looked at Niamh.

Harry nodded. "I've been learning about the mines. Do you work a seam? Or are you a trapper boy?"

Patrick snorted. "Trapper boys are the wee ones, anyone can open and shut a door. I work a seam with Martin. My sister's man." He squared his shoulders. "We put out eighty bushels a day, most days."

"That's more than any of the other teams put out. My brother is a monster of a worker and him only fifteen. Older fellows cannot keep pace with him." She lay her head on her brother's shoulder for an instant, and he smiled at her.

"But I want him to get an education." She raised her head. "I want to know how I can find someone to teach him. They won't take him at the patch school, say he's too old. I'll pay, I've saved money from the store bill." She dipped her head. "Perhaps you could teach this one, great *bómán* that he is. Could you?"

Harry looked at Patrick. The boy met his eyes straight on. "And what about you? Is that what you want?"

"Aye, sir." Patrick's voice was husky. "I can read and write. But I need more. I'll work hard."

"When would you have time? What kind of work schedule do you have?"

"That's the thing," said Niamh. "They're not working but four days a week, to drive the prices up. So he has time on his hands."

Harry knew that but he wasn't about to let on that he worked for the Youngstown operators.

"We're off Saturdays and Sundays, and different days other times." Patrick raised his brows at his sister. "Martin won't care if we're gone of a Sunday, will he then?"

Harry took note of the *we*. "Will you come too?"

She ducked her head. "I want to learn."

So that's why she'd continued to seek him out: she'd wanted a teacher for her brother and an education for herself. She wasn't at all interested in Harry, except as a teacher. And why would she be? The girl was married, she was a Catholic, their worlds were entirely different, there would never be the remotest possibility that they might some day have something more. His dreams were so outrageous that he blushed for himself at what his thoughts had been over the past months since they'd first met.

But it didn't make any difference. He wanted to be near her.

Mab rolled off Niamh's lap and flopped down next to him, panting. He scratched her ears. "We could work something out, I suppose, if you're willing to work at it. Perhaps I could meet with you once a week, say Sunday after church, bring you books, set you lessons. Then you could do the lessons during the week and we'd review them the next Sunday."

She started to speak, and he held up his hand. "There wouldn't be a charge, not at first anyway, until we see how it goes." He looked at Patrick. "Can you start in the local school in the fall? In town?"

Patrick turned red and shook his head. "Martin would skin me if I missed my shifts. And I'd be far behind the others in the classes. No, I'm thinking I need to work on my own." His voice pleaded. "I'll work hard, I will, Mr. Robinson."

"You can call me Harry. Your sister does. We'll just take this one week at a time, see how it works." He looked over the cemetery. "We'll need a place to meet when the weather's bad. Got any suggestions? Your home?"

"No!" they said in unison. "No," Niamh repeated, more softly. "I'll not bother my husband with such goings-on in the house. We'll need to find another place."

"Well, the farmhouse, then," Harry said. "There's no one left there but my Aunt Joanna and she won't make a fuss. What exactly do you want to learn?"

"I know the basics," Patrick said. "I've been to school since I was a lad, five or six, but I couldn't go regular like, I was needed in the fields."

"He's through the third book." Niamh beamed.

"What's the third book?"

"It's as far as I could go in the local school," Patrick said. "Next would be the intermediary and there was no chance for that."

"He writes a fine hand," Niamh said, "and does his sums and figuring. Dad would have him work on the accounts for the landlord even."

"What have you read? Did you have access to books? You read the Bible I suppose."

"Ah, no, not much." Patrick shook his head. "There were some scriptures in our readers, but the priest didn't want us studying those."

"We have one, sure, it's a family Bible, we put the births and deaths in over the years," Niamh said. "No one ever reads it."

"No one reads it?"

"'Tis a Protestant book. Protestants wrote it for Protestants," Patrick said. He picked a stem of grass and looked at Harry, eyes narrowed, as if judging his reaction. "It has blood on it."

"Oh. Well." Harry cleared his throat. "Maybe we should start with American subjects then. History and geography. American writers."

Patrick's eyes lit up. "That's the thing. I want to know everything I can about this country."

"I've been reading this." Harry pulled his book from a jacket pocket. "I haven't finished it yet, but it's by one of our best writers. It'll give you another idea of America, and we can talk about what you think."

"*The Gilded Age: A Tale of Today*," Patrick read. "Mark Twain." He looked up, flushed. "I thank you, Mister … Harry."

Niamh smiled at Harry, and he wished he had ten more books to give away.

"Patrick, we need to be going." She pulled at his elbow. "It will be dark soon and the boarders will be needing their dinner."

Patrick stood to go, then turned back and shyly offered his hand. "This means a lot to me. And to my sister."

Harry shook Patrick's hand. The boy looked very young. An image of him underground, doing the work of a man in the gloom and dust of the mines, rose in his mind. "Until Sunday then."

"Aye." Patrick took his sister's arm, and they dropped down the slope to the east. Harry watched until they crossed the Connellsville Road and disappeared toward the railroad tracks, a swarm of emotions roiling inside.

That July set the record for magnificent weather: the rains came only in the night leaving mornings cool and damp, afternoons breezy and warm, sweet-smelling and lush. Week days spent buried in the minutiae of the mining industry brought their own reward but Sundays loomed large. Evenings he often walked to the farmhouse, Mab snuffling at his heels or arrowing into the fields after rabbits and chipmunks. Or he pawed through the bookshelves at his mother's home and the far more generous collection at the Sturgeons' to find books and newspapers for Patrick's lessons. He told his mother and his aunts he'd been hired to tutor a couple of youngsters from the mining town, thought he'd see how he liked teaching. They asked no questions and let him be.

The cemetery, rank with summer grasses and thick with dandelions and bindweed, seemed more like a garden than a place of the dead. Niamh lay claim to a spot beneath the white pine on the east corner; Patrick and Harry sprawled next to her, books spread around them and newspapers held down by stones and fragments of marble.

"Niamh finished it, I didn't." Patrick held a copy of *Uncle Tom's Cabin* out to his sister. She took it and caressed the cover.

"I liked it very much. Especially this lovely soft binding." She smiled.

Harry smiled back at her. "Tell me what you liked."

"It's about being a mother, so. Not so much about being a slave."

"I thought it was mushy," Patrick said.

"Why so?" Harry ignored Patrick.

"Why she was perfectly happy, seems to be, with her master. Wasn't until he wanted to sell away her babe that she had to run. A mother can't be allowing something like that to happen."

"So do you think the slaves were mostly happy under slavery?"

She tossed her head. "Are the Irish happy under the English then? Is anyone whose labor is not their own? Whose children are not their own? It's an abomination and it's hard for me to believe, it is, that this country that's so fine in all other ways put up with it for so long." She handed the book to her brother. "Patrick, you're to be finishing this before next week and let Harry know what you think. Besides mushy, now."

"President Lincoln said it started the war." Patrick flopped onto his stomach, leaned on his elbows and opened the book to a marked page. "A book seems a strange enough thing to go to war over."

"There were lots of other reasons for the war. Slavery was the main one." Harry tossed an acorn from hand to hand. "My father thought slavery would die out soon, thought the war wasn't necessary."

Patrick looked up. "Did he fight in the war? Is that how he died?"

"No, he was a doctor, but he lived in Missouri. Mother says the war was particularly vicious there, worse than other places. He wrote newspaper articles."

He tossed an acorn for Mab; Niamh watched the puppy dart into the underbrush after it.

"So your da was a rebel."

"He didn't think the federal government should invade Missouri, so yes, I suppose he was."

"There are rebels aplenty in Ireland, one behind every rock. Not that it ever does anyone a lick of good."

"They fight the English, though, the way we did. Not their own countrymen."

"Oh, but 'tis Irish against Irish more like than not. Catholic Irish against Protestant Irish. Native Irish against English Irish. It's all blood, then, isn't it?"

She sat back against the tree trunk. The book lay open on the ground and she paged idly through it, stopped at the woodcut of Eliza crossing the river.

"Was he a slave-holder, then, your father?"

Harry fiddled with his pencil, doodled the outline of a crow in his notebook before he looked up. "He bought two people, a couple, Rose and Dick. Mother says he did it because their owner planned to sell them south right before the war." He tapped his pencil against the illustration; Eliza's face and her son's appeared pale in the picture. "He freed them when he could, it was illegal to free them in Missouri until the war was almost over. They went with us to Montana. I suppose they're still there."

"You knew them then?"

"Rose took care of me when Mother needed to work, especially after my father died. Dick was always there to do odd jobs. They were my first friends." He sketched in the crow's beak. "We were so isolated they were pretty much my only friends. We didn't see the neighbors much, at least I don't remember any."

"Would you have fought for the federal government if you'd been the age? Against your da?"

He threw down the pencil and ran his hands through his hair. "Ah, I don't know. Rebel against the rebel? Isn't that what sons do? Go through a time when fathers can do no right. I would never have fought for the side that kept slaves."

"I imagine it was all so complicated." She closed the book and set it aside. "Nothing is black and white"—she smiled— "so to speak. Your father understood that I fancy."

"Yes, well, no one here seems to. Once a rebel always a rebel." He rose to his feet and swiped at the knees of his trousers. "I've been assigned the task of redeeming my family name, the Robinson name, anyway. The Canons take care of themselves."

"And you're like to do a grand job of it, Harry Robinson." She too stood and shook out her skirt. "Patrick, it's late, your shift will be going down. New week starting." She turned to Harry.

"Thank you again for your teaching." She held out her hand with a smile, and he pressed it. "Patrick and I both are having the good of it. Isn't it so, Patrick?"

"Aye." Patrick scrambled to his feet, cradling a half dozen books and a sheaf of newspaper against his thin chest. "Next week it's to be algebra. I'll have the problems done by tomorrow then I can do the reading you set me." His eagerness never ceased to astonish Harry; worth the effort even if Niamh hadn't been along. Or so he told himself.

He watched them go, down the hill and back up the bank to the big road and out of sight. Then he whistled for Mab and trailed after them, feeling like a stalker, the pup romping behind nosing into burrows and the hollows at the foot of the odd tree. He kept his distance and the growing dusk hid him, made up as it was of smoke from the ovens.

At the top of the hill beyond the tracks the ovens themselves came into sight, the glow from their mouths pulsing in the murk. Figures, indistinct as wraiths, passed back and forth in front of the glow, leaned into the maw, crouched in front, their movements mechanical and surreal. Harry squatted, and the dog flopped beside him, her tongue lolling. The creaking of the larries as the dispirited mules hauled raw coal to the top of the ovens, the rumble of the rail cars, the crash and bump of ore into the ovens and finished coke out of them, echoed through the unnatural dark, muffled the way thunder is muffled by a heavy fog. An acrid scent of gas and soot borne by a sudden breeze stung his eyes and masked the smell of rank summer vegetation. Beyond the long, curved bank of ovens the workers' homes were lit, here and there, by dim spots of kerosene, watery echoes of the flames from the ovens. A firefly floated past his knee and winked out as it crested the hill.

It had been a long time ago since he and Dan and Rebecca had ventured inside the mine. It had to have changed, improved, expanded since the Company took it over. He'd read a great deal about mining, but he knew little about how it actually worked, more importantly how it *felt* to be underground without the light, day after day. The whistle blew, shrill and imperious, calling the night shift to the mine. Men were trailing by twos and threes along the rail spur that passed down the valley between ovens and mine. He looked for Patrick, saw him leave the house, pickaxe under his arm. He fiddled with his cap, fixing a wick lamp to its front. Harry folded his legs beneath him, settled on the cooling ground, watched the boy until he and the others disappeared beyond the hill that hid the entrance to the shaft.

He imagined the men dropping down the passgeways, turning off in pairs into separate headings and rooms. He remembered the cool damp of the walls, the other-wordly glow of the lamplight. The way the mountain talked to itself. It made no difference to the mountain or to the men working in its bowels that dusk was coming on and dark would soon sink over the hilltops. Day or night, it was all one to a miner. A twelve-hour shift down below would lead to a slog home, a quick wash and an exhausted sleep in a house darkened from constant soot and smoke, then it all started again. Before this summer, Harry had never given much thought to what kind of life these people lived, people who dug the fuel that kept his home warm and his dinner cooked. It seemed to him that they must be another species, one capable of living without the sound of a bird or the scent of a clean creek running free.

Mab whined softly at his knee. She wanted her dinner, and so did he. It was a long walk back into town, and in the dark. His mother would have his plate in the warming oven and would be settled in her reading chair with a book. Mattie would be sitting on the porch with Philip Murray, back in town from a recent trip to Pittsburgh. He jammed his hands in his pockets, whistled for the pup and turned south on the road, dusty from the dry summer days.

He wondered where beneath his feet the miners were, wondered why he couldn't hear or feel them, how far down they must be. Murray, though, that was a thought. Murray could get him down into the works, give him a tour. All of a sudden it seemed very important that he know what it was like for her husband and her brother to be down there in the dark, the stale air, the dust. He needed to know, to feel it. He'd ask Murray.

17

Harry remembered how blessedly cool the mine had been that time years ago when he and Dan and Rebecca had ventured in. Now, the farther he traveled down the slope, the farther behind he left the heat of the July afternoon, the humidity hovering in the ninety percentages. The damp odors were welcome, the gloom a pleasant contrast to the glare of the midday sun. As he shuffled along the uneven slate floor of the passage, the light from the entrance dimmed and the oil wick lantern on his cap flickered higher. It gleamed on the wetness of the walls and highlighted the occasional diamond-like flash of dripping water, miniature cascades that if he looked closely sent up rainbow-tinged arcs gone in an instant. The light glinted off iron rails running down the slope, disappearing into the complete darkness ahead, singing with an almost-imperceptible hum as an unseen mule-dragged cart made its way from somewhere deep in the mountain, loaded with soft black rock and sending vibrations all along its path.

He shivered and realized the pleasant chill had turned dank and the gloom pressed in so that the lamplight grew less and less significant. Ahead of him Reis, the new mine superintendent, a lean and bony Welshman, turned back and reached up a hand to the roof no more than six and a half feet over the floor.

"Roof coal," he said, "and slate on top of that. Here we're no more'n five feet below the surface. Down at the end there'll be two hundred feet of mountain atop us."

Harry lifted a hand and scratched at the rock above his head; traces of dust came off under his nails. He felt the weight of the hillside above him, brooding like a living thing, the crushing force of it held at bay by columns of timber and slate and pillars of unmined coal. He stopped for a moment and listened. He remembered vividly the moody silence of underground, broken only by rodents and gnats. Then he began to notice new sounds: the clink and bite of picks and shovels echoing dimly from side corridors, ghostly tokens of the work deep in the mountain, punctuated by the rattle of the train and the snort of mules. The scurry and rustle and squeak of rats, descendants of those they heard years ago, still made his skin prickle. A distant crack and rumble overhead like the muted premonition of a thunderstorm in the distance caused him to start and brace himself with one hand against the wall.

Reis grinned, yellow teeth in a blackened face. "The mine talks to us all the time," he said in his heavy Welsh accent. "The men down here have learned to pay attention. When the roof sets a-rumbling and begins to sound like thunder deep in the rock, they get the hell out."

"You'll let me know when that starts." Harry took a deep breath. Never would he let on to Murray that he was nervous.

The deeper they went, the lower pressed the ceiling, until both he and Murray bent over, caps scraping the occasional jagged point. A rumble sounded from up ahead and the three pressed themselves against the wall. Out of the dimness a massive long face appeared; its eyes picked up the glint of the lamplight. Harry smelled mule before he saw the rest of it. It plodded up the slope dragging four wagons piled with chunks of soft and lustrous bituminous on their way to the surface. The driver, perched on the front car, touched a finger to his cap in passing but said not a word.

Ahead, Reis turned off the main passageway into a side corridor. His lamp skimmed over the walls and lit the rails at their feet. The sound of pick and shovel grew stronger, and here and there light leaked from rooms cut at a slant off this secondary tunnel. Harry stumbled over a rock, threw out a hand to catch himself. He grasped a soft, cottony mass and turned his lamp to the beam above him. Yellow patches like tawed leather blotched its underside and fairy-like white strands of fungus like those he'd seen on his first visit wafted in the slight movement of air. He traced the beam with his fingers to where it rested on a pillar against the wall; the beam itself showed splintering and dust where the fungus ate away at it; it smelled like creosote. He picked at it and a tiny cloud of gnats spun up and away.

Reis and Murray disappeared around a corner into a thin pool of light and Harry hurried after them, uneasy to be left alone. The glow came from a lantern set on the floor of the tunnel next to a wooden box. A tiny wizened old man sat there, by the looks of him no more than four feet tall, hunched over his knees, his lunch bucket beside him on the damp floor, his hat pulled low over his eyes. The tiny being stood and saluted the newcomers with a tug on his cap, and Harry realized with a start that this was no wizened old man but a child who looked to be six or seven, face blackened into creases with coal dust, shoulders hunched and nails rimmed with dirt. He was stationed along tracks which disappeared beneath a wide door made of wooden planks and cross braces that closed off yet another tunnel and blocked the way of the mule carts.

"Morning, son," Reis said, though morning held little meaning down here. "Nicklow, is it? Your dad back there?" He nodded to the door.

The boy tugged at his cap briefly. "He is. And my brother, too." He stood and hauled at the door. It was heavy and he had to throw his weight back to open it wide.

"Got to block off the passage," Reis said. "Keep the gases out and the air in. Boy's here to open the door for the mule cars."

"Kind of young, isn't he?" Harry was well aware that boys worked underground, the labor contracts and mining news talked about them, but seeing one in the flesh was something else.

"He has to be at least ten," Murray said. "Some oeprators take a boy at seven, but we insist they're at least ten."

Harry didn't believe it.

"Makes good money," Reis said. "He'll be cutting coal himself before too much longer."

Harry looked at Murray, but the man ducked into the corridor beyond the door. He hadn't appeared to register the presence of the child.

"How're those fans working for you, Reis?" Murray took a deep breath as if testing the air and spit. "Coal dust seems pretty heavy in here."

"Yeh, air's a bit stagnant. We're a ways ahead of the current."

Harry coughed and Reis whacked him on the back. "Ye're not so used to this down here. A miner grows up in the pit, the lungs make do. He don't mind it so much."

"I suppose," Harry said, and he meant the remark to bite, "if you start at ten years old you become accustomed pretty fast."

"Oh, aye, ye do," Reis said cheerfully. "It's the way of a miner's life."

The brattice—the boy's door—swung closed behind him, and Harry found himself in a room hewn out of the coal itself. The low thud of a pick sounded, oddly deadened, rising from low down. Two men lay on their sides, backs to the room, hacking into the coal seam where it met the floor. A partly-filled wagon stood to the side, positioned to be loaded with dislodged coal. The seam itself stretched maybe five feet up the wall, aglow in the lamplight, like the rich ebony panels Harry had seen in costly Chinese cabinetry. He fancied he could make out the striations that marked the ancient trees and massive ferns, the sedges and mosses encased in their mud and sand and debris, the vestiges of primeval forests hidden for eons underground until these men in this year dug pathways and brought in lights and revealed their majesty to the world. *And we burn it. It should be on display beside the bones of dinosaurs, but instead we burn it by the trainload.*

"Frank Nicklow!" Reis called out. "Look alive! Here we have the big boss man. Show your manners."

Both men turned their heads. Harry could see that one was older, the other just a boy, about his own age, but beyond that the shadows hid their features. Both were coated in coal dust turned to sludge by sweat and the constant weep of the rock faces. The older one's teeth flashed in what was not a smile.

"Boss man, is it? Is he paying me to say hello?" Nicklow turned back to his work.

"You've just started on this room then?" Reis said. "Finished that one on number seven, did you?"

"Yeah." He struck deep under the seam with his pick. "We'll bring down these blocks later today."

"Got your boy there on the pick work."

"He's ready." The boy drove deeper with his pick, and Harry imagined he was conscious of the boss man.

The older man backed out of the cleft and leaned on an elbow. "You've brought in open flame."

"Ach," Reis said. "'Tis safe enough. The fire boss cleared it."

"Taking chances with it, up here in this one." And the man turned into his work.

The lamps the two men worked by were different from the ones Harry and his companions carried. They were enclosed and covered with mesh, and the light they shed was dimmer. Harry turned to Reis with his brows raised.

"Fire damp. Last year, December it was, you'll remember there was a blast, killed a fella, Bill Hone. It was in number five flat, next one over. He went in before the fire boss cleared it, he did. Dumb ass thing to do." Reis kicked at a loose block of coal at his feet. "Inspector finds his dinner bucket sitting right here where he left it, as if he's coming back for his bite of bread and cheese but a course he never come back. Doors wasn't closed, inspector said, gas built up. We was lucky, none of the other men'd gone in yet. You remember, Mister Murray, that's when we had to put in all those extra doors, keep 'em locked. Shouldn't be no more trouble in that way." He gestured with a thumb over his shoulder.

Harry peered around the room as if he could see the place where a man had died, alone and in the dark, and thought about the last thing the miner had seen. It must have seemed like he was already buried to be down there. He wondered if the man had died instantly or if he'd choked to death on the after-gas, aware he would never again see the sky.

"Ye'll see the flame grow tall if there's fire damp in here." Reis grinned. "And that's the last thing ye'll see." He cackled, as if it were a great joke.

Nicklow and his boy tapped short wooden blocks into the cut.

"That's called spragging," Murray said to Harry. "It props the face of the seam so he can cut the rest of the way through it."

Nicklow lay down again and wiggled his way underneath the coal face until all that could be seen was his back. The sound of the pick came faintly from the depths. Harry had a sudden vivid sense of the menacing bulk of those tons of black rock, wedged back in amongst dust and darkness, like being in a grave and forcing your way out with a dull knife.

Murray pointed to the top of the seam. "Will you blast out some of that? I understand some of it along this side's too hard for pick work."

"Aye, mebbe. Nicklow's pretty deft with the blasting."

"I ain't," Nicklow said from the deep. His voice was faint. "No need to shine me up. Blasting just wastes coal."

Reis snorted. "Frank has a pride in him. Good man." They watched in silence for a few moments, then Reis motioned them on. As they turned away, the light caught the flash of Nicklow's pickax, the dim whiteness of the son's face, the shape of the wagon, melding the shadows into a deeper and more ominous black. Like marionettes, stiff and wooden, a play put on in the underworld by creatures unheedful of the world of light above.

Harry followed as Reis turned one corner after another, led them through passageways and tunnels. Boys opened more doors and swung them shut behind them. There was an unreality to it all that had Harry half thinking he was a mole in a dream, scurrying underground in his blindness. Reis kept up a running commentary: here we are at number three butt entry, it's turned out of number seven flat. Runs across number six flat. Number four butt sealed off now, played out. We're moving toward the old works. And here we are, right-hand side of the slope, number five heading.

"There was the accident last spring," Harry said. "A man killed by a fall, we came out that night, Mr. Murray and I. Back when Keighley was still superintendent."

"Yessir," Reis said. "His own fault too. Shoulda know'd the roof weren't stable. Coulda put up posts, they was plenty to be had. He just dinna want to take the time away from digging coal."

"Why would that be?" Harry asked. "Why would anyone not take the time to brace the roof?"

Murray shrugged. "Young men think they're immortal." He grasped a timber and looked up, jiggling it. "I'll wager you do yourself. He wasn't much older than you. And he doesn't get paid to put up posts. He only gets paid for the coal he sends out."

"We tell 'em and tell 'em." Reis led the way through yet another door. The child who opened it and closed it behind them watched silently, eyes big. "But they get in a hurry. Get greedy."

"What about paying them a flat rate for doing the infrastructure work?" Harry asked.

Reis laughed. "That'll be the day. The bosses'd never go there." He glanced sideways at Murray. "Beggin' your pardon, sir."

Murray shrugged. "Maybe that will happen someday, but right now accidents are a cost of doing business."

"You could change that." He welcomed the sight of daylight; they were on the exit slope. Behind him, he heard the clink of the picks, the tap of a steady drumbeat in the rich black heart of the living mountain.

"I do what I can, Harry," Murray said. "I can't change the whole industry overnight."

Back on top, Harry shivered in the heat of the July sun, the chill in his bones deep and not entirely from the dank cold of the mine. He stared back at the two gaping holes in the hillside, little indication of the vast underground world behind them. Rails ran between the two, up and over the hill toward the coking ovens, and spurs ran into the hillside at a third opening. A shaft protruded halfway up the hill, steam pouring into the sultry air; the tipple loomed over the yard. All new since that long-ago day when he and Dan and Rebecca had explored.

Murray talked to Reis a moment, then dismissed him, and waited for Harry at the foot of the path to the road.

"Shall we take a look at the coking operation too now?"

"If you have the time." Harry turned away from the mine, and they hiked up and over the hill to the ovens.

"Here." Murray waved at the banks of beehive structures. "We can talk to some of the men if you'd like. If you're interested in this business, might as well hear what they have to say about it. I think you'll find they're satisfied enough."

Harry looked up and down the line. Men stood atop the ovens; they would be the ones responsible for guiding the coal into the mouths of the ovens from the larries. They threw sidewise glances at the visitors, and Harry thought he felt their animosity, but then he figured he imposed his own attitude on them. Why would they care? A barrel-chested worker dragged cooled coke from the face of the ovens, dumped it into a barrow and rested on his long-handled shovel. He swabbed his face with a kerchief and studied them, then turned back to his labors.

"No. I don't want to interfere. I get the idea." He turned away and moved toward the road. They'd left the buggy back by the mine.

"Harry." Murray caught up and laid a hand on his shoulder. "I know it looks like hell to you—"

"Probably looks like hell to them, too."

"It's their livelihood." Murray talked to Harry's back, since the path up to the road was only wide enough for one. "Most of these men worked the mines in their own countries in much worse conditions for much less pay. They're here because they can make a lot more and send money back to their families. Someday they'll go back to Italy and Poland and Hungary and wherever else they came from and be important men."

Harry stopped and turned. "I haven't said anything, I'm not criticizing."

"I know you haven't. I just want you to know the whole story. This is the price we pay for the kind of life we live, for fast trains and steam engines and all the good things in life."

Harry turned back and climbed onto the road. "It's a trade-off. I understand that. I hope they live long enough to go back and be important."

Murray walked alongside him now. The buggy was in sight, Murray's chestnut Morgan half asleep in the shade of a scraggly oak. "The foreigners, they're not like us Harry. They can stand those conditions."

"The Irish too? And the Welsh? And the English miners?"

"They're all miners. Someone has to do the dirty work."

"I guess." Harry was quiet on the drive home.

18

Neither the brother nor the sister ever mentioned the husband, and Harry didn't ask. He met them, usually both, but sometimes Patrick only, more and more often at the farmhouse as late summer thunderstorms invaded the valley or heat and humidity drove them inside.

Joanna asked no questions, seemed pleased to have young people in the house. Silent and watchful, she went about her chores with little comment. Every Sunday morning Harry rode back to the farmhouse with her after church and turned Mona out into the small pasture while his aunt put a pot of coffee on the stove or lemonade in the icebox and biscuits or cornbread or a pie in the oven. Harry figured Patrick came as much for the food as for the learning. Joanna and Niamh chatted some, but Niamh always followed along with the lessons, absorbing silently what Patrick studied aloud. Every week Harry came up with a sheet of math problems and Patrick surrendered the ones he'd worked on over the past week. While Harry went over those, Patrick copied out Latin sentences and declined verbs, and when that was finished, they talked history or literature.

Patrick's appetite for American politics, society, recent history was insatiable, and Harry brought study materials accordingly: the Pittsburgh papers, the *Commercial Gazette* for the Republican viewpoint, the *Weekly Post* for the Democrats. He brought in the Connellsville paper for the local mining news, and both Patrick and Niamh looked forward to it especially. Mark Twain, of course, and Walt Whitman's strange happy verses, and to balance those, a book called *Democracy, an American Novel* that had little good to say about the government. Fortified with these two contradictions, Patrick gobbled up news of the upcoming presidential election, full as it was of scandal and accusations, mugwumps and bigotry.

"That man has a child by a woman not his wife," Niamh said of Cleveland.

Patrick turned a page in the paper he read. "As do many a man in any station, but Blaine hates the Irish and so he says for anyone to hear."

Harry had spread the paper out on the kitchen table; Patrick skimmed through it and pointed to a headline. "CATHOLIC MINERS FLOP" the *Post-Gazette* blared, and he scowled at Harry. "What's he mean by that, then?"

"'The Irish vote in this township has up to heretofore been overwhelmingly Democratic,'" Harry read, "'but ever since the nomination of Blaine and Logan, these miners have openly declared in favor of the Republican nominees.' It appears the Irish have gone over to Blaine after all."

"The Irish are declared for Blaine?" Patrick said. "But that'll never happen. The Irish always vote Democrat."

Niamh took the paper. "'Father John Burns, of the Catholic Church, has espoused the cause of the Republicans,' They'll do as the priest says, they always do. The priests know what's best."

Harry read over her shoulder. "I've never understood why the working man tends to vote against his own best interests. If it were up to the Republicans only the rich landowners would vote and the laboring man be hanged."

"True enough," Patrick said. "But you'll see, the Irish will show them. Someday we'll have an Irish president."

"We will," Niamh said. "The Irish are here to stay and there's a crowd of them to vote."

Harry looked at her and said softly before he thought better of it, "As long as you're here to stay."

Niamh flushed and looked away. Patrick carefully put down the paper and made a production of folding it. "We'd best be getting back, Niamh." His voice was rough. "Martin will be off soon, and his temper is none too sure these days."

"What's wrong with Martin?" Harry said.

"Don't you know, then?" Niamh said. "They're after cutting the wages again, another ten cents a ton. And only seventy of the ovens working."

"And the miners over on the Monongahela, they went back in last week making less than when they went out," Patrick said.

"I did hear something about that," Harry said. "The operators aren't making money either, it's the recession. The price of coke is down." He sounded defensive, even to himself.

"Is that it then? I fancy it's the greedy mine owners, they do what they will with the market." Niamh stood and carried the lunch dishes to the wash basin. "I hear the recession has not stopped your friend Mr. Murray from building himself a palace on Ben Lomond Street."

Harry's head snapped up at her tone. "How do you know about that? And he's not so much my friend, in fact not at all. I only work for him."

"There's talk about him courting Miss Joanna's sister." She tossed her head and glared at him. "Sure and you'll be the master's nephew one day soon as well as his business partner."

"Niamh…" Patrick held out his hand to her.

"Ah, now, I don't mean it, do I?" She sighed and turned back to Harry with a small smile. "It just seems like they work so hard and never do get ahead, whether it's here or in Connemara."

"My aunt is not going to marry him," Harry said. "And I'll never be his business partner."

"Don't worry yourself." She patted his arm. "You'll be giving Patrick the means to get away from mining and sure I'm grateful."

Patrick pushed his papers into his jacket pocket and pulled on his cap. He ducked his head to Harry and sent him a look, and he and Niamh slipped out the back door into the warm September afternoon.

Patrick knows, Harry thought. *Am I that obvious? Pathetic.* He pumped water and washed up the dishes—Patrick had eaten three helpings of black bean soup and cornbread, and Niamh had eaten a healthy serving, too; Harry often wondered if they ever got enough to eat—and made another pot of coffee. Joanna kicked open the back door, a load of firewood in her arms, as the coffee boiled. Harry closed the door behind her and took the wood.

She smiled at him. "Where have your students gone?"

"Left early. Seems Niamh's husband might not be working a full shift today." He dumped the wood into the bin while she poured coffee for both of them.

"And he needs to find her at home when he gets there?"

"I guess. I don't think he's keen on Patrick taking lessons. They tend to tiptoe around his temper."

Joanna took milk from the icebox. "Harry, what do you know about these people? If her husband objects to their education, maybe you shouldn't be helping them?"

"I don't see how anyone can object to a boy getting an education." Harry dropped into his chair and took a gulp of black coffee. It burned his throat.

"Why did they come over here if it wasn't to get ahead? And he won't make anything of himself working in that mine."

"I don't really know what goes on over in the patch, but I hear enough to know there's a lot of dissatisfaction, a lot of unhappy people. Some of those miners can get nasty, especially when they drink. And Niamh had an ugly bruise on her cheek last week."

Harry had seen it too, and it made his blood boil. But Niamh had laughed and said she'd banged into the back door carrying a load of laundry, and Patrick had confirmed that. Harry didn't believe them but there was nothing he could do.

"What do you hear?" he asked his aunt. "The company's cutting wages again another ten cents a ton. And only half the ovens are running."

"What does Mr. Murray say?"

"Not much. I told him last week he needed to pay more attention to how the miners were treated, and he hasn't talked to me about it since. I thought he'd fire me on the spot. You should have seen how Patrick ate today. You'd think he's starving."

"A boy that age needs a deal of food, and I'll wager he isn't getting enough." She drained her cup and set it in the basin. "I'll be sure to have plenty here for him next week."

"Have you heard anything about a strike? There's some talk of it in the Connellsville paper."

"I haven't heard anything, but then I wouldn't. None of them talks to me beyond saying hello on the road." She leaned against the counter and folded her arms. "I did go into the company store last week. I was short of sugar, but it was so much more expensive there I didn't buy it. I talked to the storekeeper's wife, though. She was plenty willing to share her opinion, which by the way is not very high about any of the Patch folk."

"The paper said a lot of the Hungarians are leaving."

"That should help. The English and the Irish hate the Hungarians and the Italians, and they all hate the Negroes. But the Hungarians are the worst. They must live twenty or thirty to a house, all on top of each other. One gets sick and before you know it the whole town is coughing and wheezing."

"But where do they go? The Hungarians?"

"Back to Hungary, a lot of them. The storekeeper said as soon as they make a hundred dollars they hightail it back home and live like lords. That's why they live the way they do here, they save money by not buying food or clothes. They don't want to learn to read and they live like pigs in sties and they save everything they make."

"And meanwhile Philip Murray builds an eighteen-room mansion on Ben Lomond Street and furnishes it from New York and Paris. What an ass."

Joanna smiled. "And most folks believe he'll be your uncle soon."

Harry flushed. "Not if I have anything to say about it. She'd never be happy with him. And she isn't used to that kind of rich living."

Joanna lifted an eyebrow. "I don't believe you *do* have anything to say about it. You're in love with that girl, aren't you?"

Harry's head snapped up.

She laughed softly. "Don't look so surprised. It's fairly obvious, at least to me. I know you pretty well by now." She pulled out a chair and sat across from him and leaned her elbows on the table. "Harry, you're going to be hurt." Her voice was gentle. "That's all there is to it. You need to let this run its course, finish teaching them, then let them both go when it's time."

He folded his hands and stared at his linked fingers. "I didn't know it would be so hard. I've never felt like this before."

"It *is* hard. Everyone goes through it, and when you come out the other side, you're stronger for it. This won't last forever."

"But I want it to last forever. I'd rather love her the way things are than never see her again. I don't want to lose this feeling."

"You know all the arguments. First of all, she's married."

"Maybe he'll die."

"Harry."

"I'm sorry, but it could happen."

"Second, she's Catholic. She's Irish. She's from a different world."

"None of that matters."

"Not now, maybe. But someday it will. Take my word for it."

Something in her voice made him look up. "You sound as if you know."

She smiled.

"Was there someone for you? Someone … inappropriate?"

"Yes, there was." She blushed. She looked happy to be remembering. "I was about your age."

"Why didn't it work out?"

"Charlotte. Her name was Charlotte."

"Oh," Harry said weakly. "I suppose it wouldn't, then."

"Yes." Joanna grinned at him. "Do you hate me now?"

Harry stood, walked around the table, and put his arms around her shoulders. "Never. You're still my Aunt Joanna, and you and Mattie are my favorites." He kissed the top of her head and reached for his stack of books. "Now I need to get home. Mattie's cooking dinner, and I'm afraid Murray will be there. He hasn't been in the office all week, and he'll want to talk work."

Joanna stood. "Be kind, Harry. Remember, Mattie deserves happiness, too, and if he's what she wants, it's not yours to say."

"She's much too smart for that." Harry pulled his cap on and opened the back door. "Thanks for the food. I'll bring you sugar next Saturday."

"And coffee," Joanna called after him. She stood in the door and waved as he and Mab turned south on the Bethelboro road.

19

The rain started before Harry had gone a mile, and his mood grew darker. He kicked at a stone in the road, and Mab chased it into the ditch. It was all wrong. Niamh and her husband, the conditions in the patch, Murray and Mattie, his job. He thought about what Joanna had told him and couldn't get his mind around it. He'd heard of such things at college, between men. There had been rumors about one of the professors, and of course everyone knew about Socrates and Alcibiades, they called them "sexual inverts," but he'd never really thought about women loving women. He wondered if any of the sisters knew. He wondered what had become of Charlotte. He wondered if Mattie really did love Philip Murray or if she just wanted companionship. He couldn't imagine her marrying, she seemed so set in her ways. To have to move into a new home, adjust to another person, share decisions, relinquish charge of her finances, cook and clean for him. But then she'd live in that big house on Ben Lomond and have servants, so maybe it would be worth it. But he didn't think she would sell herself that way.

The rain was gentle and smelled fresh. Across the valley to the west, a newly-harvested hay field lay in a strip of sunshine that sliced through a gash in the cloud cover and turned the far green hills dazzling. He picked up a stick and threw it for the dog. Autumn was coming; maybe it was time to move on, start thinking about what came next. Teach school, read law, travel to Montana. He felt stuck in quicksand, immobilized, counting on something to happen but powerless to force it. An addiction waiting for a cure but he had no desire to be cured. As long as she was near, he had to see her.

✳

Mattie had dinner on the table, chicken and dumplings, tomatoes and cucumbers from the tiny garden she babied in the back, fresh baked bread filling the house with the yeasty aroma he always associated with the old farmhouse. Murray was not there, but the aunts were already seated, and his mother poured lemonade with ice into glasses.

"Where'd you get the ice?" He stepped into the pantry and poured water, scrubbed his face and hands and brushed half-heartedly at his damp hair.

"And hello to you, too," Mattie said cheerfully, slicing a too-thick slab of bread. She was broadening in the middle.

"Harry, go out back and wipe your boots. They're thick with mud. Where've you been?" His mother set down the pitcher and swiped at the drips. When he returned, she pulled him by the sleeve and brushed drops from his shoulders. "Where did you go this time?" She raised her brows at him and dropped into her chair at the table's foot.

He sat. "I've been to the farmhouse. Teaching those two Irish kids I told you about."

Agnes set down her fork and leaned toward him. "I didn't think you were still doing that. Is it all right with Joanna? Turning her home into a schoolroom for miners?"

Mary frowned and helped herself to fried chicken. "Shouldn't think she'd want those people in there, seeing she's alone and all. I don't suppose they're paying you."

Harry snorted before he could stop himself, tried to turn the snort into a cough. "They're good folks, Aunt Mary, no different from you and me."

"Of course, they are," Mattie said. "Not like those Italians and Hungarians."

"Anyone who works underground is no better than an animal." Mary's nose had that pinched look that Harry knew meant an oncoming rant. "How people can work twelve hours a day down there I just don't know."

"They don't have a choice," Harry said through his teeth.

Sarah shivered. "Like you're dead, I would think. Like you're already in your tomb. And goodness knows the way they kill them off, most of them are."

"But those Irish," Mary said, "with their popes and their incense and their idols. Drunken lazy louts they are."

"But Mary," Mattie said, "half of Uniontown is Irish."

"Including the Canons." Agnes waved her fork at her sister.

"We're no shanty Irish," Mary said. "We're Scots Irish, and so are our neighbors, good Presbyterians or better, Methodists. Not this Catholic trash."

"That's not very Christian," Elizabeth murmured. Mary didn't hear.

Sarah laughed. "What is it that Englishman said about the Irish? More like squalid apes than human beings?"

Harry pushed away his half-empty plate and stood so abruptly his chair fell over. "That's ignorant and unfair. You don't know them."

"Don't you speak to me like that, young man." Mary slapped the table. "I won't stand for disrespect from you."

Agnes threw down her napkin. "You'll stand for it from me, then, sister." She too stood. "I won't listen to that kind of talk at the dinner table. Both of you should be ashamed." She followed Harry into the kitchen and out the back.

Harry dropped to the wet ground next to the garden and yanked at a dandelion. It broke off in his fist and he threw it aside. "Who are those people? I can't believe they're related to us."

His mother sank down next to him, her skirts billowing. "They've lived a sheltered life and haven't taken the trouble to educate themselves. Sarah will apologize once she thinks about it. She follows Mary's lead."

"But Mary won't. She's a vicious, nasty old woman, and I can't keep living here with her in the house."

"You shouldn't be here, anyway. You need to be out on your own and away from all these women." Agnes pulled a radish and picked at the clinging dirt. "You might travel."

"I'd like to see Montana again. See what's happened to the old ranch."

"You might visit your father's grave." She looked over the yard, her gaze far away. "Maybe I'll go with you. I'd like to visit the Missouri relatives again."

"We could go to San Francisco. You always wanted to see it."

She huffed and hauled herself up. "But I'm really too old, and you wouldn't want an old lady along to slow you down." She pulled him to his feet. "I'd miss you if you took off for a year. And I'd hate to think you might decide to stay in San Francisco."

"I'm not sure that's far enough away from Mary."

"Probably not." Agnes smiled and kissed him on the temple.

✳

Once in his room, he stripped out of his damp clothes. He brushed his teeth, put on clean underclothes and flopped onto his bed. The window was open to the steamy post-rain humidity, settling in like a wet shawl over the landscape. A spider had spun its web in a low corner, and he tossed a flake of lint into it, but the spider seemed too enervated by the heat to pay attention. It didn't budge.

"Hell," Harry murmured. He closed his eyes and fancied Niamh laughing, Niamh playing with the puppy, Niamh stringing dandelions together in a daisy chain. He thought about the first time they'd met, felt the touch of her hand when he helped her across the stream. She probably hadn't thrilled to the touch, as he had. And he'd feared the tremor he felt would communicate itself to her, but if it had, she showed no awareness. He'd wanted to keep her hand in his, to feel its softness among the calluses, to raise it to his lips and kiss those rough spots, to swear to her that he would see them heal and never return. Those calluses, along the base of her fingers, tough on the first knuckle of her thumb, the broken nails, made him think of the ugliness of the patch town, the unending struggle against dirt and poisonous air, made him think of children who didn't eat well and didn't breathe clean air and didn't go to school.

He sat up and rubbed his eyes. He was an idiot. She had chosen her life, she'd told him more than once. She had wanted desperately to come to America and this was the only way. She rarely mentioned her husband by name, only referenced him indirectly, and he was sure she did not love him. But she never complained, never whined about her lot. She was determined that her brother would find another way, a way out of the mines and into the mainstream of American life with all its goodness. That's what she called it, its goodness. The abundance of food, the magic of steam engines, the lovely clothes, the air of prosperity—those were all the things she touched on, not in so many words, but when they talked, he knew she was enchanted with the bounty she saw in America.

And where had she seen it? Certainly not in the hell hole that was Youngstown. Not enough food at inflated prices, clothing of the plainest kind, often-washed, heavily mended. The only steam engines in the patch town world were those necessary for the operations of the mine and the ovens: fans, water pumps, the trains that rumbled by.

She would have seen the beauty and promise of America as she passed through on her way to the mines. She would have seen them on the docks in

New York when she left the ship, on the ship itself, though she would have traveled below decks in steerage. She would have seen them as she trudged through the streets of lower Manhattan, her brother in tow, carrying her one bag and parcel of food. She would have passed open-air markets full of fresh fruits and vegetables, stores with sides of beef and pork and legs of lamb on display, shops whose windows featured dresses and hats and shoes that she could never hope to buy as a poor immigrant Irish girl.

He loved that about her. She nurtured the dream that had brought so many to America, and he knew she had not been here long, but she hadn't lost it, despite the circumstances of the patch. He wondered how long it would take her to become disenchanted, to lose that freshness and sparkle that drew him to her. How long it would be before her nails became permanently blackened, her cheeks caved in and lines etched, before her eyes grew tired and dull.

But she was different, wasn't she? That was the reason she bewitched him. He sensed a spirit in her that wouldn't succumb. She would never let her hair thin and her breasts sag and her spirit grow oppressed. Niamh. *Nee-ev.* Her name was magical, a secret in itself. She was a secret. His secret. Niamh.

20

October 1884

Joanna turned up at the door of Agnes's house early on a blustering Saturday in October, out of breath and disheveled. Harry opened the door to her, his aunts at the breakfast table behind him. She leaned in to kiss his cheek and whispered into his ear. "She's at the farmhouse, she needs you. Go quickly. Mona's outside." And she turned to greet her sisters as if she'd said nothing.

Harry snatched his cap from the hook and slipped out without a word. Joanna's buggy horse stood huffing; she'd been driven hard, and yet once out of town he pushed her as fast as he dared and pulled into the farmhouse yard just as the sun broke from behind another dark cloud. The smoke from the ovens drifted over Chestnut Ridge before the chill west wind so the air was clean and fresh and bracing. He wrapped the reins to the back porch railing. The storm door was closed, but the inside door stood open to the kitchen, and he saw her through the screen. She must have heard the horse and his boots on the porch, but she sat perfectly still, her profile dark against the far window. When he pushed open the door and stepped in, cap in hand, she turned slowly toward him.

Her face was a mass of purple bruises, yellow at the edges. One eye was swollen nearly shut and dried blood clung to her nostrils. She held a damp cloth in one hand but made no effort to put it to her face. Harry stepped toward her slowly; he thought foolishly that if he moved too fast she might break. She held out a hand to him.

"Please, please find Patrick," she whispered, and he saw that her lip was split. "He'll listen to you. If he sees me, he'll go after Martin and Martin will kill him."

"I'll find him." Harry eased her back into the chair. He took the rag. Joanna had put ice in it, but it was gone now and the rag luke-warm. "Patrick won't know as long as you're here, and I won't leave you."

"I didn't know where to go," she said. "I couldn't think. Kate wasn't home and Patrick's working and I couldn't let anyone else see me—"

"You did right." There was no more ice, so he made do with cool water and dabbed at her bloody chin. "Joanna knows what to do."

"She gave me salve and a headache powder, and I asked if she'd fetch you," Niamh said. "I'm that worried about my brother."

"What the devil made him do this?"

"I said no more boarders, especially not those Huns, and he was so angry."

Harry scowled. "So he beat the living daylights out of you? I wouldn't blame Patrick. He ought to take a pickax after the man."

"Ah, no." Niamh began to cry. "I'm afraid what he'll do when he finds out. He's not a match for Martin."

"I don't know why not. Martin's a coward or he wouldn't take it out on you. Didn't anyone else in that damn town step in?"

"Kate next door went to Mass and none of the men were about. They wouldn't stop him anyway. They've never interfered before."

Harry started. "Before? How often has this happened?"

"Oh, not so wicked. He backhands me some, when he's displeased about dinner or some other little thing. This time it was like he was possessed. He's that worried, he is, about the pay cuts and the bills and all. He says we have to take more boarders, it's the only way. Only I can't do it, we already have a houseful."

"Where is he now? Did he follow you here?"

"I think he's gone off to the pub in Braddock."

"Drink won't help. Doesn't he get worse when he drinks?"

"He drinks till he sleeps when he's in a temper, then it's gone. He's fast to anger, he is, but he regrets it quick."

Harry brushed the hair from her forehead. A scabbed-over cut ran into her hair and he dabbed at it gently with the rag. She was so close. She smelled of fresh air and sunshine and salty tears. She winced and covered his hand with hers and brought it to her lips. Slowly he traced the lower lip with his finger and touched the split at its corner. She closed her eyes and smiled and her breath slowed and deepened.

"Ah, Harry," she said so softly he almost didn't hear. "You came so fast. Your aunt said you would."

"Of course, I did," he said, his voice hoarse. He opened her hand and kissed the palm softly, once, twice, then the fingertips with their broken nails. She leaned toward him and set her forehead against his. Tears spilled from the corners of her eyes, but her lips still curved. He kissed them, gently, fearing to hurt her but unable to help himself and she shifted to accept the kiss and parted her lips. His tongue touched the corner of her mouth and tasted the salt of tears or blood, slid over her bottom lip and against her teeth. Her arms slipped about his neck and he leaned in; his hands cupped her face. Then he stood, slid an arm beneath her legs and lifted her, carried her through the kitchen and down the hall to the front bedroom, the one no longer occupied with all but Joanna gone. He kicked the door closed behind him, covering her bruised face with kisses. She moaned, but not in pain. He laid her on the coverlet and dropped beside her, then he was undoing the buttons on her blouse and fumbling with the ribbon at the neck of her chemise. She pushed his coat back and he sat up to drop it to the floor. She worked the buttons of his shirt. He kissed her again and she rose up against him, her breasts pressed to his shirtfront, and his mind collapsed around sensation. Buttons opened, clothing fell away; they stroked and kissed and murmured and thrashed, and he feared he would add to her hurt. But she said only "No, no, don't stop, don't stop," and so he didn't and then finally they collapsed together and buried their faces in each other's shoulders and clung to one another.

"Oh, Harry, what have we done?" she finally said, voice low.

"What I've wanted to do for so long," he said, eyes closed, one hand stroking her hair.

"Aye, so have I."

He leaned up on an elbow and looked down at her. "If he finds out—"

"Let's not think about it. Let's not be thinking about anything besides right now, this, just here. I'm cold, Harry."

So he pulled the coverlet from beneath them and covered them both, and they settled into the pillows and smiled at one another. And then he was kissing her again and it started all over. The sunlight faded and the room grew dim with a watery glow. Rain hit the window, delicate at first then with more and more force and the sounds and smells of the storm filled the room. The autumn afternoon passed and they slept.

Harry woke to a violent pounding on the kitchen door. But before he was quite awake, he heard his aunt's voice raised over the sound of the wind.

"Patrick Kilgariff! Is that you?" he heard her say. The room was light enough for him to see that Niamh was awake, too, her good eye wide and frightened.

"It is, missus," Patrick's voice said from the back. "I'm looking for my sister." Harry scrambled from the bed and pulled on his trousers.

"Who is that with you?" Joanna said.

"'Tis my brother-in-law, Martin Gill, Niamh's husband."

Niamh stood, her back to Harry, and began to dress.

"Well, he has a nerve showing up here," they heard Joanna say, "after what he did to her. She's resting and I won't disturb her."

Then Harry heard a strange voice, a deeper voice with a rasp like an old cough. "Missus, I'm terrible sorry for what I've done. I'm here to beg her pardon and take her home. It'll not happen again."

Harry growled and bunched his fists, and Niamh laid a hand on his arm, her finger on his lips.

"Patrick, tell her," Gill said. "I've not done it before, and I'll not do it again. She'll be safe what with her brother with her and all."

Harry reached for the door handle.

"No," Niamh said. "It will be so much the worse for me if he knows you're here. He'll not have reason to think I'm anything but alone and your aunt has taken me in."

"But you can't go back to him," Harry hissed. He could see, even in that dim light, the bruises had turned a sickly green.

"What else can I do?" She pushed back her hair. "We've just made it so much worse. He'd have a right to thrash both of us if he knew you were here with me." Her face was in shadow, and he couldn't read her expression. He wanted to see love for him in her eyes; he could not find it in her voice.

"Leave him," he said. "You can stay here with Joanna, and tomorrow I'll come take you away. We'll go to Pittsburgh or Philadelphia. With those bruises, any judge will give you a divorce. We can go out west, go to Montana. It's easier there and no one will care." He was desperate now to keep her close, to keep her away from her husband.

"Don't be foolish, Harry," she said. "It's a sin in God's eyes. And I cannot leave Patrick."

"Don't go out there, then. Stay here tonight, and we'll think it all through tomorrow."

"You don't know him," she said softly. "It will be worse for your aunt and for me if I hide back here. He'll find me, he'll force his way in, she'll not stop him. Patrick can't stop him, either. And if he finds us together, he'll kill you. And probably me as well."

She pushed by him and opened the door. Harry knew she was right, that she would be in danger if Gill found out he was with her. So he remained in the bedroom, in the dark, out of sight and listened to her move down the hall.

"I'm here, Martin, and a pretty sight I am. I'll go home with you, but only if you leave Patrick alone and promise not to trouble Miss Canon."

Harry groaned and leaned his forehead against the door jamb. He longed to rush out there and beat the devil out of the man. He would find a way. He would convince her.

"You're always welcome here, Mrs. Gill." He heard Joanna push aside a chair, then Martin's voice spoke.

"Come home, *Mo ghrá*, I'm that sorry … 'Twill not happen again. I promise."

There was more, and then the door slammed and there was quiet from the kitchen. Harry sat on the edge of the bed and dropped his head in his hands. Had he been a coward? Should he have confronted Martin Gill? Were Niamh and Patrick safe with the man? But what could he do? She was married to him and her religion and the law and every rule of society said what they'd done was wrong and she belonged with her husband. Her religion and society also allowed a man to beat his wife and though most thinking people were appalled and horrified, no one really stepped in to stop it, not until it was too late and the woman was maimed or dead. And she had to want to come with him. He could not kidnap her.

A beam of light shone into the bedroom and Joanna peered at him. She took in the mussed bed and Harry's rumpled clothes and said not a word, but the expression on her face was one of deep sadness.

"Thank you," Harry said. He looked up. "At least she knows she has a place to come if it gets worse."

"What do you know about that man?" Joanna asked. "How violent is he?"

"I don't know much at all about him." He realized it was true. Niamh and Patrick rarely mentioned Martin Gill, and their worlds were so very different that there was no one he could ask who would know him. "I've seen her bruised. She said he'd back-handed her a few times but he's never beaten her so badly before. I don't know how safe she is." He ran a hand through his hair. "Or Patrick either. He's just a kid. He wouldn't be able to fight back if Gill decided to beat the crap out of him." He glanced at his aunt. "Oh, sorry."

She snorted. "I've heard much worse than that. But maybe I should keep the shotgun loaded by the back door. I don't think he'd stop from forcing his way in here to get at her because I said pretty please."

"No, I don't imagine he would. I'm sorry you're in the middle of this."

"Don't you worry about me. I can take care of myself, and if I couldn't then I'd need to move myself into town and vegetate. No, I only want to be sure that girl is safe. She's a pretty special young woman, and I think you couldn't do much better, but unfortunately, she's taken. You need to think about that and not put her in danger."

"I know, I know. I don't think about much else these days."

"You come on now and have some supper then get yourself back to town. Your mother will wonder what's become of you." She turned, took the light, and went back to the kitchen.

Harry stood and walked over to the window. It was dark now and the wind had died down, leaving behind a gentle rain. His entire world had turned upside down this afternoon, and he, like his mother, wondered what had become of him.

21

His mother's house was quiet that night. Only she was awake, reading in the front parlor, pretending she hadn't waited up for him. The lamp-light lit her face from below, leaving her eyes in shadow. He thought for a moment that she must know, he must seem different to her, as he knew so well how different he seemed to himself.

He slept almost immediately but woke in the deep of the night from a dream that fled the moment he opened his eyes, try as he might to capture it, for it had been soft and colorful. The rain had stopped, and the half-moon shone through broken clouds, silvering the edges, but leaving their centers black against the soft glow. He wondered if the moon shone in her window and onto her bed as it did his. Then he remembered she likely was not alone in that bed. He groaned.

He threw aside the covers and climbed out, pushed up the window to let the damp night breeze sweep across his bare chest. The window faced north and he concentrated his thoughts on the far horizon, wanting to touch her somehow, through air, through space, to know that their connection was so strong their minds could connect despite distance.

He needed to know that she was safe, she would heal. He needed to know what she thought of their afternoon of love-making, if she hated him for it or if she loved him for it. If only she said the word, he would take her away to the city or to the west, to Montana or California or Canada or somewhere where they could be together. He needed to know, he needed to make a plan. He would manage it. They would manage it.

"Have you lost your mind?"

For once Dan wasn't clowning. Harry could see he was shaken and angry.

"I know." Harry stood at the window of his friend's bedroom. South Street on a Sunday evening drowsed in the October twilight, waiting for evening services at the Presbyterian church to conclude. A half-dozen buggies, their horses snorting in the chill of autumn, stood at the curb, waiting. "But I can't think about that right now. She might be dead for all I know."

Dan closed his law book with a thump and pushed his chair away from the desk. "So that's what you've been up to. You were such a half-wit all summer, but I never thought you'd go this far. Now you've gone and made it ten times worse. You'll be lucky the husband doesn't come looking for you."

"Dan, you're not helping. I need to know she's all right, and I can't go myself."

"What the hell can I do?"

"Go to Youngstown, see what you can find out."

"What, just ask around? 'Say, you know the Irish girl who gets beat up every once in awhile by her husband? My friend wants to know is she still alive?'"

"Of course not. You can be subtle. They don't know you up there. They've seen me with Murray, they'll think I'm from the Company. No one will tell me anything." Harry turned back into the room and pushed a hand through his hair. "You could go up to Mt. Braddock and have a drink in the bar there, start up a conversation with someone. Bartenders know things. You're good at that."

"I'd also be good at getting beat up. Those places are pretty rough."

"You could say you were looking for work. Wear old clothes."

Dan dropped onto the bed and snorted. "And talk like a hick. No one'll believe that."

Harry sank onto the desk chair. "Dan, I'm desperate."

Dan studied his thumbnail. "What about Rebecca?"

Harry's head snapped up. "What about her? What does she have to do with this?"

"She's hurt you haven't spent any time with her since you got home from school."

"Not true. We were at the Fourth of July picnic and your father's birthday. There were other times, too." Harry looked at his hands. "Must have been."

"She wants more of your attention."

"If that's the case then it's best she not get any more. I don't want her to think—"

"Think what?"

"That I care more than I do."

"Don't wreck what you've got there. When you're over this infatuation, she might be gone."

Harry felt himself go hot. "It's not an infatuation. I've given myself to her, so I can't very well marry Rebecca. Besides, I always thought Rebecca had her eye on you."

"Well, she doesn't. And if you'd ever take your head out of your ass and look around you'd know it." Dan stood and jammed his hands in his pockets. "Look, I'll see what I can find out. It'll take me awhile." He waved at the books strewn across his desk. "I have to study, and the firm wants me in court most of this week."

"Thank you." Harry stood, too, and held out his hand. Dan took it and squeezed, his eyes sad. "That's all I ask, just find out if she's all right. Then I can figure out what to do."

Harry heard nothing from Dan all that next week. He haunted the farmhouse in the evenings and again the next weekend, cleaning stalls and pitching hay and generally getting under Joanna's feet. He hated the mournful looks she cast at him but loved her silence. Despite what he'd told Dan, he couldn't help but trail after his aunt when she finally agreed to visit the company store. It was known that he worked for Murray, and Dobson, the storekeeper, was attentive, servile. He studied the rough wooden shelves, the canned goods, the bins of flour and nails and rolls of muslin and wondered how often Niamh had stood here, choosing her purchases, weighing her husband's pay against the prices, wishing she had more choice. A sack of flour sat behind the clerk, labeled at a dollar seventy-five for fifty pounds. That was at least fifteen cents higher than Beeson's price, in town. She was good at figures, and he thought of her with a list, adding and subtracting and deciding what they could afford this week, what her husband's two dollars a day would buy, how the days of enforced idleness would eat into their food supplies. No wonder Patrick was scrawny, Niamh slender to the point of gauntness. Did she ever wonder why they'd left famine-plagued Ireland to earn starvation wages in a world that promised abundance?

Joanna counted out a handful of coins as the storekeeper handed her a wrapped package of bacon, and Harry shifted his attention back to their conversation when his aunt asked about a young woman with injuries. Dobson admitted to recognizing Niamh by sight, laughed about keeping an eye on the pretty ones, but beyond that knew nothing of her situation, nothing about her husband, had not seen her for over a week. Two older women, black head shawls framing thin lined faces, inspected the cheeses along the counter, plainly listening. Harry wanted to follow them from the store and question them, but Joanna put her hand on his arm and held him back.

"You'll do her more harm if you show an interest," she said. "Your face is an open book. Your pain shows."

But bless her heart, she followed the two and stopped them. He heard her ask if they knew Mrs. Gill. But the old women shook their heads and answered her in heavily accented English, looked away and scuttled off. No one admitted to knowing a woman with a badly bruised face.

22

October 1884

"They thought I was a union organizer." Dan stroked a brush over Bessie's flank and rubbed her nose. "Hand me that one."

Harry slid off his perch on the manger and reached for the soft-bristled brush. He'd found Dan in Doran's livery, a couple blocks down South Street from the Sturgeons' house, stabling the doctor's horse and buggy. "What did you tell them?"

"Just that I was out of work and needed a job. They weren't buying it. They said I looked too soft."

Harry snickered. "Never did an honest day's work in your life."

Dan threw the heavy brush at him. "What'm I doing now, I'd like to know? The most you do is type letters."

"So nothing about Niamh, then?"

"Not a thing. Kinda hard to bring it up without giving away the store. And if Gill finds out there're strange men asking after her ..."

He turned to see his father in the doorway in his shirt sleeves, coat thrown over one arm, his medical bag in hand.

"Harness her back up, son. We're going out." He dumped his bag in the buggy and shrugged into his coat.

Dan grinned and set aside his brush. "Mrs. Peterson's baby finally?"

"No." Dr. Sturgeon's face was grim, his voice low. He took hold of Bessie's cheek band and backed her into the traces. "There's been an accident out at Youngstown, in the mine. A bad one sounds like."

Harry straightened. "What kind? Collapse?"

"Explosion they said. The night shift just went down, there're a bunch of men trapped."

Dan tightened the girth and stood. "I'll go with you."

"I'd appreciate it," Dr. Sturgeon said. "We need to set up a field station."

"So will I." Harry piled in the buggy with the other two and set the medical bag on his knees. He tried to think what shift Patrick and Martin Gill worked, if they worked days or nights. He kept seeing Niamh's bruised and battered face in front of him, Patrick's thin limbs and half-starved look. Thought about how far the boy had come in his lessons, how well his Latin had progressed. Felt again Niamh's soft body under his, heard the Irish words she whispered in his ear that rainy afternoon, words he couldn't understand but that spoke volumes.

They felt the confusion and the panic well before they pulled up at the entrance to the mine. Dozens of men and women, children, too, milled about the air line portal on the west side of the slope. Harry spotted Reis, the superintendent who'd guided him through the mine, and pointed him out to Dr. Sturgeon. Reis stooped next to the adit, one hand on the timber heading, bent as if to probe the mountain's depths. He made no move to enter. The atmosphere was heavy with acrid smoke and the scent of dread. Women stood back from the opening, some with babies, children huddled against their skirts, faces strained and stark with shock. Their eyes flitted over their neighbors as if to take inventory of the men. Who was there and safe. Who was not. The crowd fell silent as the doctor stepped down from the buggy, the children as well as the mothers. Harry scoured the faces, searching. She wasn't there.

The sun had dipped behind the western ridges, the twilight murky and thick. Lanterns dotted the crowd, throwing lurid, moving shadows across rails, caked mud, weeds. But the mouth of the mine was shrouded in shadow—no one wanted to bring a flame close for fear of after-gas. Several men carried safety lanterns, but they made little impression on the growing gloom. Harry shivered. The entrance to hell must look like this. He spotted Murray talking to a tall lanky man whom Dr. Sturgeon said was Stinner, the district inspector. Harry and Dan moved close enough to overhear.

"Gas," Stinner said. "I thought at first it couldn't be too bad because it was late in the afternoon, but the night shift went in around three so there's a full crew in there. Reis and Cole say there are ten, maybe twelve working over there on the right-hand side." He gestured. "I'm having the Clanny lamps cleaned now. We'll go in soon as we get supplies."

Reis's plaintive voice carried: "We checked for gas," he said. "We checked for gas, I swear we did."

"Who've you got to go in with you?" Murray said.

"Got a couple volunteers." Stinner looked around. Men watched him, faces darkly apprehensive, uncertain. "They're afraid of the afterdamp, and I don't blame them."

Harry stepped forward. "I'll go."

Murray turned, raised his brows. "No. You don't know what you're getting into."

Stinner looked from one to the other. "I can use every man I can get."

Harry locked his eyes on Stinner. "Tell me what to do."

Murray looked him up and down, then shrugged and turned away. Dan said his father needed him to help with the injured and slipped into the crowd. Harry followed Stinner toward the mine where a pile of supplies had been stacked: bolts of muslin, buckets of nails, hatchets, safety lamps. Someone gave Harry a stiff helmet and a kerchief to wrap around his mouth and nose and showed him how to handle the safety lamp. Six men gathered around Stinner—the only names Harry caught were Bosley and Hanlin—and the crowd parted to let them through.

They entered the mine by way of the boundary-line air course, along the right-hand side of the slope. The gloom was intense, the atmosphere filled with shifting, gritty clouds of particles like swarms of countless hard-shelled insects. Harry could taste the coal dust on his tongue, smell the heavy earthy scent of pulverized stone and something underlying it, bad egg he thought. He ducked as a stream of gravel rattled out of the ceiling, stumbled over rubble underfoot. Stinner, at the head of the meager column of rescuers, held a map and referred to it at every turn. Twenty-five yards in they found a wood door smashed to splinters, then a second. And a third. The damage increased the farther they dropped into the mine. Stinner assigned Harry and a Welshman to tack sheets of muslin across passageways to stop the flow of gas and bad air from room to room. They'd begun on their second when a cry echoed from the tunnel ahead.

"Here!" And then "It's Nicklow, Frank Nicklow, over here." Harry remembered the name and a cold shiver went down his spine. He tacked the last corner of the barrier and stumbled along the rails to the next room. It was not the one he'd been in when he met Nicklow and his son, he didn't think, but the maze confused, the flickering lights in the dimness disoriented. The kerchief over his nose irritated him, the helmet pinched and his eyes watered. The shadows thrown by the searchers hunched and wavered, grew and shriveled against the walls in a macabre dance.

Nicklow sprawled across the threshold of his room, a hand stretched into the corridor as if reaching for someone. His helmet was gone, his safety lamp upturned by his side. His eyes were half open in death. Harry had never before seen eyes whose light had gone out; it seemed to take all humanity out of the man. He would have expected the pallor of death, the bluish lips that he'd seen on a corpse laid out in a parlor, but Nicklow's face was ruddy, almost cherry red in the lamplight, with white splashes on his neck, as if the sun had scorched his skin, left it aflame.

"Asphyxiation," Stinner said. "Nothing else turns 'em that color." He squatted next to the body, dipped his head for a moment, then lifted his hand and softly closed the dead eyes. "Leave him for now, we need to get to the living." He stood and pushed on.

Forty feet farther on they found Nicklow's older son. William, Harry recalled, the boy's name was William. He lay along the side of the tunnel, crumpled against the rock wall, his head toward the entrance as if he'd died trying to reach fresh air. Had he known he was dying? What little Harry knew about suffocation made him think unconsciousness took over so quickly that the dying were oblivious. But what if that weren't true? What if, even in a state of senselessness the mind struggles for life, the heart begs for reprieve? Especially in a boy as young as William Nicklow. A boy that age thinks life is forever. Harry knelt next to the body and tentatively touched a cheek. It was reddened the way his father's was and the pressure of Harry's touch left a pale spot in the color. William was close to Harry's own age, he guessed. He wondered about the boy's mother, if she sensed her son and husband were dead.

They moved onto the next flat, number seven, where they found a man named Taylor and another that one of the men thought was George Cunningham, then a man they identified as the mule driver, along with two dead mules whose bodies blocked the road and forced the group to take valuable time clearing a path. Then another father and son, and the pumper and the track layer. And then a man still alive.

They nearly missed him. He lay curled into a pocket carved out of the wall at the near end of number seven flat. His skin was the reddened color of the dead men, but he'd bound a kerchief over his mouth and nose. Stinner knelt next to him and put a finger to his neck.

"He's alive, boys." His weary voice lifted in quiet wonder. "Let's get him out of here. He won't last much longer in this air."

One of the searchers, a big man with a massive chest, crouched and lifted the boy, for he was little more than that and slight. The boy's head fell back. Harry drew in a quick breath. It was Patrick.

"I know this man," he said. "I'm going with you."

Stinner frowned. "We need you down here. Somebody's got to carry bodies."

"I'll be back," Harry said. "I'll bring more men down with me, we'll take out the ones up front." The big man was already halfway up the flat and Harry scrambled after him.

It was full dark now, and the crowd had grown. It shifted and murmured as they appeared at the mouth of the mine, and Harry wondered how long they'd been inside. There'd been no news since he, Stinner and the other searchers had disappeared inside, and Harry saw fear and pain on every face. As soon as the big man appeared at the entrance with his burden, the crowd surged forward and Harry was engulfed by a crush of frantic bodies, eyes anguished, sweat reeking of terror. They pulled at his sleeve, called to him, pressed in on him. The big man shouldered his way through, shouted for the doctor, yelling "This boy is alive! Give way!" Harry felt the energy in the crowd surge. If one man could come out alive, then others could, too. Cries of "What have you seen?" "Who have you found?" filled the air. People shouted names at him but he couldn't distinguish one from the next. Then Murray stood before him and grasped him by the shoulder.

"What's in there, Harry?" he asked in a low voice. "How bad is it?"

Harry watched the back of the big man disappear through the crowd, wanted to follow after, wanted to find Niamh. "There are dead men in there, Mr. Murray. We found seven or eight, some of them boys no older than that one there. I don't know names." He shook Murray's hand off. "I know some, but I won't be the one to give the news to the families. You and Stinner can do that."

He pushed away and elbowed a path through the crowd. They called to him and he shouted again and again, "I don't know, I don't know who they are. Yes, there are dead men in there, I don't know." And they finally let him be to follow Patrick.

The yard was lit by lanterns and torches now, a miasma of fog and smoke from the still-burning coke ovens a half-mile away muddying their flames and rendering the whole scene ghastly. He searched through the crowd for Niamh, but in the lurid shadows it was nearly impossible to distinguish faces. An old army tent had been set up and furnished with trestle tables for the injured and dead, and Harry's temper lightened some to see Dr. Sturgeon in a rubber apron, swabbing the surfaces. Dan used forceps to pull instruments from a boiling kettle and line them up in a metal tray. With surprising gentleness, the big man laid Patrick on a table. Dan's father leaned over the boy, felt his pulse, lifted an eyelid. He glanced at Harry, showed no surprise and turned back to his examination.

Then Dan was at his elbow. "Is it one of them?" His voice low. "Her brother? Husband?"

Harry nodded and glanced around. "Brother." There were few people in the tent, a couple of women whom the doctor would have pressed into service as nurses; two men set up the last of the tables. "Have you seen her?" then remembered Dan wouldn't know her, had never seen her.

"Can't make anyone out in this mob." Dan looked at his friend, then grasped his elbow and pulled him over to a table. "There's coffee here, Ma sent a flask. Looks like you could use some."

"Thanks." Harry took a cup and gulped a mouthful of bitter black coffee. "Folks out there could probably use some."

"Yeah," Dan said. "They're in a fright. Must be horrible not to know. What did you see down there?"

"Dead men. They'd suffocated in the after-gas. They're all red, like Patrick only worse. God, what a way to die, Dan." Harry set down the empty cup and pushed the heels of his palms into his eyes. "You wouldn't believe what it is down there, like the worst hell you ever imagined, light jumping around and shadows and the smells—smells like an open sewer and you don't know if the smell is what'll kill you and the mountain's up there pressing down and you think maybe you're a rat and you'll die down there without ever seeing a star again or a tree. Or feeling a cool breeze…" He pulled his hands away. They were wet, his face streaked.

Dan put an arm around his shoulders. They both looked at the table where Dr. Sturgeon worked over Patrick. The boy's chest rose and fell, shallow breaths, his eyes closed.

"I'm going back down," Harry said. "I told Stinner I'd bring in more men to carry out the bodies. They're still looking for anyone alive."

"I'll ask around, see if I can find your girl," Dan said. "She should be here with her brother anyway. Pa won't need me unless a bunch of live ones come in."

Harry turned to go, turned back. "Dan. I'm glad you're here. Really glad."

"Yeah." Dan nodded. "I know."

It was close on midnight before the last body was carried out of the mine, fourteen in all, most of them the cherry-red color of the asphyxiated. The men who'd worked on the south side of the passageway had been burned. Several of them lived, some even walked out. But two were charred almost beyond recognition.

Harry worked alongside miners and cokers whose speech he couldn't understand, men from Poland and Italy and Wales and Hungary and Ireland and England. If any of them wondered why a town man sweated among them, they didn't ask, probably never even noticed. The dead and living alike were taken to the hospital tent, the living to be treated with salves and debridement, the dead to be washed and claimed by their families.

He and the big man set down the last body on a table already crowded with two others. Harry took off his kerchief to swab his face and turned to look for Dan and the doctor in the glare of lanterns. Not ten feet away Niamh sat next to Patrick, who lay unmoving in the same place they'd left him hours ago, but now covered with a blanket, a cloth over his forehead. She held his hand, smoothed her fingers across his forehead. While he watched, she looked up, as if she felt Harry's eyes on her, but her look was glassy. She showed no recognition, and she turned back to her brother. Harry sank onto the ground, his back against a wooden crate. Someone handed him a tin cup of water and he closed his eyes against the waking nightmares.

It was close on three in the morning when Dan and Dr. Sturgeon came to fetch him, to take him home. Philip Murray had disappeared long ago, whether to return to town or to huddle with his managers, Harry didn't know and didn't care. He had no desire to see the man again that night.

"There's nothing more for us to do here." Dr. Sturgeon wiped his hands on a filthy towel and glanced over the bodies laid out on tables. "The Company's sent its own doctors down from Connellsville. I don't think it wants outsiders in here."

"The dead men," Harry said, "do they know who they all are?"

"I think everyone's been identified," Dan said. "Or at least accounted for. A couple of the bodies were pretty charred. But they've figured out who they must be." He put a hand on Harry's arm, pulled him away from his father, who'd stopped one last time at the cot of a moaning man with burns along his left side.

"Harry," he said, "one of them is Martin Gill."

"Gill."

"They're almost sure. Couldn't be anyone else. I asked around. He's the only one not accounted for, and one of the women, said she's a neighbor, said she recognized a St. Christopher he had around his neck. Said he never went without it."

Harry's head buzzed with exhaustion so that the news made little impression. "Didn't bring him much luck, I guess."

Dan looked at him steadily. "No, it didn't."

"Does she know?"

"The neighbor woman was to tell her. They didn't want her to see the body. She hasn't left Patrick all night."

Harry lifted tired eyes in the direction of the far tent, where lanterns still burned low and shadows like grotesque vultures moved between light and tent walls. He could not see her from where he stood, but he knew she hadn't moved. "I should be with her."

"No." Dan shook his head. "Now's not the time. Let it all sort out. Go home and leave her be. She won't be thinking beyond tonight, there's plenty of time for thinking about later."

Dan was right, and besides, Harry was too tired, too numb, to consider what had happened to Niamh and to himself that night. There was too much death around him to think of life, too much grief to think there could be joy. He let Dan guide him to the doctor's buggy. By the time the doctor had climbed in and Dan had set the horse on the road back to town, he was asleep.

23

Niamh twisted on the wooden chair, her back cramped from the long vigil. She held a prayer book in one hand, but it was closed, not enough light to read now. The soft worn leathery feel of it was a comfort. It was late, must be going on two in the morning. The clock was silent, stopped as was proper in the presence of a death. It was odd not to hear the breaker whistle announce shift change, the mine quiet, the men at loose ends. Even the ovens were still. Without coal to turn into coke, the beehives were cold, the chargers and levelers, the daubers and the pullers and their mules all idle. Everyone was out of work, and some said the dead men were the lucky ones.

The coffin rested on chairs borrowed from Kate's house and set up in the desolate front room. Niamh had wrestled her own bedstead and mattress into the kitchen so Patrick would be near the warmth of the stove. Kate herself dozed at the foot of the bier. In truth it was more than dozing. She snorted through her nose and buzzed in her throat, but her sleep was so deep she didn't wake herself up. Niamh's mind moved at the rate of cold molasses, so weary was she. And Kate had to be even more fatigued. She'd spent hours caring for the wounded and washing the dead without rest or food. She was not yet forty, but she looked to be well into middle age, her hair shot through with gray, hands reddened, cheeks a mass of wrinkles. Life in the patch did that to a woman.

It had been more than twelve hours before they brought Martin back to the house, his body wrapped in a bedsheet and carried on a plain wooden plank. There were fourteen men and boys to be delivered to their homes and boarding houses, and only one Black Maria, the boxy enclosed carriage that every wife and mother dreaded to see trundling down the patch streets. Kate's husband James and another coker set the plank with the body on the bare wooden floor of the front room, leaving its care to the widow and anyone she could find to help her. Niamh had been preoccupied with Patrick and only glanced at the shrouded body, lying in the dim predawn light like a giant cocoon. She would think about what to do with it later.

Patrick still breathed, but shallowly. His pulse raced, his skin flushed with the effects of the after-damp, but Dr. Sturgeon had told her if the boy lived through the night he would probably not die. His eyes were half open, his gaze fixed on nothing. Niamh was determined that he would not die, would not be snuffed out so carelessly like a potato bug crushed by a careless footstep. She fussed over him, salved his burns and scrapes, which were minor, swabbed his forehead to check fever. The doctor said there was little she could do for the gas poisoning but keep him in fresh air; the brain and the lungs would heal of their own. Or would not.

So when Kate Byrne finally arrived, sometime mid-morning on the day after the disaster, she found Niamh huddled on a stool in the crowded kitchen by Patrick's bedside, and the body of her husband still on the floor in its soiled shroud, untouched and neglected.

"Ach," she muttered, crossing herself, and Niamh lifted her head, eyes dazed. "You poor chick. You've none to help you with the laying out." Kate bent and twitched back the shroud from Martin's face. "Ah, the poor man. He did not deserve this then, did he?"

Niamh put a hand to her belly. Her insides roiled, and she felt light-headed. The smell from the body grew stronger in the small room, a smell of rotting cabbages.

"At least you've opened the window," Kate said, "so the poor man's soul could get away. You'd best be closing it now, so he doesn't slip back in."

"I cannot," Niamh said. "Patrick must have fresh air and I will not close it off from him."

"Then you'll be having your husband's spirit pestering you and the boy, you will." The woman stepped out the front door and called to someone across the yard.

Niamh stood. The dizziness had passed, and she thought she ought to have a piece of bread to settle her stomach, but the effort seemed too much. Kate returned, trailed by her two daughters and the younger boy, all three strapping young people who had no trouble lifting the body to the kitchen table. Kate sent Niamh for the sewing scissors and snipped away at the bedsheet.

"Eileen," she said to her daughter, eyes on her work, "you'll be putting on the kettle and make us tea. And Brandon, you're to bring over the kitchen chairs from our house. See that you don't bang them about. Mary Margaret, help your brother," and she made her way around the table to the other side.

"Now you, Miss," she said to Niamh, "you best prepare yourself for the sight. It'll not be pretty, but you must remember the soul is gone and this just the clay that's left behind." She dropped the piece of shroud she held and crossed herself again.

Niamh held back until the bedsheet was cut away and the body lay before her on the table. Kate was right: there was nothing of Martin here, this thing that he used to be was not Martin. He'd been burned about the head and shoulders; one leg was crushed. Kate cut away what was left of his clothing, periodically touching a vinegar-soaked handkerchief to her nose and mouth. Niamh turned, her head fuzzy and her limbs moving of their own accord, and fetched the washbasin. Eileen had filled it from the bucket in the corner, added hot water from the kettle and dropped in flakes of lye soap and a flannel rag. The washing and dressing of the body proceeded in silence, and after all was done Niamh remembered none of it. A wooden coffin had appeared outside the front door—the miners and oven men had hammered together fourteen in the past few hours—and the Byrne children helped their mother lift the remains into it. Martin had been tall and no one had bothered to take measurements, so the fit was faulty and his legs required bending at the knees, feet forced into a corner. Niamh removed the shoes she'd put on him, his Sunday shoes, and thought idly that it was well they would not be buried with him. Patrick would have use for them.

Then the coffin, set between Kate's kitchen chairs, was nailed closed because the body was not fit to be seen, and candles, new purchased from the company store and hardly affordable, were set at each corner.

"You must stop the clock and turn the mirrors to the wall. And close the curtains." Kate washed her hands at the basin, and Niamh answered that she had no mirror, and the curtains were not to be closed so that Patrick would have fresh air, but she did stop the clock. Kate had said no more and left to get her dinner at her own house, promising to return to share in the vigil.

Now in the wee hours, the candles had burned more than half down. They would require replacing before the coffin left the house. Patrick tossed, restless, on the bed in the corner. The window remained open though the October evening was sharply chill, and both Niamh and her friend were wrapped in shawls and blankets. Each time Niamh rose to check on her brother, she tripped on a trailing corner of blanket or dropped the wraps and shivered, teeth chattering. She was relieved that he seemed to have no fever, but he had not awakened, and she began to worry that he never would.

Exhaustion was fast gaining on her. She'd been awake now for more than forty hours and had eaten only toast and tea. The odor from the coffin permeated the front room and she thought she could smell it still in the kitchen and even upstairs in the bedroom. The lodgers had appeared in the afternoon along with other visitors come to pay condolences but had not returned for dinner or to sleep, out of respect, Kate said, so there was no one else to watch but the two women. And someone must keep a watch. The neighbors had brought food but the offerings were meager, and Niamh had little to add to them in the way of a traditional wake, and no beer or whiskey at all, though several of the men who stopped by had found whiskey somewhere. All over the patch, families waked husbands and fathers and sons, some families with two bodies in the front room since at least three fathers had died with their sons. The visitors, Niamh thought, could only bear so much contact with the grieving and the grieving could bear only so much of the visitors, it being readily apparent that each visitor felt naught but relief that he or she did not wake a family member of his own.

Kate gave out a mighty snort but still did not rouse, and Niamh stood, dropped her blanket and shook out her skirt. She made the sign of the cross, kissed her fingertips and touched the crucifix that hung over the empty space where the bed had stood. The candles guttered, two already burned out, but they shed enough light that she found her way to the water bucket without stumbling. She dipped up a cupful, drank some and poured the rest over her hands, scrubbing them over her face. Patrick muttered in his sleep and she went to him. He looked peaceful in the dim light. The flush had abated, his breathing deepened. She pulled the quilt to his chin and closed the window. She'd be able to build up the fire in the stove, now, though her coal supply was low, and she knew she'd need to be frugal with it.

She slipped out the back door, careful not to let it bang behind her. The coal bin stood next to the privy and in the blue light of the waxing moon she could make out half a dozen lumps of coal. When it was gone, she'd be hard put to buy more. Her account at the company store, what with the candles and the coffin and the sweet chocolate she'd bought to tempt Patrick, threatened to grow unmanageable and there would be no more pay days. She stooped to scrape the coal into her basket and at the same time sensed she was not alone. Someone hovered just outside the railings around the frost-blackened vegetable garden, a shadow in the moonlight, but she knew him.

"Harry," she said, her voice low. "You shouldna be here."

"I wanted to see how you are." He held his hat in his hand and fingered the brim while he came around the fence. "No one will tell me much about Patrick or you … or your husband."

"How long have you stood here in the cold, ye daft man? It's near to dawn."

"Since midnight, I guess. I've been at Joanna's. Came here once it was dark and things quieted down."

"It's not decent that you're here. If anyone were to see you there'd be the right devil to pay."

He looked stricken, and she felt sorry, but she was too exhausted to worry about it now.

"All right, I'll go, but first tell me how Patrick is."

"He's alive and sleeping, and beyond that there's no knowing how he'll be. Martin is dead as I'm sure you've heard. Now go away with you."

Harry settled his hat on his head, turned, then swung back. "Niamh, if you need something, anything at all, go to Joanna. Promise me."

"I cannot promise anything, now can I? I cannot know what I'll be doing from one minute to the next." She dumped the six meager lumps of coal in her basket. For the first time since Martin died, she felt the tears well up. She would not have him see them and she'd as soon not see him either just now, it seemed so wrong. But all she said was, "Harry, I do thank you, and I thank you for coming. Now go home to your bed and leave me be for now. There will be time for talk later." She turned away from him and hurried up the path. Once in the kitchen she closed the door into the front room where Kate stirred and Patrick slept, and she stuffed the coal and kindling into the stove, blew on the sluggish coals and waited till a flame flickered and caught. She pulled the rocker close to the warmth and sank into it, pressing her fingertips against damp eyes. "Forgive me," she whispered. She leaned back, closed her eyes, and rocked. "Forgive my, Father, for I have sinned." The rocker stilled and her thoughts faded, an emptiness growing from somewhere deep within touched by a melody, old as the hills of Connemara.

"*Anois teacht an Earraigh beidh an lá dúl chun shíneadh,*" she murmured, hardly knowing she did. "*Is tar eis na féil Bríde ardóigh mé mo sheol…*"

✳

Harry watched her go and something tore inside him. Her hair was disheveled, her hands black from the coal, but she was beautiful in the moonlight, not quite human, beyond human. He shook himself. Lack of sleep, the mental burdens of the past day encroached, weakened him. But he loved her and as he took the road toward the farmhouse, all he could think of was that now she was free.

24

The office of the Youngstown Coke Company had to make do without Harry for the rest of that week though Murray roared and fumed about how much work there needed to be done in the wake of the accident. He ordered Harry to keep away from the mine and the patch town and let the inspector do his work, but Harry ignored him and slept Tuesday at the farmhouse. His aunt did her level best to get news about Patrick and Niamh, but once again the patch folk closed ranks against outsiders.

On Wednesday, Stinner examined the mine again, along with the mining boss, the fire boss and half a dozen others. Harry invited himself along, and Stinner asked no questions. He probably assumed Harry represented Philip Murray, and Harry did not disabuse him of the notion. The rest of the men showed him barely-disguised hostility and snarled comments in his hearing about the high-and-mighty Company and greedy bosses. And when he asked Stinner and some of the others about the wounded, he got only stony silence.

Then on Thursday he was summoned to the coroner's investigation as a witness. The courtroom was full by ten in the morning, though the coroner and jury hadn't yet put in an appearance. The smells of sweat and coal dust merged with furniture wax and the peculiar parchment smell that clings to authority. Brown-skirted women in kerchiefs and shawls filled the gallery, miners in suspenders and brogues crowded the benches behind the bar. The talk that swirled around him was a polyglot of languages and accents, Hungarian and Polish, Italian and Welsh, Irish, British, southern American, Appalachian twang. He'd put on his Sunday suit and wished he hadn't. He ran his hand through his slicked-back hair. In the front row, left side, backs firmly to the crowd, sat three men in bespoke suits, briefcases on their knees and ties knotted in identical four-in-hand perfection. These were the representatives of the company owners, attorneys from headquarters in Ohio. They stared straight ahead and whispered among themselves; one man laughed when his colleague whispered in his ear, the sound strangely loud in the murmur that filled the room.

Harry found a seat in the far back and pushed himself into a row of men who, from their accents, appeared to be American-born. From the black looks he got, they thought he was a Company man taking names. He scowled back and scanned the room, picked out several of the men who'd been among the rescuers on Monday. Stinner, as principal witness, sat in front of the bar along with a man Harry thought was the fire boss, and a third man he knew was the mining boss. Cole, he thought the name was. Stinner and Cole stared at the floor, silent, solemn. The fire boss glanced at the gallery and to the side, ducking his head, twitching the papers in front of him. Philip Murray was nowhere to be seen.

A second dais had been installed in front of the judge's usual bench and a long table with chairs for the coroner and the jury set up. The seven filed in, Markle and Bowman, storekeepers in town, a lawyer named Wycoff, and three men Harry didn't recognize. Last was John Batton, a slender, sandy-haired doctor not yet thirty years old who had taken the coroner's job because no other doctor wanted to touch it.

The fire-boss, Ramage, was first to be called and as far as Harry could tell, the man may as well have stuck his neck in a noose. He said he had no experience with fire-damp, didn't examine all the air-courses, hadn't been instructed on trap doors, didn't pretend to be an expert. The company bosses had fired their seasoned fire-boss in September and stuck Ramage in the job raw. An underswell of comment rose, angry and hissing, and the coroner glared at the gallery. Ramage never looked at the jury, testified staring at his hands, and the coroner barked at him to speak up. Harry had a hard time hearing. Someone down the row stage-whispered a translation in a guttural, Eastern European language. When Ramage finally stepped down, a low rumble ran around the courtroom and Batton banged his gavel.

Cole followed and made it all worse. He said the company got rid of the regular fire-boss to cut down on expenses, required only one inspection a day instead of two, said no boy had been posted to close the trap door, and didn't think Ramage was particularly competent. The courtroom by now was stifling, heavy with body odor and tension. The men on the benches shifted and muttered, the women in the gallery hissed. Stinner took the stand and tied it all up with a bow—the company knew there was gas in number six heading and yet the fire-boss was told not to bother with it. Further, there'd been two other fatal accidents at Youngstown in the past twelve months and the company had sued to be allowed to ignore Stinner's safety orders.

Bannon didn't bother calling on Harry or the company's lawyers.

"Those men were as good as murdered." Harry set his glass down and got to his feet.

Murray tented his hands in front of him and looked up with tired eyes. "It's a cost of doing business, I've told you that before."

"Human cost," Harry said.

"Yes, human cost. One the miners are fully aware of and are prepared to pay."

"You know that?"

"I'm sure of it. Would they be better off in their old countries, starving? What other jobs would they be able to get over here?"

"They should at least be able to count on coming out alive at the end of a shift. If those men had been American born, the company would have made damn sure there wasn't gas in there."

"Harry," his mother said, "language, please." She put a careful stitch through the material that lay across her lap. Mattie sat silent, hands motionless in her lap.

Harry turned on her. "What do you say, Mother? Mattie? Is he justified in sacrificing a certain number of men every year so the company can make a profit?"

Agnes set down her sewing and looked past him, out the window at the autumn dusk. "Your father thought that that's what the war was about. Powerful men sacrificing weaker men for profit. It appears we've not learned any lessons."

Murray flushed. "I was not aware you harbored that opinion of me."

"Oh, Philip, of course she doesn't mean you personally. We know how much those deaths bother you." Mattie leaned toward him, put her hand on his where it rested on his knee.

Agnes glared at them both. "The men who own the companies, make the decisions, never meet their workers face to face or visit the patch towns.

They don't understand or don't care about the human cost. They build their mansions in Philadelphia and Pittsburgh and New York and allow their workers to live in shanties that are falling down around them."

"You, madam," Murray stood and leaned over Agnes, "certainly benefitted from the building of *my* house."

Harry jumped in. "If you and your partners had invested in decent housing for the miners and paid for a competent fire-boss before you spent money on your mansions, then those men wouldn't have died and their families wouldn't freeze in the winter."

Murray turned to Mattie, bowed stiffly. "My dear, you need to choose. I'll not set foot in this house again."

"At least you won't face gas burns and falling rock," Harry said.

Mattie got to her feet. "Philip, don't leave angry. We're just saying that you're in a position to make changes for the better. They'll listen to you." She laid a hand on his sleeve. "I fear another war," she said quietly, "I truly do. There's not much difference between how these people are treated and how the slaves were held. Think about it."

Murray brushed off her hand and settled his hat on his hand. "That's a bit farfetched, my dear. I'll do what's necessary to be done, but don't look for big changes. That's just not the way it works." He bowed his head stiffly. "Good evening, ladies." He ignored Harry and left.

Agnes picked up her sewing again. "Good riddance," she muttered. Mattie left the room and disappeared up the stairs. The door to her bedroom slammed.

25

Martin was in the ground not twenty-four hours when Mr. Dobson from the company store appeared at Niamh's doorway with the record of the Gills' account.

"Mrs. Gill." Mr. Dobson removed his hat. "My condolences on your loss." He wore a high-buttoned sack coat with trousers that didn't match. Niamh realized she had never seen him in a coat. In the store he wore shirt-sleeves with black garters and spectacles that sat low on his nose. Now his spectacles sat high, his eyes bulbous. They peered over her shoulder at the front room.

Niamh leaned against the doorjamb and folded her arms. "But you'll be telling me I owe you money." She didn't want him peering into her home, such as it was. Patrick sitting up in the bed, staring at nothing. The breakfast pot unscrubbed, the floor unswept. Her own pallet still on the floor, blankets scrambled from a restless night.

"Yes, you do. And the company will need this house. Housing is for married men with families." He smiled as if that were good news.

"I have a man in the house, my brother. And there are lodgers, the three of them." They had all three returned late last night, two of them drunk and singing, the third stealing sideways looks at her as he shuffled his mates into the loft. At least she'd not had to cook for them or heat their bath water these past three days. They'd spared her that.

"That'll buy you some time, but you should plan to be out by the first of the year. And this account needs paying before then." He ducked his chin and gazed at her as if she'd been a naughty girl.

She swallowed the venom she wanted to spew and pressed her lips tight. After a moment he settled his hat on his head. "Good day to you then, ma'am."

Niamh watched him go. Of course, she knew about the debt, she handled the family's money as did all Irish wives. It was nearly a hundred dollars, and how would she ever pay it? Patrick showed no sign of being able to work any time soon, Martin's wages were gone, the lodgers barely paid the cost of their food and the coal it took to heat their bath water. Patrick would need medical attention, and she still owed for the care he'd had so far. She had a suspicion, too, that she didn't know how to handle. Her stomach had been unsettled even before the accident, she'd not been able to keep the morning meal down. And her courses were late.

Patrick came out of the mine with an illness, not just the afterdamp or the burns that were superficial and easily treated with ointments. Sometimes Niamh would close her eyes and try to imagine herself under the earth, deep in a grave the way Martin was, the way Patrick must have felt when he lay under the hill in the dark. To die and be resurrected again, like Lazarus. She wondered if Lazarus slung the same empty stare when he was brought back that came from Patrick's eyes. To be dead and then alive again—no one can be unmarred after that. Niamh nursed him the only way she knew, kept him clean and tempted him with cheese melted into potatoes and coffee fondant when she could get the extra coffee. His burns faded and healed and his skin took on a whitish, translucent glow like milk-glass, and his gray eyes settled into the uninhabited expression of a child who has yet to learn about the world.

The lodgers had been quietly respectful of the widow and her damaged brother and slid in and out of the house as if any extra noise would disturb some fog of woe that was necessary to be kept intact, until Niamh was thoroughly disgusted and told them for the love of Mary, act natural, we won't be breaking. And so they tried, but they still treated her like she would shatter at the first loud noise.

Since Patrick now slept in the kitchen where she could keep an eye on him, herself on the pallet in the corner, Niamh decided she could take in another and even two more, to help make up the loss in wages. So she let Mr. Reis know she would house two men who'd been hired by the company to replace the dead miners, and late in November they moved in. The new men were from somewhere in the east of Europe, Poland or Hungary or some region more obscure, and their language was harsh to her ears and coarse. The Welsh lodgers called them hunkies and let Niamh know in no uncertain terms that they were not pleased to be sharing their loft with them. But she needed the money and so she ignored their grumbles and communicated with the foreigners as best and as little as she could. Within two weeks the Welshmen were gone, they'd rather live five to a room in a Welsh household than in a pigsty. So she took in two more single men and a man whose wife came along, since Kate said it would be scandalous if not dangerous if she were to be alone in the house with none but foreigners and a *taise*. But the foreign wife kept to herself or spent her days at the homes of her country-women, and often cooked for herself over a small brazier upstairs.

Thankfully, the three men were rarely in the house. She fixed their lunches and fed them a dinner or a breakfast depending on their shifts, but when they weren't sleeping or eating or working, they were off to the tavern or a meeting. She heard rumors of action against the Company because of the accident, some means of forcing them to make improvements in safety. Kate told her one morning that her husband put no stock in the Company's promises to abide by the mine inspector's orders to hire a qualified fire-boss or more trapper boys. But Niamh figured it was closing the barn door after the horse got out, anyway. And what could the miners do? The appearance of the Huns from Eastern Europe made it clear that there were plenty of workers to be had. Any work stoppage to force changes would just mean hiring scabs, so she paid the rumors little mind.

26

Harry never went back to the offices of the Youngstown Mine and Coke Works. Murray left town directly after the inquest; he hadn't bothered to contact Harry, and Harry forfeited his last week's pay. If Mattie saw the man again, she kept it to herself; his name was never mentioned again among the aunts. A for-sale sign appeared in front of the just-finished mansion on Ben Lomond Street, advertised through a competitor of Agnes's from Connellsville.

He walked daily to the farmhouse, but Joanna knew as little as he did. He haunted the cafés and stores in Uniontown thirsty for gossip, but there was precious little information to be had. The citizens of the city had little interest in the day-to-day doings of the patch. They were interested in whether the mine was active and the ovens lit since the profits of the several companies operating in the valley affected the well-being of the merchants and professional men of the town. But as for news of the families disrupted by the accident, there was almost none. There had been funerals, the Uniontown and Connellsville papers covered those, but so many were buried at once that the individual dead were not mentioned. Even in death, he thought, the miners were a faceless lot, lumped together in a single mass. Dan's father knew very little. After the Company had brought in its own doctors to tend to the injured men and made it clear Dr. Sturgeon's services were no longer necessary, it sent him a generous payment for his efforts the night of the accident. And that was that. By the end of the second week Harry had exhausted his patience and his sources, so he set out for Youngstown himself.

It was late afternoon when he left Uniontown. The sun would not set for another hour, but by the time he crossed Shute Run, the light had faded, and snow began to fall. It drifted down in great soft flakes that danced in a light breeze through the gathering dusk like sentient creatures. He knew a rush of joy and stopped to raise his face to the sky. The cold snapped and popped, the waters of the creek sang. Before he'd gone far on the road to Youngstown, the surrounding fields lay cloaked in a blanket that softened the harsh ridges of black mud along the embankments. It was full dark, the dinner hour, when he turned from the ridge into the Youngstown hollow. A kerosene glow beamed from the windows of the patch houses, and even the coke ovens, the few still in operation, gleamed through the dark with a promise of warmth and light. The squalor of the settlement, the mud and cinders and casual trash of daylight were hidden, sounds muffled in the evening still.

A curtain twitched in the window next door when he rapped at Niamh's house. He took a deep breath. He was just a friend, here to convey his condolences, see how the family coped. It took a second rap before the door opened to him and he was flustered to find a strange man on the other side, dressed in sooty work clothes that stank of smoke.

The man stared, silent.

"I'm here to see Mrs. Gill and her brother." Harry snatched his hat from his head and held it in front of him.

"*Gillné asszony?*" the man said. He squinted at Harry in the low light. His accent was strong, Eastern European. Behind him the front room was dim, lit by a lantern set on the floor next to a half-barrel washtub. A man crouched in the tub, silhouetted against the light while he washed his chest and listened to the conversation. On the wall above the washtub, a crucifix hung, the twisted face of Jesus outlined in glints of lamplight and sharp black shadow.

"I'm a friend of the family. From the farmhouse over in Bethelboro." He paused but the man continued to eye him. "My aunt lives in the farmhouse and she's met Mrs. Gill. Wants to know how she and her brother get on." The man showed no comprehension.

"Who is it, Mr. Halass?" With a shock, he saw Niamh bend over the washtub to scrub the man's bare back.

"Visitor," Halass said. "Is stranger."

The bather stood up, naked, and began to towel off. Niamh ignored him and came to the door. Her eyes widened when she saw Harry.

"It's all right, Mr. Halass. I know him." She waited until Halass turned back into the room, then she stepped onto the porch and pulled the door behind her.

"Harry, what are you doing here?" She frowned.

"You shouldn't be in there—those men are bathing. They're naked!"

She snorted. "I've been washing backs for more than a year now. It's my job, isn't it. The boarding missus washes backs."

"But you're a widow now. What if they take advantage? They're foreigners."

"Harry, they're much too tired to take advantage, and I can deal with them in any event." She waited. He stared at her. "It's part of what I must do, don't you see. It's a boarding house. Now why are you here?"

"I hoped you'd be glad to see me," Harry said. "It's cold, do you have a coat?"

"Of course, I do. But I need to go back in. Supper's on the stove and I have four men and Patrick to feed."

"Niamh, I needed to see you, know that you're all right. Find out how Patrick is." He reached for her. "I've missed you and I've been worried."

She backed away but her expression softened. "It's good of you, it is, Harry, to worry about us but there's no need, not now. We're managing for now, 'tis day to day."

"Is Patrick better?"

"Ah, his burns are healing but his mind is still in a fog. He's not yet come back from the fear. It'll take some time, the doctor says."

"Niamh, I can take you away from here. We can be married and I'll have a home for you and Patrick in town. We can get him the best medical care—"

Niamh glanced at the window of the next house. "Harry, step away with me here." She took his arm and led him off the porch to the garden area between her house and the neighbor's. In the shadow of the buildings, Harry pulled her into his arms and bent to kiss her, but she turned aside and rested her head against his chest. "Not now, Harry. Don't ask me that now, I can't make that decision yet. It's just so raw, it wouldn't be fair, not to you and not to me."

"What will you do though? Where will you go? The Company won't let you stay here."

"No, not indefinitely. But I don't know yet, do I? It will depend on Patrick, whether he gets better and can go back to work."

"He won't have to, not until he's ready, if you come with me. I can take care of you."

"Can you then, Harry?" She pulled back to look into his face. "Can you afford to house a wife and a feeble-minded boy? What would your mother say and your aunts? Your friends? There are others to think of, Harry, besides us. It's too big a step to take so quick."

"It doesn't matter what they think." Harry ran his hands up and down her arms. "We can convince them all. They'll love you once they know you."

She shivered and he let her go, slipped off his coat and made to sling it around her shoulders. She backed away.

"No, I'll be getting back inside." She turned to look behind her, as if there may be an audience there, turned back again. "I'll not say no, Harry, because now is not the time for big decisions. But please, let me be for a time, let us see how it is with Patrick. Once things settle a bit, we'll perhaps know our minds better."

Harry blew out the breath he hadn't realized he'd been holding and nodded. "All right, if that's what you need. But keep in touch, somehow, let me know that you're well, how Patrick is. How long you'll be able to stay here." He let his fingers touch her cheek, soft and gentle. "Niamh, I love you and I can't bear not knowing how it is with you."

She took his hand and turned her lips into his palm.

"You're a good man, you are, Harry Robinson," she whispered. "I'll not cause you pain if I can help it." She stepped back. "Don't come back until I send for you, promise me that." She waited until he nodded, then turned and disappeared around the corner of the house. He heard the door open and snick close.

"*I'll not say no, I'll not cause* you pain—" It was little enough but it was all he had for now.

27

November 1884

Agnes collapsed the Tuesday before Thanksgiving. She'd shoveled snow from her front walk, then turned and continued along the sidewalk to the second house she owned, a boarding house whose tenants expected the walks to be cleared. Harry was away, selling Joanna's pigs to a cousin who lived over toward Brownsville, and by the time the message reached him and he fought his way home over snow-clogged roads, his mother was asleep, and Doctor Sturgeon stood in the kitchen, repacking his medical bag. The aunts hovered.

"I've given her chloral to help her sleep," the doctor told Harry. "Mattie's sitting with her for now."

"It isn't so bad, then?" Harry asked.

"Let's go sit down. And no, I don't think there's any immediate danger." He gestured toward the aunts. "The ladies have heard this already, but they may as well hear it again."

When Harry first stepped into the kitchen, he'd taken heart to see no one was in tears. The mood was somber, but he sensed relief in the air. It occurred to him that the group of women clustered in the kitchen, the four of them along with Mattie and his mother, were like a single body with a multitude of appendages. Since Belle had died more than twenty years ago, and Agnes had come home, the sisters had formed a solid front to the town and to life; if one ailed, they all fell ill. If one were to die, each of the others would dwindle.

"It's her heart." Dan's father pulled out a chair and sat at the kitchen table. "Mary tells me she had rheumatic fever when she was a child. I knew she had a heart murmur, I've kept an eye on it since she came back from Montana."

"Heart murmur?" Harry's head snapped up. "I didn't know she had a heart murmur."

"She didn't want you to know, didn't want any of you to know. It hasn't been a problem up to now."

"But now it is?"

"It might be and it might not be. These things can get worse over time, as the heart ages. It's probably a stenosis—"

"What's that?"

"Scarring, from the fever. The scar gets thicker over time and eventually changes the rhythm of the heartbeat. I'm hearing that now, and there's a second murmur, a different kind that indicates the problem is beginning to worsen."

"So…" Harry creased the tablecloth between a thumb and forefinger. His own heart beat fast and he felt lightheaded. "So, what can we do about it? She isn't going to die is she?"

"Eventually, I imagine," Doctor Sturgeon said with a soft smile. "But not today." He leaned back in his chair and crossed an ankle over his knee. "She could die tomorrow or she could live another twenty years. We just don't know. But we can do quite a lot to make twenty years possible."

"No more shoveling snow," Harry said. "I should have been here to do that for her."

"Not your fault, Harry," Joanna said. "She should have known better."

"Agnes always thought there wasn't anything she couldn't do." Elizabeth sniffled, her eyes red. "She always acted like she was a man."

"She did what needed doing," Mary said.

Elizabeth burst into tears and fled from the room.

"Oh, for heaven's sake," Sarah muttered and went after her.

"Right." Sturgeon nodded. "No more shoveling snow. And at least for now, until we find out how far the disease has progressed, she needs bed rest and sleep. Mattie says she's never slept well so I'll leave the chloral here. If that doesn't work, we need to go to opium."

"She won't want opium. That'll worry her even more."

"I don't want to go there either, but she needs to sleep. She needs to rest. Once she's up and about she'll need to cut back on her work schedule."

"That'll be a hard sell," Harry said. "She doesn't sleep because she's always got schemes running through her head. Lists and projects. She never sits still."

"She's sixty years old and she needs to accept that." Sturgeon stood, rolled down his shirt sleeves and reached for his coat. "Ladies, remember what I said about food and quiet, and call on me any time night or day if you need to."

He took Harry's arm and steered him to the front door. "She needs you here, Harry. Your aunts are wonderful caregivers, but right now I think you're the one who can set her mind at ease. And you can take on some of the estate agent work that she'll fret about."

"I guess I can take over the business. I'm out of a job anyway."

"Do that. And let me know if there's anything I can do to help." The doctor clapped him on the shoulder and slipped into the growing dusk.

Harry closed the door behind him and stood, hands braced and forehead pressed against the cold wood. She couldn't die, she'd never showed the slightest sign of weakness. The whole world suddenly looked different, vast and uncertain and precarious. He'd seen death, even horrific death, in the mine just weeks ago. And gentle death. Dan's grandfather, the old Senator; though he mourned the old man at the time and still did, he'd understood it. But death hadn't touched him, not really. He lived in a bubble of health and well-being, not on the edge. Not like the miners and their families, not like Niamh.

Joanna appeared behind him and laid a hand on his. "She'll be all right, Harry." She leaned in and kissed his check. "She's a tough lady and won't let this stop her. She'll outlive us all, you know that."

Harry winced and smiled. "If she has anything to say about it, she will. I need to go up and see how she is."

"She'll be glad to see you there when she wakes. You can be thinking about how you want to handle this, help her with the business. And what you want to do in the long run. We'll have a conference this evening. Figure it out."

Harry nodded and turned to the stairs. "I'm glad you're here, Joanna. You always seem to be in the right place when I need you."

"It's been quite a year."

"And it isn't over yet."

Agnes slept for nearly twenty-four hours, and while she slept, her son and her sisters rearranged their lives and hers. Joanna offered to give up the farmhouse—it was time, she said; the work was too much, the coal fug and dirt discouraging—to help with the family finances while Agnes was unable to work. Harry promptly offered to move into the boarding house down the street. Life in a house with six spinster ladies held few attractions for him. And to find a job in town that earned a decent salary.

"Time for you to have your own bachelor quarters anyway," Mattie said.

And when Agnes found out about all these changes, she nearly collapsed all over again.

"I'm not an invalid yet. And I'm certainly not dead." She threw back the covers and heaved herself to the bedside.

Mattie grabbed for the breakfast tray and steadied the half-full juice glass. "No one thinks you are, but you need to be careful." Harry took the tray from his aunt and set it on the bureau.

"I can be careful without giving up my business and sitting in a rocking chair for the rest of my days."

"Mother, that's not what we're saying. Doctor Sturgeon says your heart murmur is worse. You just need to slow down."

"And my slowing down means you'll work two jobs and Joanna has to give up the farm? She loves that farm."

"Joanna's been thinking about giving up the farm anyway," Mattie said. "It's changed so much out there it isn't even the same place any more. It's unhealthy for her just to breathe the air, and the well is fouled. John Jones wants to buy it and we need to take advantage of that while we can."

Agnes stood, swayed, and sat back down again. She shook her head.

"Mother, you need to stay in bed. For a while."

Agnes started to speak.

"Just for a few more days. Until Doc Sturgeon says you can get up."

"Otherwise," Mattie said, "you'll drop dead and you won't be any good to any of us. I'll have to marry Philip just to keep a roof over our heads."

Harry snorted. His mother rolled her eyes and swung her feet back under the covers.

"All right, but I don't want any big changes made until I've had my say. And Harry," she turned to him, "be sure you don't do anything in the business without asking me. I almost have the Gilmores talked into the house on Stockton, and I don't want that to fall through."

"I'll take care of it, Ma." Harry leaned over and kissed her on the head. "It's quiet over the holidays anyway. I promise not to close any big deals without asking you first."

"I know." She leaned back into her pillows and closed her eyes. "I really am tired, I suppose. And short of breath. But if I moulder here thinking about what's going on inside me, I'll just bring on another attack."

"Harry and I will keep you occupied, and the other girls will be sure you're well-fed and comfortable." Mattie patted her hand. "Properly fed. Nothing rich."

"And Thanksgiving's on Thursday. Everyone's so busy."

"No pecan pie for you." Harry took the breakfast tray and elbowed open the door. "But I promise I'll check with Doc about candied yams."

28

"She's probably no longer there." Joanna pulled a book from the shelf, dusted it and tucked it into the crate. "If Patrick can't work, she'd have been evicted."

"They wouldn't do that—wouldn't throw a widow and an invalid out into this weather," Harry said. "And besides, she would have let me know. Or let you know." He hefted a filled crate, toted it to the back porch and set it under the eaves out of the icy December sleet. Across the valley, fog and mist mixed with fumes from the coke ovens and pressed into the hillsides like a layer of sludge. Back inside, he pulled another book off the shelf. "She would never leave without telling us."

"You don't know how she'd react, Harry," Joanna said. "She's from a different place, she has other ways than we do. She'll want to be with her own kind, and there's nothing for her or Patrick here."

Harry stopped with the book in his hand and sat on the floor, back against the worn leather armchair. "But she doesn't have anyone else in America." The book he held was Whitman's *Leaves of Grass.* "She has nowhere to go and I'm guessing no money." He polished the *Leaves* and tucked it away. "With you in town and strangers living here, she'll be stranded."

"So you plan to rush in and save her, I suppose."

"Well, yes. If she'll have me."

"She has friends in the patch, Harry, someone will have relatives in Philadelphia or New York or Boston. A hasty marriage now between you would be a disaster."

Harry studied his coffee cup. The coffee was tepid and bitter, and he didn't really want it.

"It wouldn't be hasty. We've known each other for nearly a year—"

"Five months."

"Counting from March. And I know she never loved him."

"She would be marrying you as much from desperation as from love and that doesn't bode well for a marriage."

"And you would know." Harry regretted the words as soon as he said them.

Joanna, silent, packed a last book into her crate. The parlor was nearly emptied by now, the bookshelves the last to be cleared. Only a few pieces of furniture waited for a hired crew to cart it into town. The barn had been cleared, the animals sent to the Jones farm.

She fitted the crate's top and tapped nails in before she spoke.

"Do what you will, then, Harry. But think about what she needs, too. How well will she fit in with your life here? Her religion is different, her background, her education—it isn't just a matter of needing a home, any home. She needs one she can feel comfortable in. And what about Patrick? Are you prepared to take him in, too?" She pushed herself up from the floor and stretched her back. The persistent pain from shoulders to hips that had dogged her for the past few months was a big reason she'd agreed to give up her beloved farm. "Maybe what she needs from you is financial help to go back to Ireland."

"She'd never take that from me," Harry said. "And you don't know her the way I do. She's not just another ignorant Irish girl, she's smart and curious and adventurous, and I know she'd take to our life. It's what she's wanted, what she came here for."

"And Patrick?"

"He'll heal, it'll just take time. It's only been six weeks. Doc Sturgeon says there's a good chance he'll come round, get his old self back."

"And pigs will fly." Joanna picked up the coffee cups and took them into the kitchen. Harry followed with the last crate and stacked it on the others. Eight crates of books, a lifetime of collecting for a family of readers. Some of the books, a very few, had come over the mountains with old Mordecai Lincoln nearly a hundred years ago. There was history in this house, stories in every nook, tears and laughter in every crevice. Harry had always felt the ghosts of his forebears here, the tug of connection back through the years that tied him to this place, this land, centered and defined him. This farm meant he belonged somewhere, he existed within an established order that started long before his birth and would continue long after his death, so that his life had meaning beyond its span.

And now that connection was to be severed, and he would struggle to build new associations in its place. What that would be he didn't know, but family—his mother, his aunts, his relations, most of all the children he expected to sire—was the key.

He looked toward the coke valley again, but the fog was so heavy that not even the closer hills were visible. Ireland, he realized, must mean the same to her.

After her early rally, Agnes relapsed. And she was not a good patient. The bell by her bed jangled regularly, summoned Mattie or Elizabeth or Harry up the stairs with water or toast or a different book or the latest *Harper's* or *Home Companion*. She was adept at hearing the arrival of the post or the newspaper, both of which Harry brought home with him at noon and immediately upon his shedding his coat in the foyer the bell would sound. He was required.

When Joanna moved in, Harry moved out. He relinquished, with a touch of sorrow for the passing of years, his refuge under the eaves to Joanna and Mattie, and hauled his belongings down the street to the boarding house his mother had bought when Harry left for college. It was an investment, she'd said, for his education and true to her flair for business she made money on the rents. But he took all his meals with his family and spent much of his spare time in the house, attending to his mother's needs and his aunts' whims. He wound up two of her pending estate deals—completed the sale to the Gilmores and signed a new lease with the renters—and by the first week in December had arranged to take over a teaching job at his old school on South Street.

29

January 1885

To Harry, the South Street school may as well have been the county jail. The term began the first week in January, and his third-floor school room was alternately frigid and stifling. The twenty-year-old furnace, the pride of the school board when the school was built, quit at the most inconvenient times and poured heat into the upstairs rooms without rhyme nor reason. On his first day he sweated through the back of his shirt though the temperature outside his window hovered at twelve degrees. The boys in his first period Latin class wore multiple layers which they added and removed at will. They appeared much more comfortable than he was and knew they had the advantage of him. The girls seemed impervious to temperature variations. They giggled among themselves as they took their seats, sending sidewise glances his way and whispering. He'd been warned that a roomful of eleven- and twelve-year-olds fresh from holiday vacations would be a challenge, but no one, not the school board members who had hired him nor the headmaster who took charge of the older students in the room next door had any suggestions for how to manage them.

At five minutes to eight in the morning he stood at the front of the room. Behind him hung a slate board, freshly scrubbed and supplied with three sticks of new chalk and a rag for erasures. An imposing desk sat angled in the corner. One of the local mothers had polished it to a spit shine, though scratches and scuffs hinted at years of use by nameless teachers long gone. Two double-hung windows looked out on the schoolyard where bare branches clacked against one another in their icy coats. He counted. Twelve boys, eight girls. They would be with him for three hours in the morning for Latin, literature, and rhetoric instruction. Then the older students would come in for advanced Latin, and this group would accost the headmaster for mathematics and geography. Then, blessedly, the last two hours of the school day would be devoted to the subject he loved the most and the reason he agreed to take this job, the study of natural history. But for now, Latin. He surveyed his charges and wondered what in the blue devil he'd got himself into.

He'd worked up a week of lesson plans ahead of time and within five minutes of calling the class to order, turned to write the basics on the board: *sum, es, est, sumus, éstis, sunt.* The chalk squeaked and a female voice said "eeeewww!" Snickers all around; the back of Harry's neck prickled. He turned to the room. Three of the young ladies in the first row were huddled together over a notebook, pointing silently to something drawn there and trying very hard not to giggle. The boy in the corner stared vacantly out the window and tapped his boot idly against the leg of his chair. It made an annoying, low-key *thunk* in a rhythm only the boy understood. In the back of the room three of the bigger boys snatched at each other, some primitive game involving annoying one's mates that Harry remembered from early grade school. The rest simply looked bored.

He took a deep breath. Either take control or walk out the door. The latter was not an option. He leaned over the girls and lifted the notebook, glancing at the rude poem scrawled there. He stepped to the corner and smacked the vacant boy on the ear with the notebook. Back to the front. "All right then," he said, his voice up a notch. "I am *Mr.* Robinson, and these are the rules."

"One plus one is two. Two plus two is four." *Shouldn't that be* are *four?* Harry thought. *Or not? Is that a plural subject?* Seven-year-olds probably didn't need to worry about it. From the back of the room he watched Rebecca move along the slate, pointing to the sums she'd chalked up. The singsong recitation was mildly hypnotic, the childish voices sweet and melodic. But it was lunch time and he was hungry, and he wondered how Rebecca bore the tedium. One small boy in overalls stuck his finger in his nose and dug around. His lips didn't move. Two others laid their heads on their small desks, eyes drooping. These second-graders weren't much different from his first-year high school students. And if he didn't take steps to prevent it, they would be in his class in another five or six years. The thought was unsettling.

Just as his own eyes grew heavy and he began to fear he might snore, Rebecca wound up the math lesson, and her pint-sized charges gathered lunch pails and lined up at the door. Mrs. Thompson, mother of one of the youngsters, shepherded them toward the lunchroom, and Rebecca was free.

"How do you put up with it day after day?" He stood and stretched his arms over his head, the crick in his back unresponding.

She looked surprised. "I love it. I love these children. It's wonderful to watch them grow and learn."

"What about the kid who picked his nose? And those two half asleep who weren't paying any attention?"

"Don't tell me that wasn't you fifteen years ago. And look how you turned out."

"My point exactly. What's for lunch?"

She laughed and opened the window where two metal pails nestled in the cold. "Ham sandwiches, deviled eggs, apples and German chocolate cake." She handed his to him. "Remember tomorrow's your turn."

"Tomorrow we'll go to Mother's and eat whatever Elizabeth's whipped up. And it'll be warm."

"Ummm." Rebecca settled herself at one of the miniscule desks and let Harry take the teacher's chair. "Harry, you really don't like this teaching, do you?"

Harry chewed and swallowed. "No. I don't. I don't have the patience. And the money isn't particularly good." He picked up his apple and studied it. "I'm thinking about the law. I can go back to Morgantown for the course at the university next year. Dan and I can go partners." He bit into the apple. "I sure can't see supporting a family on a teacher's salary."

Rebecca stilled, then bit into her deviled egg. Her cheeks were pink, and Harry thought she suffered from the heat of the furnace, though it felt cool to him.

"But you enjoyed teaching the Irish boy from the mine, I thought? You were good at that, from what Joanna tells me."

"That's different. He was smart and motivated, and it was more like debating with a friend. We had real discussions, about history and politics and slavery and all kinds of things that you can't have with a roomful of adolescents."

"It's a shame what happened to him." She picked at her sandwich, pulled the crust away and crumbled it between her fingers. "How's he doing, do you know? And his sister? Are they still in Youngstown?"

158

Harry crumpled the sandwich paper, stood up and moved to the window, his back to her. Her classroom was on the first floor, and the snow was halfway to the sill. The Presbyterian church next door was dark, gloomy in the mid-day gray of January; skeletal trees lined the walkway. The preacher, bundled in scarves and woolens, pushed a shovel along the pavement, clearing the last of the snow. He didn't want to talk about this, not to Rebecca. The whole business was a mess, such a mess.

"I don't know. I haven't heard from them since right after the accident. I no longer have a reason to go out there, and I don't know anyone who does."

"Do you need an excuse to visit them?"

"It doesn't feel right. And she told me not to come until I hear from her." He turned around. "I think it makes things difficult for her, my being connected to the company and all. It's pretty tense out there."

The look on Rebecca's face was stony. "Harry, do you have feelings for her? This isn't just about the boy, is it?" Now she stood, went to the board and began to erase the sums. "Dan says—"

"Oh, for the love of God, what business of Dan's is it to go talking to you? It's no one's business but mine."

She turned to him, cloth in hand, eyes snapping. "Dan and I are your best friends, Harry, and we worry about you. You moon and moan around like a—you're being puerile, that's what you are. Puerile." She threw the cloth on the desk. "I need to fetch my students." She was gone.

"Puerile," Harry said to the walls. "Huh. Where'd she get that?"

30

"Köszönöm." The man smiled at Niamh, flashing the gaps in his teeth. She thought he was János, but she couldn't be sure; she had never been able to tell the him apart from his brother. The other was György, and they carried the same surname, which as far as she could make out was roughly *Halász.* They'd written it out for her when first they'd moved in, but their handwriting was as foreign as their accent and she couldn't quite make it out. She called them both "Mr. Halass," which amused them no end.

She poured them their morning coffee and left them to the potatoes and eggs she'd fried up. There would be no meat until pay day, when the boarders' wages were tallied at the store and she was able to buy against them. She'd saved some for Patrick, a rasher of bacon that was about to turn, and when the Hungarians left, she fried it up for him. He sat in the rocker where he spent most of his days, gazing out the window as if waiting for a visitor, though when someone, a neighbor or one of the bosses, did pass by, he didn't appear to see them. He fed himself now; he hadn't done for the first month after the accident, so when toward Christmas he began to lift his bread and bacon to his mouth, she'd had hopes that he was improving. But it was now into January and he'd come no farther. She helped him to the chamber pot or the privy, washed his face for him, and fed him soup, since he couldn't manage the spoon. Sometimes she would sit before him and take his hands in hers and look in his eyes, hoping to penetrate their depths, see what lay behind, search for a spark of that lively, curious, hungry mind. But she found only emptiness. He would look back at her mildly, his eyes the blank of a window with the light reflecting off it, showing no recognition, no lack of recognition. Nothing.

Now he ate his bacon without taking his eyes from the snow piled a foot deep outside the window, the watery light washing over him as if he were underwater. She took the coverlet from the bed and spread it over his knees, tucked it around his chest, and tipped a cup of warmed-over coffee to his lips. He drank, and she thought she saw the shadow of a smile, but it must have been a reaction to the warmth. Her own stomach roiled with the smells, not so bad as it had been early on, but still too much for her to eat aught but a little boiled potato.

"I'll be leaving you here with Kate." She set his plate and cup on the counter that served as her kitchen. "I've to stop by the store and see if the post has come." She talked to him always, told him every little thing she did and planned to do, hoping the sound of her voice might spark a reflex, awaken an instinct. And when she ran out of commonplaces, she told him the tales of Ireland that she learned as a lass, and when the tales ran out, she sang to him. The singing seemed to soothe him, especially the old songs in the Irish she remembered her father singing in the evenings when she and Patrick were but babes. If she watched him carefully while she sang, she could see him settle more deeply into his chair and his eyelids would droop as though he looked inside himself, and his lips would soften.

Today, though, she had no time for singing or story-telling as she expected an answer to her letter to New York any day, and she could not risk the storekeeper reading it. She had no faith he would not, there was no such thing as respect for privacy in that establishment, and since the accident and her widowing, the odious Mr. Dobson had shown an unseemly interest in her person.

"My dear, bundle up, there's a good girl." Kate blew in on a draft of frigid air and let the door slam behind her. "'Tis a day for the fire, so it is." She flapped snow from her shawl and batted it from her skirt, leaving puddles on the wood floor. "Will you be long then, lass?"

"Just the half-hour. Thank you kindly, Kate. He's eaten his meal, should be fine for the time." Niamh wrapped a woolen muffler around her neck and ears and shrugged into Martin's old canvas coat, buttoning it over her thickened waist. "Can I bring you anything from the store?"

"No, dearie, I haven't the scrip for it, not till payday, and maybe not then. Sure, the idling ovens are eating into the larder." James Byrne was a coker and since the summer, fewer than half the ovens were lit, such was the low demand and the bad times.

Niamh stepped into the cold and eased the door behind her. There was no wind, thankfully, but the deep iciness of the air sliced like a shard of glass and the brilliance of the sun in a stark blue sky seemed to aggravate the chill. The pristine snowfall from last night was already covered with a layer of soot, the working ovens spewing the fine powder that had become second nature to the patch dwellers. The swath of land fronting the houses had long been churned to mud, frozen overnight into stiff ridges and stumblers that lay in wait to turn an ankle. The path to the store took her close to the working ovens where clusters of children and not a few mothers huddled close to take advantage of the heat despite the sticky mud.

Two women were at the counter when she entered the store and she had to wait her turn. The stove roaring in the corner warmed the small space. Dobson stood in his shirt sleeves, hands flat on the counter, listening with little patience to his customers. They carried on in a language that sounded croaky to Niamh's ears, not quite what her Hungarian boarders spoke but similar. They might have been Romanian, didn't sound Polish, definitely not Italian. By means of gestures and nods and an odd little clap of hands wrapped in fingerless gloves, they made their needs known, and Dobson piled up three or four tins and a couple of small packages. He opened a ledger, flipped through it and marked in it, and only then did he push the purchases toward the women. One scooped them all into a string bag and they turned away, taking no notice of Niamh. She hoped they would stay and warm themselves so she would not be alone in the store with Dobson, but they did not. The door opened and closed behind them and the store for a moment was silent.

"Mrs. Gill." Dobson pushed his black garters farther up his arms. "And what can I do for you today? Your credit's good again. As you know." He stared at her, eyes narrowed.

"What do you mean by that?" She hadn't paid since before the accident, there was no money to pay with.

"Your friend paid for you." He looked away, picked up a rag and swabbed the counter. His sneered.

"What friend?"

"Don't play innocent. The company man, the one from the farmhouse."

Niamh frowned. "He couldn't have. He knows nothing about what I owe."

He smirked. "He must owe *you* something. And he's paid it off."

Niamh flinched. How could Harry have done that without telling her? He must have known how it would be interpreted. And once Dobson knew, or thought he knew, he'd tell all sorts of people. Her stomach, once again, reacted. She thought she might throw up. She stood back from the counter. "I'm expecting a letter, if you please. Have you anything for me?"

She regretted the choice of words immediately. "Have I anything for you?" Dobson leaned over the counter and squinted. "Oh, I have, certainly, and you could improve your credit a great deal and enjoy the experience to boot." He laughed and straightened.

"Mr. Dobson, have you a letter for me?"

Dobson stared at her again, then turned to the back counter. "I have and there's two cents postage due on it." He held up an envelope. "And if you have two cents, I'll be staggered." He held the letter up, out of reach.

The door opened and the cold pushed in, along with a miner whom Niamh knew as a Mr. Riley. Riley glanced at the scene at the counter, then turned away to warm himself at the stove. She took courage from his presence.

"Why, Mr. Dobson, sure and I can see the postage has already been paid and I don't owe a thing. You must have missed it, smeared as it is."

Dobson glanced at Riley and squinted again at Niamh. "So it is," he said finally, and handed it over. Niamh snatched it and spun on her heel.

"You're welcome," Dobson called after her. "And don't forget, your credit can use some work."

"Give my best to Mrs. Dobson." Niamh shoved her way through the door and let it bang behind her.

Once outside she retreated to the line of ovens, sank down on an upturned barrow, and ripped open the letter. Kate's New York cousins, it said, were well and pleased to hear from her. But they would be unable to accommodate Mrs. Gill as the rooms they lived in were full to bursting with wee ones and a family group just arrived from the Old Country. Also, there was little work in the city for a mother with child; the only work was domestic and the families that hired would never take a woman with a babe and an ailing brother. They were very sorry they could not hold out more hope, perhaps toward the summer if the times improved and there may be sewing to be done. They would let her know.

Niamh felt the tears start up and blinked them back lest they freeze. She'd been so much more emotional lately, not the composed, impassive self she'd schooled herself to be ever since she'd agreed to marry Martin and come to America. Now every small event—scorched toast, spilt soup, the black dust that seeped into everything—unnerved her and moved her to tears. Only once had she given in to them, one evening soon after Christmas when she'd filled the washtub for the boarders' baths, and her back ached, and Patrick had refused his dinner. Then she'd sunk into the rocker and wept in deep gulping sobs. When the Hungarians came in, they were embarrassed, she could see. One of them, János she thought it was, patted her clumsily on the shoulder, and they slunk upstairs without their usual bathing and let her be.

And on top of it all, Harry had paid her bills. He'd kept his promise not to seek her out and she had not sent for him. She would not, could not, send for him in desperation, it wasn't right. And the thought of him raised feelings in her—dark feelings that tangled with the horror of that long night in October, the sight of her husband's charred flesh and Patrick's empty eyes—that eclipsed the warmth and safety she'd once known in his company. Now he'd cast a shadow over her life in the patch town. Some of the mining wives would refuse to believe she had sold herself—sure, not Kate—but others would think she was no better than she should be. From there, they would say, it was an easy step to selling herself to survive.

And that no Irishman or woman could abide. Such things didn't happen in Ireland and even in America, when poverty drove widows to drink and theft, when asylums and poorhouses were filled with abandoned wives and their children, it was a rare thing to hear of a *cailín* crossing that line. The priests, the confessionals, saw to that. And yet she had, hadn't she? She had stepped over it willingly, hungrily, out of loneliness and pain. In the eyes of God and the church she was already a fallen woman.

It was no good, then, to hope for a new start in that vast city that had thrilled Patrick so long ago, a lifetime ago. Not until spring, and likely not then. How she would get there in any event she didn't know. By then she'd be large with the child and no one would take her in, not with Patrick in tow and him not much more than a looby, God knows. And the money, where on God's green earth would she get the money for the train? She might take in more boarders, but the Welsh and Irish refused to live with the Hungarians and the Hungarians. The house was bursting with Hungarians already. And the Company wanted its house back.

Maybe somewhere closer, Uniontown maybe. Harry lived there and she didn't want to see Harry. But it was a great large city and perhaps there'd be a job, for a few months anyway, and God willing their paths would not cross.

31

No Negroes, No Irish Need Apply. The words caught her eye before the rest of the hand-lettered sign registered. It was in the corner of the display window of a shop on Main Street; it advertised *Help Wanted: Shop Girl.* She knew how to figure prices, add and subtract in her head, didn't she do it daily to make ends meet? But her nails were grimy and broken, her skirts shabby, shoes worn. No one wanted such a sales girl. She turned away.

The downtown bustled with women in wool caped coats, men in velvet-collared overcoats, working men in fustian or corduroy. Carriages trundled up and down the street, kicking up chunks of ice filthy with mud and horse droppings. A door opened, sending forth the aroma of fresh bread, and her stomach growled in response. Muffled church bells sounded, striking three. She'd had no lunch, had been on her feet since early that morning. It was all she could do to force herself into the lobbies of fancy hotels, to knock at the alley doors of shops. Uniontown seemed to her as imposing as New York had been, even more terrifying. Then, she'd had Patrick. She could do anything with Patrick beside her.

She pulled the collar of Martin's old canvas coat around her ears and stuffed her hands in the pockets. If she accepted Harry, she too might browse the shops of Main Street in a lovely plaid coat and fur muff. Since well before noon, she'd inquired at four hotels, a grocer and a milliner. The grocer employed only family, the milliner simply looked down her nose and said no. The hotels preferred maids to live on the premises but when she told them she'd be bringing a brother with her they turned her away. Even when she offered that he might do odd jobs for nothing more than the use of a room, though she didn't know if ever he could. She must find a place to live, then, before she applied for a job, a place that would take them both. But any rooming house would require she have a job before it let to her. And very soon her condition would betray her. No one wanted to employ a woman so plainly with child.

The next sign caught her eye. It hung in the middle of a second-floor window in the peculiar rounded building on the corner of Main Street. It read "A. Robinson, Estate Agent" and pictured the silhouette of a house. She wondered if Mrs. Robinson were there; strange it was to be so near her. Harry's mother loomed large in her imagination, a woman of business, someone who'd traveled into the vast interior of this country and lived to return. Someone who lived unencumbered by a husband, free to chart her own course. She wanted to see this woman for herself.

A small sign on the inner door said to "Come in" and so she did, without knocking. It was a single room, the window largely blocked by the sign she'd seen from the street. Paper covered every surface: desk, oak filing cabinets, a small corner table, the floor, the hard wooden guest chair. Behind the desk sat an older woman whose dark hair, liberally streaked with gray, was pulled gently back from her face in a knot that spewed loose strands. She appeared much weaker than Niamh had expected; she'd looked for a robust, vigorous woman.

"Can I help you?" Mrs. Robinson set down her pen and pushed her spectacles up with a single finger. Her eyes were curious: plainly Niamh was not there to buy or sell a home.

It occurred to Niamh that she hadn't a plan. Exhausted with the day's trek, discouraged over her job search, she hadn't thought. She'd simply wanted a look at Mrs. Robinson.

The thought occurred to her that Harry might easily have been in the office and she felt a flush of relief that he wasn't there. "I'm looking for a job, so." She reddened. Her accent came out strong, she may as well have been right off the boat.

The woman looked around the room. "I know it's apparent I could use some help, but I'm not hiring right now."

She said nothing about how absurd it would be for Niamh to take a position as estate agent. Or even as a clerk.

"No, I'm thinking ..." Niamh hesitated. "I'm thinking you might know of people new to town would need a maid. A chamber maid or a scullery maid," she finished in a rush. Brilliant idea: an estate agent would know if someone wanted for servants.

"I see." Mrs. Robinson sat back and gestured to the guest chair. "Just drop those papers to the floor and have a seat. I'm sorry I don't get up. I've been ill."

Ah, so Harry has had his troubles, too. The care of his mother would weigh on him. Niamh sat, folded her hands in her lap and studied the woman. The face was lined, cheeks shadowed, skin pasty. But her eyes were bright and lively. And interested.

"I'm that sorry you've been ill. It must be difficult to run a business when you've a doctor to obey."

Mrs. Robinson laughed at that. "That's a unique way of putting it, and you're absolutely right. I don't always obey him, though." She turned her pen in her hands; there was a blot of ink on her forefinger. "And I have a son who steps in when I really can't exert myself."

Niamh feared she blushed at the mention of Harry. This woman couldn't know who she was. Unless Miss Joanna had told her.

"So you're hoping to find a position as a maid? Have you worked as one before?"

"No, ma'am, I have not. But I've been a boarding missus, out at the patch. I've cooked and cleaned for my husband and the boarders." Niamh turned her wedding ring around on her hand. Her fingers were reddened still by the cold outside, she had no gloves. "I'm a widow, you see, and must make my way."

Mrs. Robinson's smile faded; she tilted her head. "We have that in common, then. I too am a widow and I've had to make my way. Do you have children?"

Niamh hesitated only a moment. The child was not yet born and may never come to be. "No ma'am. But I have a brother and I have the care of him."

"How old? Does he work?"

"No ma'am, not at present. He was injured in the mine a few months ago. He's improving though, he'll be able to work again soon." God willing.

"The explosion at Youngstown, I suppose. I'm so sorry." Mrs. Robinson tapped the pen against her lips. "You would need someplace to live, as well?"

"I would, yes, a place for myself and my brother. We'd make do with a single room, we would, at least to start. Until he's up and about again."

Harry's mother was silent for a moment. Niamh felt her measure being taken, her soul weighed. She wished she were anywhere else; this had been a mistake.

Mrs. Robinson pulled her chair back to the desk and rested her forearms on it.

"I haven't anything at present, dear, but I will certainly keep you in mind if I hear of any position. I know a few people who take in boarders, but I'll need to speak with them before I can send you their way. If you'll leave your name and let me know how to contact you, I'll let you know if anything comes up."

"They're bringing in more and more of those hunkies and paying them starvation wages. James won't be standing for it, he won't." Kate twitched her apron, studied her hands. She didn't look at Niamh. "So we'll be moving on to the mines in Ohio, there in the Hocking Valley. Soon as the weather lets up and we can save the fare."

Niamh stared out the window. The glare of sun on snow hurt her eyes. First the letter, then the failures in Uniontown. Mrs. Robinson would never contact her, she had to know who the Irish girl with the damaged brother was. Harry or his aunt must have told her. Now Kate would be leaving. The Company would hire in more Huns; a new family would settle next door. Since Ellie Finnell's husband was killed, no Irish families or even single men had moved in. Several had left after the accident.

Kate poured water into the basin and scrubbed at the oatmeal pot. "Some of the miners will be leaving, too. James says the Company's after bringing in one of those cutting machines." She snorted. "Doesn't take a genius to run one of those things, any hunkie can do it. A good Irish miner who knows how to cut the coal by hand won't be any use once those things take over."

"And that means the Company will be able to drive wages down even more." Niamh swiped a damp cloth over the table. "My boarders weren't even miners where they came from, they were farmers. Or I think they were."

Kate rinsed the pot and dried it on a flour-sack towel. "'Tis time you left here, lassie. Go into Uniontown." She turned, hands on hips and peered at Niamh. "You must ask your gentleman friend."

Niamh's head jerked up.

"Oh, don't act so surprised. The gentleman from the company, the one who's come sniffing about. James says he's a spy for the operators." She pulled out a chair and sat, leaning forward. "I've heard the rumors about you that *diabhal* Dobson's passing. You'll not do yourself any more harm by going to him, then, and sure it's your only hope."

Niamh twisted her fingers together. "He was teaching Patrick, he's only a friend to us."

"I'm thinking he wants to be something more. You needn't do ought that you'd be shamed of, but you'd be a fool not to have the use of it."

Niamh stood, carefully pushed her chair under the table. "I married once for advantage, and see where it's got me. I'll not be so quick to do it again." She opened the stove and stirred the coals, shivered as a wave of warmth washed over her face. "I'll not beg and what can he do for a woman with a half-wit brother and a babe on the way."

"You'll not marry him then."

"Out of desperation? No."

"Do you have a choice?"

"I don't know," Niamh said. "I truly don't know."

32

"You'll not be meeting in this house." Niamh dried the last dish and set it down with a sharp click on the counter. The Hungarian, János or György, she didn't know which one and she didn't care, smiled his shy smile. She scowled at him, sure he only pretended not to understand.

"No meetings!" She waved her hand toward the stairs up which four other Hungarians, three women and a man, had disappeared. This was the third night this week that her house had hosted some kind of gathering, as many as ten or twelve Huns and their women crowding into the upper rooms, their strange guttural language seeping through the ill-fitting floor boards. Just this morning she'd found a handbill lodged behind a step; it was printed in a language she didn't recognize, Hungarian or maybe Polish. She'd shown it to Kate, who clucked over it and lowered her voice, as if someone might be listening, but there was only Patrick. And Patrick was in his own distant world, not listening to anything but the voices in his head.

"There's been talk of a labor action," Kate had said. "James's been dithering about whether to go with the others to a meeting Saturday next. They'll be talking about a strike, they will, if the wages don't go up." She turned the paper over and frowned. "Sure and I wish we could get off to Ohio, but the weather…"

"I heard there was a meeting on New Year's Day." Niamh sank down on the stool and flipped over the flyer. The language on the reverse was Italian, no Welsh and no English. "I thought nothing was decided."

"The Huns are after taking the matter into their own hands, James says, and sure they'll be pushing the others into a strike."

"And they've been meeting in my house to plan it all," Niamh said. "I'll be evicted for their trouble, and nothing I can do."

"And haven't we talked about this, dearie," Kate said. "You'll be living day to day here out of the goodness of the Company's black heart and Patrick never able to work."

"I have nowhere to go," Niamh had said softly.

Now it was dark, and Patrick lifted his head at the anger in her voice, his eyes darting between her and the Hungarian.

"*Csak egy születésnap, igen? Család.* Family, yes?" He smiled at her again, as to a child.

She decided he was János. György never attempted English words. "Not family." She jabbed a finger at him. "Miners, meeting about a strike. I don't care what you do about your work, but you can't do it here. I'll be evicted, you understand?" She leaned toward him and spit the word. "*Evicted.* Then you'll be finding a new place to live, you will."

But János was already halfway up the stairs and paid her no mind.

Patrick watched with flat eyes.

"Patrick," she sank onto the floor next to his rocker and laid her head on his knee, "what are we to do? Where are we to go?"

He stroked a gentle hand across her hair, but when she looked up at him, surprised, he gazed not at her but out the window, into the dark.

The rumors began filtering in early Friday. Kate turned up at Niamh's door mid-morning, mending in hand and eyes flashing.

"And wouldn't you know but it's the Huns started it, up to the north. And did they wait on the convention? No, they did not." She planted herself on a kitchen chair and spread her sewing on the table.

"What convention?" Niamh was up to her elbows in dishwater.

"Sure it's the meeting called for tomorrow, up to Scottdale, to decide on what to do about the wages and the company store and all the rest of it." She scrunched her eye at the needle and threaded it. "Himself"—she said, speaking of James—"is to be a delegate. But the Huns can't be waiting for that and they've gone out up there."

Niamh turned, wiping her hands on the sack towel. "So I'm thinking that's why János and György never came back last night."

"And serves the company right it does. Bringing in those cheap foreigners to replace honest English-speaking labor. And wouldn't you know but it comes back to bite?"

But Niamh feared she and Patrick would be the ones bitten by the Huns' actions. The operators would survive the strike and when it was over, they would dismiss and evict anyone involved. She would be tainted by association and yet she needed the boarders at least into springtime. The weather trapped her in the patch, the mercury below zero most mornings and any warming attended by snowfall so deep even the rails were disrupted. A strike now was the height of madness; no Irish nor Welshmen would have started such a thing.

But as the next few days showed, they may not have started the strike, but they readily joined in, for the most part. And those who didn't were set upon by those who did. The Huns, led by their women, marched from Mt. Pleasant to Stonerville, stopping at the Alice works long enough to chase away several coke drawers who had chosen not to go out. They forced out the men at Morewood and Enterprise, pushed toward Donelly, beat a young man at Mayfield who claimed he hadn't known there *was* a strike.

The first Niamh knew the strike had migrated from Westmoreland County into her sector was early Thursday, the twenty-second day of January, when a mob of Huns, hundreds of them, poured down the Connellsville road and into Youngstown. The weak light of sunrise had begun to filter over the east ridge and the first shift—those men still working and all of them English speakers—straggled along the path toward the mine. A handful of drawers manned the ovens, though only a third were in operation. And it was cold. Though the weather had eased since the first of the week, the temperature lingered close to zero still. Crusts of ice surrounded the well, the ruts in the paths crackling and treacherous.

Niamh, Kate and Maggie Raftery labored to thaw the pump; with temperatures viciously low for days and ice caked thick on the handle, they wrestled for their water.

"You'll be wasting water to pour it from the kettle," Kate said. "It freezes as fast as you pour it, no matter it's just been boiled."

Niamh was cross and put out with their criticisms, being as she was the only one making an effort to get the contraption to work at all.

"It's snow I've boiled, anyway, not fresh water. This filthy snow is nothing we can use, so full of cinders as it is." Just then the pump handle creaked and moved, no more than an inch. But it was a start.

"What's that then?" Kate straightened and turned toward the road. They were up on the hill, high enough over the hollow where the ovens and rails squatted to be above the worst of the smoke and cinders. But so few of the ovens were in operation that morning that the sky was almost clear, a slice of icy blue visible to the west.

"What's what?" Maggie pulled her shawl more closely about her shoulders and grasped the pump handle along with Niamh. Maggie's hands were bare and red; she was sure to aggravate her chilblains. She had no gloves.

Niamh heard it then, a roar almost like surf but fast dissolving into voices coming from the north. From their vantage point on the hill, a stretch of the Connellsville road was visible before it disappeared behind the knoll, and into that space surged a rabble of singing, shouting women. The noise echoed across the valley as the mob neared, and the porches of the houses clinging to the hillside filled with women and children scrambling for a view.

"Mother of God, what on earth!" Kate said. Maggie dropped the water bucket and crossed herself. Niamh craned to see between the houses below.

Two large women led the way, both bearing flags, one American and another, red and white and green, that was strange to Niamh. They waved those flags over their heads as if they conducted a marching brass band. Behind them the crowd surged, men and women both, many with clubs and coke-forks on their shoulders, some few with rifles or muskets. The head of the procession disappeared behind the knoll and the singing swelled, off-key and sporadic, the words foreign.

"Will they be going to Uniontown then?" Maggie clutched at the front of her shawl and shivered in the sharp breeze.

"Ah, no," Niamh said, "they're turning in here. And now we're to be shut down completely."

The miners halted, uncertain and nervous. The cokers at the ovens stepped back. Most threw down their tools and retreated toward the houses as the strikers surged into the open spaces in front of the ovens.

"My Andrew's safe at home at least," Maggie said. "And where is James, Kate?"

"Down there at the ovens," Kate said. "He'll not do anything rash, but our men will look to him to tell them what to do." She dropped her bucket and pulled her collar around her ears. "I'm going down."

Niamh put out a hand. "It won't be safe down there. That crowd is angry, there's no telling what they'll do."

"I won't be away from my man. I'll not stand up here and watch him attacked." The snow crackled under her boots as she picked her way down the slope toward the ovens.

Now the mob packed the road between the mine and the ovens like a muddy brown river at flood. Niamh watched Kate reach the rails and pick her way across, stop and scan the ovens for sight of James. Then the head of the column reached her, and she disappeared into their midst. The strikers converged on the working ovens and the men who stood before them with coke forks or wheelbarrows in hand.

Niamh saw a Welshman she knew by sight point his coke-fork at a striker; the striker swung a club, the fork spun out of the Welshman's hand, and he disappeared beneath a pile of burly Huns. It took great strength to pull coke from the ovens, but one strong Welshman was no match for a dozen or more Huns.

Others of the Youngstown men backed off, threw down their tools, moved away from the ovens and watched as the strikers kicked at the blocking that sealed in the cooking coal. The Hun women fanned out along the valley floor collecting tools and equipment—forks and hoses, wheelbarrows, brass cocks, anything loose—and tossed them into the fires.

Maggie clutched at Niamh's hand and squeezed. "Will they be burning our homes do you think?" Her eyes were wide and frightened.

"No, sure they won't. They want us on their side, and besides not a few of them live here, too." Niamh searched the crowd for familiar faces, her boarders and their friends who'd used her home to plan all this, but the crowd shifted and turned too quickly. "But they'll beat anyone who refuses to stop the work. I hope James is sensible."

"Andrew," Maggie said. "I must go see to Andrew. He'll not be going down there if I can help it." And she scurried off.

Another wave of strikers appeared on the road from Connellsville. Most bypassed Youngstown. They headed south towards Lemont and Stewart, maybe farther south beyond Uniontown. Somewhere in the county, Niamh had heard, the sheriff with a posse of armed men from Pittsburgh waited for them. They would find a lively welcome before they went much farther.

Below her, a gang of strikers had found a crowbar and pried up a half-dozen rails, threw them into the fires and moved on to destruction elsewhere. From her perch on the hillside the scene seemed unreal, like a force of deranged nature, a flood filling the valley floor and surging back and forth, side to side. The noise became a chant, faded into the background. Then a shot sounded, and the roar swelled, punctuated by screams mostly from the women on the porches, and Niamh ducked into the house to peer out at the melee from the relative safety of the front window.

The whole donnybrook lasted no more than twenty minutes. The gunshot had done no harm, but one Welshman was badly mauled and others suffered cuts and bruises. The ovens were effectively shut down, the miners turned back to their homes.

The mine bosses and supervisors were conspicuously absent.

33

February 1885

Evictions began on Monday, the second day in February and the eighteenth day after the strike began. Temperatures hovered in the low teens and filthy black snow covered the ground; nothing fresh had fallen for a week. North of Connellsville, Sheriff Sterling and his deputies set out the goods of a family who was not at home. They were Huns, it was said; the man had been a leader in the strike, and where they were when the deputies carted out their few extra clothes and their dishes and bedding, Niamh and Kate did not hear. They did hear, though, that a crowd gathered in silence to watch the eviction, but no one interfered.

Farther south, at Broad Ford, four families were turned out into the muck and the frigid temperatures, and at Summit two more. The rumors and stories ran ahead of Sterling and his men down the Connellsville Road to Wheeler and Uniondale, Hill Farm and Parrish. All anyone seemed to know for sure was that the sheriff, and the coal operators who had ordered the evictions, targeted the leaders of the strike no matter their nationalities. But it appeared that the Huns were being singled out above others.

"So I'll do the tossing first," Niamh told Patrick. He looked up at the sound of her voice, but his vacant stare showed no understanding. He rocked and hummed.

"They'll find no Huns here if they come looking, they won't, and we'll take in only the Irish and the English from now on. The English are bad enough, God knows."

She had not seen any of the men, the Halász brothers or any of the others, for days. The only woman, wife to one of the sons, Niamh had ordered out with shouts and gestures first thing that morning. Where the woman went Niamh didn't know and didn't care; she'd carried a bundle of clothes and odds and ends, and Niamh hoped that would be the last she would see of her.

The two upstairs rooms required a mickel of cleaning. Niamh was never really sure how many had been living there—they came and went and often fed themselves, not willing to pay her what she required to provide meals. All she'd cared was that they turn over enough to cover her own rent and keep a roof over her and Patrick's heads for the winter. But the reek had grown since they'd moved in, and now she saw why: the rooms were worse than the filthiest hovels she'd seen in the Irish countryside. Vile straw ticks for bedding. Unidentifiable meat hanging from rafters. A small coal-burning brazier, cold now, holding a half-empty crock of soup, congealed and slimy. She began by donning her coat and mittens, opening the rear window and heaving the bedding into the mud and snow below. The food, wrapped in a threadbare blanket, followed along with the cook pot, the brazier and a half-dozen articles of clothing that she cringed to touch. And then there was nothing left. As many as ten or twelve people had slept there, sometimes eaten there, over the past two months and all they had to show for their presence went out the window in ten minutes.

The clean-up required the rest of the morning and most of the afternoon. She boiled pot after pot of water, hauled it upstairs, and used the last of her lye to scrub down the walls, the floors, and what little furniture there was, two iron bedsteads strung with rope, a table, and a wobbly bench. By the time she finished, the house was frigid but the smell was gone, or else her nose was too cold to pick it up, and she would need to use up the last of her coal in the cook stove to warm the downstairs for Patrick.

She was standing in the back room upstairs room yanking at the now-stuck window, when the front door opened and heavy boots stamped on the bare floorboards. The Huns were back. But they'd never used the front door before, always came through the back and immediately up the stairs. Whichever door they used, they needn't think they still lived here.

But it wasn't the Huns. She stumbled into the kitchen to find Dobson from the company store and two other men, Americans and strangers. One of the men, a big yellow-haired New Englander with a flat Boston accent, scooped the blankets from Patrick's bed and dropped them onto the front porch. The second man dumped the last chunks of coal out of the basket onto her clean floor and filled it with her few precious books, the Mark Twain that Harry had given them, a geography that Patrick had bought from a Welshman, the *Key of Heaven* prayer book and Martin's *Catholic Piety*.

"No Bible, of course." The man sent Dobson a "wouldn't you know it" look.

Dobson leaned over the bed and unfastened the crucifix that hung there. "Damned papists." He studied the figure of Jesus in agony, turned it over as if he expected to find exit wounds. "Put your own Irish pagan twist on it. What's all this here?" He pointed to the Trinity Knot and flicked a fingernail against the circle behind the crossbars. "All this trash and filth, think it'll save you?" and he tossed the piece of polished oak into the basket.

"But I've got rid of the Huns." It was all Niamh could think of to say.

"And now it's time for you to be gone, too," Dobson said. "Clear out the kitchen, boys, including that lazy fella in the chair." He pointed at Patrick, still in his rocking chair, a quilt wrapped around his shoulders against the deep chill.

"But where are we to go?" Niamh said, her voice high now and shrill. "My brother is ill, he can't be put out like this. I can take in more boarders. I've cleaned for them and everything."

"The company's been patient enough with you, Mrs. Gill. We need the house for men that'll actually do the work. Not widows and lazy boys and agitating foreigners." He turned his back on her and ran a hand across the top of the window as if searching for a hidden stash.

Niamh pinched her lips together as she watched her kitchen utensils dumped unceremoniously into the wood box. The blonde ape yanked at drawers in the low chest where she kept her clothes and Patrick's, and the small stash of coins she'd managed to set aside.

"Get out!" She leaped at him and shoved. "I'll do it myself, you great *gabhdán.*"

She dropped to her knees and pulled her old valise from under the bed. The bureau drawers were warped, and she struggled to open the top one, rattled it and yanked until she felt the tears begin to well up. She bit down hard on the inside of her lip; Dobson would not see her cry. Finally, the drawer gave way and she bundled up Patrick's extra shirt and smalls, her own underclothes and nightdress, her extra stockings and the one good frock she'd brought, the dark blue wool that had been her wedding dress. It had been folded away ever since, no use to her in the patch town. She slipped the coins into her pocket; there were pitiably few of them.

Patrick stood in the door to the front room, a puzzled look on his face. "Niamh?" he said in his soft voice.

She snapped shut the valise and went to him, put her arms around his thin chest. "We need to leave here, dear. Let's get you into your coat."

Patrick nodded; the trust in his eyes all but broke her heart. He let her wrap him in Martin's coat, and she knelt to tie the laces of his boots. Dobson's man tossed her valise into the slush and mud and cinders off the porch.

"So the boy's an idiot." Dobson stood, a shoulder against the kitchen door jamb, thumbs through his braces. "I'd heard something of it, didn't know he can't even tie his shoelaces."

"Thanks to your precious company that can't be bothered to make the mines safe for man nor beast," Niamh said.

"All the more reason to get you out of here. Company can't afford to house widows and half-wits."

Niamh ignored him. She wrapped a scarf around her brother's neck, her movements heavy, the scene a dream. The voices of Dobson and his men and the crowd gathering outside sounded distant and hazy. Even the biting cold seemed apart, something happening to someone else, with no power to touch her.

She was surprised at the size of the crowd that had gathered. Kate stood on their shared front porch, eyes narrowed and jaw clenched. A dozen or more Irish and Welsh families, mostly women and children, crowded the yard, trampling the frozen mud into mire, no Huns to be seen. Dobson had timed the eviction so that most of the men were in the mine or at the ovens. They were eerily silent, little to be heard but the sound of shifting feet and icy wind. Someone coughed and spit. Niamh picked up her valise, fished out her prayer book from the coal basket and slipped it into Patrick's coat pocket. She would take nothing more.

A rock flew through the air and hit the New Englander on the shoulder. He dropped Patrick's rocker and whirled to face the crowd.

"Who threw that?" He fisted his hands.

The crowd stirred, muttered. Maybe they would defend her, Niamh thought, force Dobson to leave her the house for one more night, give her time to find someplace to go. Yes, and maybe someone would hand her a hundred American dollars to set up shop and rent a house. Wasn't that the American dream, though?

Dobson stepped onto the porch, a yellow paper in his hand. He waved it at the crowd.

"All legal, now, got a writ of ejectment here, sheriff will be along shortly. You all go on about your business. We want no trouble here."

"Come inside, dearie." Kate put an arm around Niamh's shoulders, turned her toward the other side of the house. "You'll stay here tonight, and we'll come up with a plan for you." She took Patrick's hand and pulled him along. Dobson and his men disappeared inside Niamh's home.

"We'll be keeping these things for you, Niamh." Maggie stepped out of the crowd and picked up the coal basket with the books. "Till you're settled somewhere."

Niamh looked over her household goods, everything she possessed in the world. She shrugged. "Keep them. Or toss them. I don't want any of it." She turned into Kate's arm and slipped into the house.

In the morning, the priest from Connellsville came for her.

34

Towards midnight the snow began to fall, dropping in heavy wet flakes that coated tree limbs and outlined the eaves of the patch houses in lace. Before sunrise, though, it stopped, the temperatures dropped, and a skim of ice crusted the drifts and hillocks in the valley. Fewer than half the ovens were fired up and around them the snow and ice melted and turned the mud of the yard into an even stickier gumbo that weighed down the boots of the men and the hooves of the mules. The smoke from the ovens rose straight into the air, no breath of wind spreading soot or cinders abroad.

Niamh rode next to Father McDermott, Patrick wrapped in blankets in the wagon bed. As they climbed out of the valley onto the Connellsville Road and turned north, the first rays of a brilliant cold sun shot over Mount Braddock and washed the western fields with orange-gold and lavender, etching the shadows of trees and fence posts with precisely penciled strokes. The hills to the west floated in mist, purple and distant, and the quiet of the morning, without breeze or birdsong, was absolute.

A memory intruded, of a winter when she was a child, no more than five or six, when a great storm raged over the whole of Ireland for twelve days, shrouded the hills and vales in blue-white. The snow was so deep the rock walls appeared to be tunnels made by large rodents winding their way beneath the surface. Sheep, stranded, froze in stony corners, and roads were impassable even to mule-drawn sleds. And because the harvest had been meager the past two years and hunger haunted Connacht once again, there was fear abroad that *An Gorta Mór* would return.

Niamh remembered the hunger, though that was not possible. The Great Famine had ended a decade before her birth, but the images, the scars, were seared into every Irish peasant's soul like an inherited disease. Her mam never spoke of it, but her da sometimes did, and though he had survived by his wits (he would have her to understand) and prospered in the following years, he told tales of starvation, forced emigration and eviction. Niamh, wide-eyed, asked him what it would be to starve.

"*Dia linn*," he would say. "The hunger is terrible, it surely is. But the worst thing is to lose your home." And here he would cast his eyes about the four-room cottage that he had expanded with his own hands. "Your home is everything, your bond to the past, to your kin. 'Tis the thing that says you're a man, not an animal, the place where if ye starve, you'll starve like a man." He pulled on his pipe and wreathed his head in a smoky mist. "If you're huddled in a ditch with your babes wet and cold about you and naught for a roof but the hedge itself, why you may as well starve, *a chailín,* and the quicker the better."

The terror of the notices and the bailiff's men, the hook and the battering ram, became for Niamh the stuff of nightmares filled with families huddled in ditches beside their demolished cabins, sheltering beneath sticks and a sod roof only to see even that slight refuge pulled down. She had begun to notice, among the fields and byways of Carrowbaun townland, overgrown foundations and the faintest trace of paths, to imagine emaciated peasants huddled before the doors of teeming workhouses where nothing was on offer but infection and death. Eviction from one's home, no matter how temporary or unsatisfactory that home may be, was beyond horror, the most fundamental evil of all.

Niamh said not a word to the priest on the drive to Connellsville, and after several attempts to convince her God would provide and the Holy Mother held her in her hands, he gave up and concentrated on clicking to the horse and avoiding the icy ruts. By the time they reached Connellsville, Niamh was too numb with cold to appreciate the welcoming lights of the Rectory. She stared with dull eyes at the neighboring church. It was where she'd been married.

"You'll need to stay here until I can find quarters for you." The priest stepped down into a snow bank that came to his knees. "Drat this weather."

"There must be others who've been evicted," Niamh said. "Where do they go?"

"Ah, she speaks!" McDermott said. "Various places. Some go to relatives or friends. A fellow named Harton over toward Fort Hill has some tenement houses he's offered." He lifted her down and set her in the street.

"Why would he do that?"

The priest smiled. "He's a good man. Doesn't like to see families out in the snow."

Niamh reached into the wagon for her valise. "I didn't know there were any left. Patrick, come now, time to get down."

Patrick smiled through blue lips, pushed back his blankets and clambered down, dragging the bedding with him.

"Does he require payment?" Niamh asked. "And is there any work there for me? Or here, for that matter. I'll not take charity."

"What is it you can do?"

"Most anything. Clean. Sew. I'm not the best cook, but I can put together a meal for a houseful of boarders. It's just that I need to have my brother by me at all times or someone to tend him while I work."

Father McDermott bundled up Patrick's blankets and took the boy by the arm, pushing a path through the snow to the door of the Rectory. "We'll find you something." He glanced back at her over his shoulder. "The church and the Irish take care of their own."

Niamh sat on the last bench in the nave, not so very far back from the sanctuary since the church was small, fashioned from an old Methodist church a decade before. The narthex, an enclosed front porch, let in a frigid February draft that touched her neck with icy fingers and set the votive candles a-flicker.

Patrick sat next to her, wrapped in the neck scarf she'd knit him for Christmas and the canvas coat, too big for him since he'd lost so much weight in the past three months. His eyes wandered about the church like those of a child, delighting in the beauty of morning sunlight through the single window of colored glass, the flare of altar candles on polished brass, the rising and kneeling of the celebrants.

Niamh had come to love these early masses in the few weeks she'd spent in Connellsville. Father McDermott arrived at the church at five-thirty every morning and so did she, Patrick in tow. She stoked the fires in the two coal stoves and swept the walk, cleaned the melted wax from around the votive candles while the priest prepared the Mass. Though the church was crowded on Sundays, so much so that the parish had begun to talk of raising funds for a new church, the weekday masses drew only a few women and old men, many Italians whom Niamh was unable to chat with after services. The resulting stillness and solitude during that hour, the scent of candlewax and incense, the soft light of dawn or the pearly glow of snow clouds soothed her soul and cleared her mind for the day ahead.

This morning the singsong Latin of the Psalms and the prayers in Father McDermott's rich bass touched a particular chord in her. Most days after Mass she would make her way to the Rectory to fix the priest's breakfast and tidy his parlor while he finished in the Sacristy and took his place in the Confessional. But today she determined it was her turn to clear her conscience. She laid her hand on her belly and fancied she felt movement. Couldn't be, it was much too early. The flutter she felt was nerves: she had sinned and God continued to punish her for it.

The Gospel ended and Father McDermott stepped down from the Altar, bowed to the Cross and disappeared into the Sacristy. Patrick stirred; Niamh patted his hand and continued to sit, her rosary in her lap, practiced fingers telling the beads. She closed her eyes as the half-dozen congregants passed down the side aisle and out the door. She hoped they would see her deep in her devotions and pass by without conversation. One old woman lit a candle, crossed herself and muttered a prayer. Niamh listened for the sound of the door to the Confessional but it did not come; she would be the only one today. The church emptied and she felt the silence press in.

"Bless me Father, for I have sinned. It has been, um, eight months since my last confession."

Niamh rested her forehead on her folded hands so she wouldn't need to look at the shadowed outline of the priest on the other side of the screen. He had been so kind to her and so sympathetic. She heard him rustle as he settled himself on the stool and cleared his throat. He'd taken a chill and worried that his cough would disrupt services, so she fixed peppermint tea several times a day and insisted he drink it.

"I have had …" she stopped. Tried again. "I have been angry with the mining company."

"I imagine you have been," he said. "You'll need to work on forgiveness as time goes on, to be sure."

"And I've resented the burden of Patrick. I've been angry with God that he's done this to Patrick."

"Ah, resentment I understand. Being angry at God—well, we'll talk about that. Are you thankful, though, that Patrick lives in spite of all?"

"Oh, I am, Father, I would not have him dead. But Father, I did not love my husband."

"Are you pleased then that he is dead, child?"

"No, no, it isn't that." She stopped. Her throat felt thick, she was afraid she would be violently ill.

"There's more then, isn't there?"

The words came in a rush. "Father, the accident was my fault, I killed all those men. And made Patrick what he is. It was my fault. I sinned, and I'm being punished and that was part of my punishment but not all because you see I'm with child, I'm going to have a child."

The priest stirred. She peeked at him and saw his hand brush over his face.

"I don't see how your being with child, which is a natural result of marriage even if there was no love involved, caused the accident. It isn't a sin to bring a child into the world without love if the child is wanted and there is respect between the parents."

"But you see—I had carnal relations with another man. It was before my husband was killed. And I don't know, I think the child is not my husband's."

There was silence from the other side of the screen. She felt, more than saw, him sit straight and turn full face toward her. Finally, he took a breath.

"Well, child, that's a grave sin indeed. And is this man another miner?"

"No, Father, he's a man from town, from Uniontown."

"And is he in a position to marry you?"

"He is not already married, Father, and he's said he wants to marry me."

"Then I suggest you take him up on it, and quickly."

"His family will object and he's not of our faith nor would he agree to convert. And he's very young, he's not settled on a profession. And there's Patrick to think of."

"And you don't love him."

"I don't know, everything has happened so fast, I don't know what to think."

"You seem not to love very easily." His voice was dry.

Niamh ducked her head and whispered, "Sure, it isn't about love, is it. It's about survival."

Father McDermott sighed. "God forgives, as well you know, and He may grant you a lifetime in which to atone. Devotion to your brother and your child is a good start. I'll continue to pray for your soul, and we'll see what we can do about your earthly situation. Dry your tears now, girl, and empty your mind of all but the glory of God."

He turned to the side again and she saw his profile dip in prayer.

"*Deus, Pater misericordiárum, qui per mortem et resurrectiónem Fílii sui mundum sibi reconciliávit et Spíritum Sanctum effúdit in remissiónem peccatórum, per ministérium Ecclésiæ indulgéntiam tibi tríbuat et pacem. Et ego te absolvo a peccatis tuis in nomine Patris, et Filii, et Spiritus Sancti.*"

"Oh my God," Niamh said, the words coming automatically, "I am heartily sorry for having offended you and I detest all my sins, because I dread the loss of heaven and the pains of hell. But most of all because I have offended you, my God, who are all good and deserving of all my love. I firmly resolve with the help of your grace, to confess my sins, to do penance and to amend my life. Amen."

Without another word, the priest slipped out of the tiny closet, his footsteps echoing on the wooden floor. She cried, then, in deep choking sobs.

35

March 1885

Spring came early that year, or rather a false spring to tease the senses and swell buds imperiled by the threat of a late frost. Within a few days of the first of March the snow had melted from paved streets and walkways and the ice from muddy lanes, leaving behind clumps of cinder-blackened snow caught in desiccated weeds and ankle-deep mud.

Harry sat in his mother's office behind a desk stacked with neat piles: contracts in the left corner, advertisement copy in the right, correspondence to be answered in a wooden box in the center. The first task Harry had finally convinced his mother to allow him to do was to organize her office. He'd filed and sorted and boxed until the visitor's chair was available for clients, the table empty enough to spread out blueprints and the file cabinet cleared for a vase of hot-house flowers. Whenever his mother spent her limited hours there, she returned home complaining she couldn't find a thing.

The tall gas lamp behind his chair was lit in the gathering dusk. He had lessons to plan for tomorrow's classes and two purchase offers to review before he closed up. Spending three or four hours in the office at the end of each school session made for long days, but it was the only way to keep the business healthy. And he wanted activity. It kept him from thinking.

He stood to open the window to let the heady spring breeze waft away the gas lamp's warmth and caught sight of Dan crossing the street. He crumpled a paper and hurled it out the window at his friend's head.

"Come on up, the coffee's not yet cold."

"I found her!" Dan grinned up at him and disappeared around the corner toward the building's entrance.

"Found who?" Harry wrestled with the tetchy window sash. Then he realized what Dan had said.

He dropped into his chair and stared at the papers on the desk. All of this—his teaching job, his mother's business, his family's needs—in a few short weeks he'd slipped into a rut of duty. He hadn't forgotten her, far from it. At night, he tossed in his bed and remembered how she'd looked beneath the tree at the cemetery, how she'd chatted with Joanna during lessons. How she'd felt beneath him. Wondered where she'd gone and whether he would ever see her again. The days, though—then his mind was a fog where she was concerned. A paralysis, hemmed in by other demands.

Now Dan had found her.

Dan slipped into the office and shut the door. He pulled off his cap, dropped into the visitor's chair, and tossed a newspaper onto the desk.

"I found that first." He jerked at his tie. "Actually, Al Williams found it. The junior partner in my law firm? He represents a fellow in Lemont in an eviction case. He's been reading all the news stories."

Harry picked up the paper. It was a month-old edition of the Connellsville *Courier*, and the article Dan had circled was headed "Houseless and Homeless."

The work of evicting the striking miners and coke drawers commenced on Tuesday. That day Sheriff Sterling and a few deputies visited the Valley works and set out the goods of a family that were not at home. A writ was in the hands of the sheriff to evict another family at the same works, but the critical condition of the miner's wife caused the officer to desist. In the afternoon the posse went to Youngstown where they set out a widow and her ailing brother in the snow. From there they went to the Mahoning and added two more families to the list.

Harry looked up. "It's her." He stood, jammed his hands in his pockets, and turned to gaze out the window. "I don't believe it. I can't believe they'd do that."

"Yes, you do," Dan said. "You know they wouldn't hesitate. No one in the patch would tell me anything at first, so I went to the sheriff. He said everyone evicted found a place to stay. The paper says the same thing."

"So where is she now? You said you'd found her."

"She went with the priest to Connellsville. She's living up there in the Rectory. The priest is keeping her for now."

"You saw her?"

"No, I haven't been up there. I finally convinced that neighbor of hers,

Mrs. Raftery, to talk to me. She didn't much want to tell me where she was, but I told her your Aunt Joanna was asking."

"I'm going up there." Harry moved back to the desk and stacked papers.

"Not today, though," Dan said. "The last train's left, and what about your classes? You have school tomorrow."

Harry sat down and ran a hand through his hair. "Damn, I can't just not show up."

"Take the Saturday train, it's only two days. She'll still be there," Dan said. "Where would she go?"

Where would she go indeed? Harry stood in the study of the Rectory, hat in hand. Father McDermott leaned back in his desk chair. A housekeeper had shown Harry into the room and closed the door behind him.

"She left late last week." McDermott eyed Harry curiously. "She's gone to Philadelphia. A couple from the parish was making the trip, and she took the opportunity to go with them."

"Did Patrick go too?" Harry asked.

"He did." McDermott picked up a paper knife and tapped it idly on the desktop. "Won't you sit down?"

Harry perched on the edge of a wooden chair and leaned forward. "Where in Philadelphia? Had she arranged a job?"

The priest hesitated, then appeared to come to a decision. He put down the paper knife and he, too, leaned forward. "She'd made plans, but I don't know that I am at liberty to share them with you. She wanted no part of her life here over the past year."

Harry frowned. "But that doesn't include me. She'd want to see me."

"How do you know that?"

Harry looked away. He couldn't very well tell this man that they'd fallen in love, they'd slept together. He turned back. "What did she tell you?"

"Anything she said would have been under the seal of confession."

Harry nodded. This exasperating religion with all its rules. "I plan to marry her. I can take care of her. And Patrick."

McDermott studied him again. "How old are you, son?"

"Old enough to marry. Old enough to know."

"How old?"

Harry felt himself flush. "Twenty."

"And you're willing to take on a wife, a child, and an invalid brother?"

Harry's head jerked up, eyes wide. "A child?"

The priest raised his brows. "You didn't know? She's with child."

"When?" Harry said softly. "When is it ... when will it come?"

The priest thought a moment. "July, I would say. Sometime in mid-summer."

Harry leaned back in the chair and rubbed a hand over his eyes. "And you say she's in Philadelphia? Can you give me any more than that?"

"I would," McDermott said, "if I could. But truly, I don't know. I can give you the name of the family she left with, but what she's done since I cannot tell you."

"Did she have money?"

"She had some, not a lot, but enough to keep her for a time. And she has friends, people connected to this parish who are willing to help. People connected to her family in Ireland."

Harry nodded and pushed himself up. "Well. Thank you for the information. I'll take that name if you would, and I thank you for your help to her. And to Patrick."

McDermott scribbled a name on a piece of notepaper, thought a moment and added a street name. "That's as much as I know. I wish you ..." He hesitated. "I wish you success in whatever it is will be best for both you and Niamh. She's a strong woman; she'll do as she thinks is right."

Harry took the note. The priest held out his hand. "God be with you."

Harry grasped the extended hand and shook it. "I hope so, Father. I truly hope so."

36

By the time Harry reached Philadelphia, spring had disappeared and winter had returned. A sleet-laden wind off the Delaware River knifed through the stoutest coats of workers and idlers on the docks. Harry ducked into the shelter of a side-door, mashed his hat to his head and wished it covered his ears. Across the walkway loomed the mouth of the covered wharf where the *Illinois* was docked, its two high masts dwarfing its funnel. Passengers flowed into the passageway like miners trudging into a mine, to reappear on deck, distant and indistinguishable.

It was sheer chance that he was there at all, in time, that the ship hadn't yet sailed. From the time the train deposited him in the Philadelphia depot four days ago, his search was laced with frustration. The clannish Irish seemed to be in league to hide her, the swarming city impenetrable.

He'd walked the three miles from the station to the address on Baker Street the Connellsville priest had given him, where the Irish herded together in barely habitable tenements, fragrant with boiled cabbages and small children. But the family she'd traveled with had left for New York, and no one remembered a widow and her slow-witted brother. Then two miles back to the Schuykill River wharves, where the dockworkers slanted sideways looks at him and simply shook their heads if they responded at all. But one colleen took pity on him after he bought a bag of hot chestnuts and paid double the asking price. She sent him to the Kensington neighborhood on the east side of the city, to St. Michael's Church not far from the moorings where the Europe-bound ships lay. If anyone were to know where such a one would be, she said, it would be Father O'Connor.

Once again, he took a horse trolley across the city. The narrow brick church, its two unmatched spires grimed by smoke from surrounding mills, was covered in scaffolding and the priest himself stood in the center of

Second Street directing the work of three brick masons and dodging noisy traffic.

Yes, indeed, he remembered Mrs. Gill and her brother, and no, he wasn't about to give a strange young man directions to find her and please go away, can't you see I'm busy with God's work here?

It was late, and it was cold, and Harry had had enough run-around. O'Connor had turned his back to gesture at an upper cornice, shouting over the din of coal carts and rumbles from the carpet factory across the street. Harry grasped the priest's arm, spun him, and thrust his nose into the man's face. "Give some thought to your flock, Father."

O'Connor sputtered. "Leave me be, man, or I'll have the law on you." Red-faced, he rubbed his chest. He looked unhealthy.

He released the priest's arm, none too gently. "More important than the building."

O'Connor's face said clearly he didn't agree, but he brushed himself down and stepped back to the curb. Harry followed, dodging a pile of steaming horse droppings. The breeze swirled the priest's robes along the pavement and plastered a sheet of newsprint against his shin.

"She's gone, as far as I know." His accent was faint; not a new arrival himself.

"Gone where?"

"Back to Ireland. Or if not yet she soon will be." He waved his arms at his workers and they peered down and shrugged.

"Do you know how? Which ship?" Harry wouldn't believe he'd missed her. "Was she alone?"

"Blast it," O'Connor said. "You missed a row. Over there!" He shouted through cupped hands. When the workers turned their backs on him, he shook his head at Harry. "Of course not, the boy was with her. And from the looks of her she'll have another one soon enough."

"Do you know where she was staying? Who she was with?" Harry's voice was bleak, needy, but he didn't care. The priest narrowed his eyes.

"The child is yours, is it?" He waved a hand in front of his face. "You're like all the others those lasses have the misfortune to run into over here. You have your filthy way with them then send them off without a thought. And now you're worried? You should have thought of that when you took her to bed." He coughed into his hands, then into a grimy handkerchief he pulled from his cassock. "Ah, it's the heart." He pounded his chest.

Harry's gaze took in the grimy street. Several businesses stood dark and shuttered, closed in the wake of hard times last year. Other doors opened; workers spilled into dirt alleyways, tossed shawls about their shoulders, jammed shapeless hats on their heads. Their chatter rose in the chill evening air in a variety of accents, British, mid-Atlantic, the soft drawl of the American south. And Irish. Activity picked up in the pubs tucked among the mills and row houses; men and women both, children as well, ducked under the low headers in ones and twos. She'd been here, may still be. He wouldn't believe he'd missed her.

The priest mounted the steps of the church. "If I were you, I'd inquire at the immigration station, down on Washington Avenue. She might be on the passenger lists. Outbound, of course." He looked down at Harry for a moment, then made the sign of the cross and disappeared through the heavy oak doors.

At least I've been blessed again, much good that'll do me. Blasted papists. He pulled from his pocket the map of Philadelphia he'd bought at the train station and counted the blocks. Washington Street was more than three miles away, along the waterfront. He started walking.

By the time he reached the Immigration Station, the American Lines ticket office was closed for the night. He roamed the darkened streets searching for a boarding house or an inn, kicking himself for not planning ahead, and ended up in a tiny room above a bar whose exuberant clientele sang off-color sailing songs far into the night. By six a.m. he had planted himself outside the steamship company's offices and dozed until a bleary-eyed clerk opened the windows at eight. Then it was a matter of begging, threatening and finally bribing the man to check his passenger lists for a Mrs. Gill and Patrick Kilgariff. It was coming on noon before he found them.

Niamh and Patrick had bought steerage passage on the *Illinois*, set to sail in three days time. The clerk showed him the entry: nothing but names and amount paid, no information that would lead him to her. He had nearly three days to search.

He spent those days wandering the working-class neighborhoods of Philadelphia scanning faces in the marketplace and on the streets and in the bars. She was here somewhere, the next street over, or across town in a cramped tenement. She would no longer be asking for employment, no longer concerned about where she and Patrick would live. He wondered about her health, whether the pregnancy was difficult. He'd heard Irish women bred without the pains of the higher classes. He hoped so.

He had never looked, really looked, at places like this. Uniontown had its poor neighborhoods, but nothing so seedy or crowded as the Philadelphia mill districts and docks. He'd always imagined Niamh in his own neighborhood, her nails clean, dressed the way Rebecca dressed, where stoops were swept and horse droppings cleaned up daily. She didn't belong in a place like this and yet most everyone he passed spoke in the lilting accent that was hers, carried that hungry look that had pained him to see in her the last few times they'd met.

He spent the second morning on a bench outside the great wooden doors of St. Michael's, watching the worshippers come and go, hoping for a glimpse of a familiar face, hers or Patrick's. The women wrapped themselves in dark black shawls, the men hunched into heavy wool coats and flat caps against the wicked March wind. Children clung to skirts or huddled in strong arms. Their big eyes passed over him in mild curiosity, then moved on. The adults stopped just inside the vestibule, dipped fingers in a basin of water and touch them to foreheads, making the sign of the cross before disappearing into the dim interior. Niamh was not among them.

The final evening before the *Illinois* sailed, he dragged himself back to the bar and his tiny room. He'd walked miles all day, knocking on doors, haunting shops, striking up conversations with street vendors. Wherever they were staying, they were well hidden. The noise from downstairs swelled, the Irish accents a mockery. He shrugged back into his jacket, stuffed his watch and cash into his pockets and slipped downstairs.

By the time he'd finished two pints and a plate of fried fish and boiled cabbage it was coming on eleven. The crowd had thinned to a half dozen weather-beaten old men, dockhands, by their conversation. The serving girl cleared Harry's dishes, pulled the shades over the front windows and built up the fire with a last shuttle of coal.

"A round," Harry said. The long day and the beer had just about done him in but he couldn't bear the idea of the dreary room and straw-tick mattress. He slapped a bill on the bar and turned to the fireplace. The publican set out a row of small glasses and pulled out a bottle of whiskey. The workers hooted and slapped him on the back, and he found himself in the big armchair by the fire, glass in hand, the Irishmen calling for stories.

The whiskey made his head heavy and the fire warmed him so that he sat slumped in an armchair, half listening to the musical voices, a low buzz from which the word "Niamh" slid like a dream.

He started and came awake, eyes darting about the room, but there were only the workmen, sipping their whiskies and smoking their pipes. They listened sleepily to the tale being told by an old fellow with wispy white hair and heavy black eyebrows, the tale of Oisín and Niamh. It was a story Niamh had related once as she sat beneath the tree in the cemetery with Patrick dozing in the sunshine and Mab asleep at her feet. It was the story of Niamh Chinn-Óir, an Otherwordly woman who carried away Oisín, the son of Finn MacCool, to the land of Tír Na nÓg, where no one knew sadness and everyone lived forever.

"But Oisín missed Ireland and his father," said the old man.

"Aye, hmm, yes," murmured the others, the sound melting into the hiss of the fire.

"She agreed to let him return to Ireland," the old man said, "and sent him off on her white charger. But she told him, 'Do not get off this horse, and do not let your feet touch the ground, or else you will never be able to return to Tír Na nÓg again.'"

The old man stopped there, knocked his cold pipe on the hearth stone and set back in his chair. Harry sat up.

"Aren't you going to finish the story?" he asked.

The old man took a leather pouch from his shirtfront and extracted a pinch of tobacco. "We all know how it ends, so," he said. He looked at Harry from under his brows.

The others began to stir and nod. Two of the men stood and stretched, another turned to a fourth and said something about the morrow's work. They were done.

"I'd like to hear it," Harry said, though he knew the ending.

"Well then," the old man said and he scratched a match against a horny thumbnail, held it to his pipe bowl and sucked. Through a cloud of smoke, he said, "Of course he touched the ground and didn't he age three hundred years and died soon after and never went back to Tír Na nÓg again." He turned away and stared into the fire.

Harry sat for a few more moments, then dragged himself up to his room.

❉

Which is how he came to be huddled on the Wednesday in a doorway across from the American Line docks as dawn broke through the dingy smoke and fog of a dreary Philadelphia morning. He would wait for her here.

He swiped at his reddened nose with a handkerchief and worried about his unsavory appearance. It was not the best way to present himself to her. He studied every face, every passenger who approached the wharf, willing her to appear. But even then he didn't recognize her at first, a slight figure in an old canvas coat, melting into the crowd. But Patrick stood out, his sweet, childish face atop his delicate frame unmistakable. Niamh's thin coat did little to hide the protruding belly. Her face was puffy and pink from exertion, her hair pulled back, severe against her neck. She grasped Patrick's elbow in one hand, a battered valise in the other.

Harry stepped in front of her. He held his hat in his hands, hair whipping.

"Niamh."

Her eyes widened but otherwise she showed no surprise.

"So you've found me then." She set the valise down and held out her hand. "Patrick, it's our old friend." She tugged her brother around. No recognition showed in Patrick's eyes, but he smiled, his gaze vacant. Niamh took Harry's hand.

"We've paid passage back to Ireland you see." She waved toward the ship. "I'm so looking forward to seeing my mam and dad again." She smiled, contented, sure.

"The baby. Is it mine?"

She dropped his hand and looked down. When she looked up, her eyes were clear and direct. "No," she said.

He knew she lied, but all he said was, "I want to marry you. I'll take care of you and the baby and Patrick. Stay."

For a moment she said nothing, but her eyes held his. "I cannot, Harry. I won't stay in this country any longer." She looked away, then back. "Will you come with us, then? You'd like Ireland." Her voice challenged him.

He'd been so willing to take her away, to Montana or San Francisco. All that seemed a long time ago now. And Ireland. Across an ocean.

He gazed up the boardwalk, not seeing the crowd. "I can't do that. I'm needed here, this is my home. It could be your home, too. Give us another chance."

"No, Harry, this won't ever be my home."

The stream of passengers flowing onto the ship had thinned, and a whistle blew. She picked up the valise.

"It was a pleasure to meet you, Harry Robinson." Her voice was low, he had to bend to hear her, and now she didn't look him in the eye.

Her brother stood a few paces apart, his face vacant, the intense, intelligent hunger he'd shown during their lessons gone. He hummed, a low, tuneless burr that bored into Harry like the hum of a distant steam engine. Niamh turned toward him and took his arm. Patrick looked down at her and smiled, bland, simple.

"And that's all," Harry finally said. "As if nothing ever happened."

"Nothing really did, then, did it?" She turned back to him. "We were friends, and I hope we'll always be friends."

"Even an ocean apart? Even if we never see each other again?"

Niamh hesitated. "Harry, if you come to Ireland, I will welcome you."

"You know I can't."

"I know you won't."

Then there was nothing more. Niamh motioned to Patrick and tugged her coat over her thickening waist. She leaned in and kissed Harry's cheek.

"It was a pleasure to meet you, Harry Robinson," she said again, softly. She turned, grasped Patrick by the elbow and disappeared onto the wharf.

February 1930

Dan Robinson parks on the street behind the house. No one has shoveled the drive and the Plymouth is up to its hubcaps in snow, a thick blanket covering the roof and hood. Soon, if this keeps up, the car will disappear entirely. The walkway from the rear door had been shoveled but another couple of inches already coats it like frosted sugar. He should clean it off before his mother comes home; he'd seen her downtown in the Titlow Hotel's lunchroom with her bridge cronies. He hopes whoever is driving her home can manage the roads. It's less than a mile, though, and he isn't really worried.

The door into the mudroom is unlocked, the kitchen cool. Mother turned down the thermostat before she left; his father had installed separate heating circuits a few years ago so the entire barn of a house wouldn't eat up electricity. He calls out to his father but gets no answer.

The light filtering in through the big kitchen windows and the vast entry next to it is watery, shifting, the shadows deepening each minute. He flicks a switch and lamps turn on, waver, hold steady. The lines haven't come down, at least, and the electricity still works.

"Rebecca?" His dad's voice rasps, full of phlegm.

"No, Dad, it's me, Dan. Mother isn't home yet."

His father's eyes are closed, and he's dozed off again by the time Dan sheds his coat and makes his way to the front room. The room is dim, shaded by the overhanging porch roof and the leafless red oaks crowding the front lawn. Dan remembers when those oaks were saplings; Father planted them as soon as the house was finished and they moved in. Dan was eight at the time. He loved to help water the fledgling trees, carrying buckets to the far reaches of the property while his father played a hose over the closer ones. Now they are forty feet tall or more, able to fend for themselves. Unless the ice gets too bad.

He picks up the newspaper scattered across the floor and sits in the rocker that his mother uses in the evenings. But as soon as he finds the business pages and starts in on the latest bank collapse, his father stirs and sits up, coughing and hawking, spits in a ceramic mug kept at hand for the purpose.

"So," the old man says, "what happened this time? Did the judge buy your argument?"

Dan folds the paper and drops it back to the floor. "Didn't get a chance. He postponed again. The defendants said they need more time, guess they can't find a witness they want."

"Witness?" His father breaks into a raspy cough. Dan stands, searches for the water pitcher his mother always leaves full and pours a glass. His father waves it away. "What witness could they possibly need they don't have?"

Dan sits again and snorts. "They didn't share that information. I'll see what I can find out tomorrow. You'd think this was a murder trial, the way they're going about it. It's just a case of fouling someone's water supply."

The old man glares at his son. "Could be murder, if the county hadn't tested that well when they did."

"I know, I know. It's serious. The company messed up this time, and I'm betting we'll finally be able to force them into doing some major repairs."

"Yes. Well." His father is quiet for a moment, lets his eyes roam across the room.

Dan glances at a box of papers next to his father's chair. The old man's been sifting through memories from the past. He hopes he hasn't tossed anything valuable. Somewhere there are clippings about John that Dan wants to keep. All five of the brothers had returned from the war alive, three unscathed, John and Dan wounded. John died of his wounds, though he fought the pain for ten years; Dan figures he'll die of his, too, but not for a while yet.

"Bring me that picture, son, will you?" His father points to a framed photograph on the mantelpiece. It's of Dan's grandmother, Agnes, when she was young, sometime after she was married but before she came back to Pennsylvania. He has a clear memory of her, though it doesn't match the picture before him. In the picture she has dark hair with a shine to it, parted in the middle, high cheekbones and heavy-lidded eyes that look directly into the camera. Challenging. Daring you to say "No" to anything she wants to do. Long slender fingers casually grasp a book as if she's about to tap it impatiently. She doesn't smile, but maybe that's because it took so long to take the exposure. She smiled often when he knew her, though she was sick, even bedridden, most of those years. She had a bad heart, and it slowed her down once she turned eighty. But that didn't stop her from ruling her family from her sickbed. She died the same year they moved into the big house on Prospect Street.

The old man takes the picture now and studies his mother. "She had beautiful bone structure. Look at those cheeks. Even toward the end, they just got sharper." He looks into the fire and taps the frame against his knee. "Did I ever tell you the time, she was probably seventy, maybe even more, had to be the late nineties, she hopped on that bicycle Johnny had and rode past my office just as I was leaving for lunch with a new client. She waved and yoo-hooed and took off down Main Street with her skirts flapping around her knees. She and Aunt Mattie had a good laugh about it."

Dan grins. "I suppose she could have died of a heart attack right then."

"I read her the riot act when I got home. She paid me no mind." He sets the picture on the side table and rubs dust from the top of the frame. "She was quite the old girl. Never gave up."

Dan smiles and nods. The room is dark, and he reaches to turn on the reading lamp behind him. His father's eyes are closed again; he falls asleep easily. *He'll not make it into his eighties, not like his mother.* He feels a twinge, a physical pain at the thought. *Probably won't be long now.*

His father breathes gently, begins to snore. Dan folds the newspaper, sets it aside for his mother. The contents of the box are scattered on the arm of the chair, on the floor at his feet, on the side table. He sorts news clippings from the debris. They're mostly from the Great War, the pictures of Dan and his brothers, the stories of John's deeds in Europe. Lieutenant John. Dad was so proud.

He opens a child's pasteboard autograph book. Obituaries from the local papers are pasted on black pages: his grandmother, John, Dan Sturgeon, the friend for whom he was named. And Aunt Mattie, the last of the sisters, dead these fifteen years.

He tucks the clippings and the book into the box. Those are the ones he wants to save. The election certificates, probably not; he sets them aside. He picks up a folder and opens it. There are clippings here, too, dating from way back, the mid-eighties, about a mine disaster. He skims the story but doesn't recognize any names, any reason why his father would keep this particular story. There were lots of disasters over the years.

Underneath the clippings are a photograph and a letter, the letter written on thin paper with a crabbed hand that strikes him as foreign. The photograph is of a young woman, dark-haired, dressed in the style of twenty years ago or more, high-waisted skirt and high-necked blouse. Heavy-lidded dark eyes stare directly into the camera; she's unsmiling. Her rounded chin is thrust a little forward, defiant; her cheekbones are high and sharp.

He looks from this picture to his grandmother's. There's no mistaking the resemblance. They might have been sisters, twins even, but for the difference in dress and hairstyle.

He flicks open the letter. It's dated 1918.

> *Dear Harry Robinson,"* he reads.
> *I thought you had a right to know about our daughter. I hope you can forgive me for keeping her a secret all these years. I thought it best and still do, we've had a good life here in Galway, we've worked for the local landowners, the Gregorys, and my daughter has had many advantages. She lives in Dublin now. I've never told her. I will leave it to you to decide whether to contact her. Please do not contact me.*
> *I named her Agnes.*
> *- Niamh*

Dan watches his father sleep in the big armchair. He's tiny, old, wasted. He hears the back door open, the sound of a car spinning its tires as it pulls away on the icy drive. He should have cleaned the walk. His mother calls from the kitchen where she'll be brushing snow off, changing her overshoes. He slips the photo, the letter and the clippings into the folder and drops it onto the fire, watches it curl to ash.

※

A Taste of the Irish Language

- luipreachán - Leprechan
- praties - Hiberno-English word for potatoes, deriving from Irish *prátaí* (Munster) or *fataí* (Co. Galway)
- Sliabh Eachtaí - Slieve Aughty, or Mount Aughty Mountains, a range in western Ireland
- poitín (*Pwu*-teen) - Also, *poteen.* Illegal liquor made of potatoes
- Pádraig Mór - Patrick the Greater (Mór, literally: large)
- airneán (*Ar*-nyuh) - Night visiting
- béaloideas (*Bale*-uh-dus) - Folklore, traditions
- seanchaidhe (*Shan*-ha-tya) - Storyteller
- *Shan*-ha-tya
- leathbhád (*Yow*-vo-d) - Half-boat
- bairín breac (*Bar*-i brak) - Also, barmbrack. Quick bread with sultanas and raisins
- daoine sídhe (*Dee*-nuh shee) - The faeries
- púca (*Poo*-ka) - A spright which may bring both good and bad fortune
- uaisle (*Oosh*-la) - Gentry, a polite word for the fairies
- mo chroí (Ma *Khri*-a) - My heart
- a stór (Uh *store)* - My dear
- Méabh (Mayv) - The warrior fairy queen
- bómán (*Bo*-man) - Dolt, noodle, numbskull
- mo ghrá (mo *Gro*) - My love
- taise (*Tah*-sha) - A doppelganger spirit; it takes on the appearance of someone who has just died or is just about to die. A taise will usually appear to the loved ones of the individual and will appear to be perfectly normal, if somewhat distant or distracted. Rarely malevolent.
- cailín (*Call*-ene) - And *a chailín* (vocative). Girl
- diabhal (*Del*-'l) - Devil
- *gabhdán (Go*-don) - Gullible person

- An Gorta Mór *(An Ger-ta Mor)* - The greatest hunger
- Dia linn *(Di-a linn)* - God with us

Niamh's song:

Cill Aodáin
(Kill A-den)

Anois teacht an Earraigh
beidh an lá dúl chun shíneadh
Is tar eis na féil Bríde
ardóigh mé mo sheol
Ó chuir mé i mo cheann é
ní chónóidh mé choíche
Go seasfaidh mé síos
i lár Chontae Mhaigh Eo.

Now with the springtime
the days will grow longer
And after St. Bride's day
my sail I'll let go
Since I put it into my head
I shall never stay put
until I shall stand down
in the center of County Mayo.

Antoine Ó Raifteirí (1779-1835)

Acknowledgements

Thanks to my readers and book group: Toni, Janet, Sally, Lana, Helena, Deborah, Katharine and Kathy. And thanks especially to Taylor Chapman-Sutton for her expertise in the Irish language. And a huge thanks to Amphorae Publishing, especially to Kristina Makansi for her skilled editing. And as always, thanks to Dan for his on-going support.

About the Author

Deborah Lincoln has lived on the Oregon Coast for eleven years. She grew up in the small town of Celina, Ohio and earned a bachelor's degree in English from Michigan State University and a master's degree in Library Science from the University of Michigan. She and her husband have three grown sons.

Of her passion for historical fiction, she says: "I'm fascinated by the way events—wars and cataclysms and upheavals, of course, but the everyday changes that wash over everyday lives—bring a poignancy to a person's efforts to survive and prosper. I hate the idea that brave and intelligent people have been forgotten, that the hardships they underwent have melted away like a rim of ice on a warm spring day."

Agnes Canon's War is the story of her great great grandparents, two remarkable people whose lives illustrate the joys and trials that marked America's tumultuous nineteenth century. *An Irish Wife*, follows Agnes Canon Robinson back to Agnes's hometown in Pennsylvania.